STONE
COLD
KILLING

An addictive crime thriller with a fiendish twist

D.E. WHITE

Detective Dove Milson Book 4

Joffe Books, London
www.joffebooks.com

First published in Great Britain in 2022

Cover art by Nebojša Zorić

ISBN: 978-1-80405-577-9

ALSO BY PAMELA CLARE

Romantic Suspense:

Cobra Elite Series

Hard Target (Book 1)

Hard Asset (Book 2)

Hard Justice (Book 3)

Hard Edge (Book 4)

I-Team Series

Extreme Exposure (Book 1)

Heaven Can't Wait (Book 1.5)

Hard Evidence (Book 2)

Unlawful Contact (Book 3)

Naked Edge (Book 4)

Breaking Point (Book 5)

Skin Deep: An I-Team After Hours Novella (Book 5.5)

First Strike: The Prequel to Striking Distance (Book 5.9)

Striking Distance (Book 6)

Soul Deep: An I-Team After Hours Novella (Book 6.5)

Seduction Game (Book 7)

Dead by Midnight: An I-Team Christmas (Book 7.5)

Deadly Intent (Book 8)

Contemporary Romance:

Colorado High Country Series

Barely Breathing (Book 1)

Slow Burn (Book 2)

Falling Hard (Book 3)

Tempting Fate (Book 4)

Close to Heaven (Book 5)

Holding On (Book 6)

Chasing Fire (Book 7)

Historical Romance:

Kenleigh-Blakewell Family Saga

Sweet Release (Book 1)

Carnal Gift (Book 2)

Ride the Fire (Book 3)

MacKinnon's Rangers series

Surrender (Book I)

Untamed (Book 2)

Defiant (Book 3)

Upon A Winter's Night: A MacKinnon's Rangers Christmas (Book 3.5)

Lullaby, rock-a-bye, won't you sleep,
Sweet little baby sleep so deep . . .

PROLOGUE

I can see now I made the wrong decision.

"You can't live like this! Don't leave me . . . You won't ever be able to come back!" His words were snatched away on the icy wind that slashed my bare arms and stung my face.

I staggered a little on my high heels before slamming the car door firmly behind me, not bothering to argue any further. Everything had been said, and the waves of pain and regret had filled the car. I was glad to escape, and also terrified he would talk me round.

The storm had whipped sea spray across Beach Road, and it spun and danced in white foamy tendrils. I started walking faster, hearing the car finally pull away, the driver revving the engine as though in anger.

The darkness was broken by the fast-moving clouds, creating a velvet patchwork of shaded greys above the sea. At 2 a.m. there was nobody to see a woman fighting her way through the storm in a party dress. The sea drew my gaze as I passed the corner, the waves rearing and crashing down on the stones, the hypnotic push and slide of the water.

Two months later, I found out I was pregnant . . .

I allow my mind to fast forward the memories now, the drugs taking hold, moving me to a better place, and a more restful one.

I can picture her in my mind as if it were yesterday . . . I find myself cradling my arms against my chest as though she is still settled safely in the crook of my elbow. My talisman, and the person who would change my life.

She was so beautiful, my baby girl. So perfect and innocent. I had drifted off again, warm and safe in my soft bed.

That was the main feeling, I remember quite clearly: that I was safe and the future I had agonized over was finally clear.

I didn't trust anyone easily, but this seemed like another chance, a gift from the universe . . . I would do whatever it took to give my baby a good life and I also knew I couldn't let anyone down, not again.

I blinked as another needle pricked my arm and I slid away on a soothing flood of reassuring words. Someone was holding my hand, and I knew I trusted her, too.

I had done it! Despite all my fears and anxieties about the birth, she was here, and she was perfection.

An unfamiliar sensation was giving me strength. Confidence. Her gift to me. My gift to her would be the best life I could make for the both of us. I had made promises I needed to keep.

But later, in the nights that followed after I left my safe haven, when I woke up and my baby was crying, when the other children were restless, and I was cold and alone, it became harder to hold on to my promises.

In my head, the voices still soothed, but in my chest panic and grief tore at my heart. I could feel myself slipping again. The promises became less urgent, the future less colourful.

Each day I would start again, fighting to retrieve my strength, my good intentions. I needed to do this, make myself think hard about the life we would have. For my other children and the lives they don't have. But first I always needed to rest a little.

I believed everything I promised myself, but in the end, I couldn't bring myself back from the brink. Lying on the couch seemed to be the best I could do most days. They knew I had failed them. I saw it in their eyes, their blank expressions, and in the bruises on their soft skin.

I am lying down now, but I'm not on the couch. I can taste salt on my lips and feel the wet pebbles beneath my cheek. The sea ebbs and flows, calming and merciless. I'm back at the place where I made the wrong decision.

How long has it been? In my mind, I've never stopped searching for that future I promised us. But maybe you can search and search and never find what you are looking for. You let people down, and you let yourself down.

When do you give up? I close my eyes and the sea washes up and over, soothing away my nightmares.

CHAPTER ONE

The baby was in the middle of the road.

Cocooned in a car seat, tiny face suddenly, violently, illuminated by the headlights.

"Shit!" Detective Constable Dove Milson yanked the steering wheel to the left, stamping on the brakes, sending the car into a skid on the wet tarmac.

Her colleague, Detective Sergeant Steve Parker, in the passenger seat, grabbed his phone as it skittered along the car interior. Dove got the vehicle under control, and as soon as she had parked safely on the grass verge, both police officers leaped out into the torrential spring rain, booted feet sinking in the mud. Further ahead, beyond the child, and around ten metres from the road, a crashed car sat askew in the ditch.

"You get the baby and I'll check the car!" Steve said, moving swiftly towards the vehicle, shrugging on his rain jacket against the weather.

Dove reached the baby first, moving the car seat to the safety of the grass verge, before gently putting a hand inside the seat. She dashed her hand across her face, wiping away the raindrops that blurred her vision, "Hey baby . . . What's happened to you?" Her hands were shaking, and the first rush of adrenalin left no room to consider anything but her training. No blood, but no noise either, which was worrying. The face was warm to the touch, the eyes closed.

"Nothing in here! Some blood on the driver's side though, and the airbag's blown." Steve, after a preliminary check of the car, had run over and crouched beside her. "How's baby?"

Dove, unable to tell if the baby was breathing, had unfastened the harness and lifted the baby. She swiftly recoiled in shock, dropping it back into the car seat. "Jesus Christ, Steve, it's a bloody doll!"

It was eerily lifelike, and when she picked it up again, the eyelids rolled back, revealing a direct blue gaze. The doll was around the same weight as an infant, Dove thought, still shaking in shock. It *felt* like a baby, too. She peered at the body, turning it carefully in her hands. It was dressed in a yellow romper suit, and the facial features, the hands and feet, were all delicately moulded, glass eyes now staring into the distance. And it was warm to the touch.

"It's bloody good." Steve was clearly shaken. "I've heard of these real-life dolls, but I've never actually seen one before."

"Yeah. Freaked me right out. It was just like holding one of my nieces when they were tiny!" Recovering, she set the doll back down and moved the car seat further onto the grass verge, turning it towards the crash scene, mindful of any approaching traffic. As she rested the seat securely against a tree trunk, something rolled out of it.

Half expecting a baby's dummy or even a toy, she slipped on a pair of plastic gloves, stooped and picked the object up, turning it over in her hand. "It's a beach pebble?"

Steve shone his torch directly on the object. It was smooth and round, with the edges accentuated as though they had been filed down or even carved, somehow, to create a heart shape. It was painted red, but the paint was worn and faded. "A heart."

"As if this couldn't get any weirder . . ." Dove said, still peering at the small object in her palm.

"I'll update Control," Steve said, looking back at the car. "There's a lot of blood. I don't like to think we've missed something, and if our driver *is* lying injured nearby, we need to get a search done ASAP. It's hard to see in this light and this bloody rain. What happened to the spring heatwave?"

"This is it." Dove grinned at his grumbling. "I'll bag it and we'll hand it in later."

He pulled out his phone as Dove slipped the pebble into an evidence bag and tried to stop herself from staring at the baby. Who drove around with a baby doll in a car seat? It wasn't like it was a child's toy . . . And the eyes were so real, with each tiny lash delicate and spiked.

As Steve finished his call, noise in the woods beyond the crashed car made Dove glance up sharply, narrowing her eyes against the rain and the dusk. Cracking twigs, and a swift shadow. She shoved a handful of wet dark hair from her eyes and pushed it behind her ears, under her rain jacket hood. Her heart was pounding. "What was that? Our driver?"

"*Hallo*? Are you okay? It's the police!" Steve called as they both headed for the path into the woods, just to the left of the deserted car.

Dove slipped slightly on the narrow wooden bridge that spanned the ditch, recovered her balance with a soft curse. The smell of petrol and rubber lingered on the cool evening air and below the bridge a ditch bubbled and gushed with dirty brown water, barely visible among the tall, lush weeds of the hedgerow.

They stopped on the edge of the wood, a vast pine forest. The tall, swaying conifers providing a darkness for anything or anyone who wanted to remain hidden. Ahead, leading slightly uphill, were various narrow twisting animal paths, and further to their right, a decent-sized track marked with tractor wheel ruts.

"Do you need help?" Dove called.

The silence that followed was broken only by the monotonous drip of raindrops. Every sound was magnified by the vast tree canopy and Dove could hear her own breathing, the squelch and whisper as she shifted her boots in the muddy grass.

"Did you check in the weeds in the ditch?" Dove asked suddenly, glancing back at the doll. It was giving her the creeps. "They're tall enough to hide a body . . ."

Steve shook his head, wiping a hand across his face and pulling his hood further down to shield himself from the relentless rain. "Um . . . no, but be my guest if you want to head down there."

"Why would you be driving around with a baby doll strapped in a car seat?" Dove asked, surveying the vehicle again as they walked back across the narrow bridge, boots echoing on the wood.

"No idea, but maybe it makes them happy."

The car bonnet was crunched inwards where it had hit a tree, spun 180 degrees and slid nose-first into the ditch. Huge raw muddy tyre tracks showed the progress from the road through the lush green of the weeds and grass.

A car drove slowly past, the driver taking in the scene of the accident. Dove raised a hand to indicate all was well and he gave a thumbs up in response, driving carefully onwards, vanishing around the sharp bend.

"Good thing you moved the baby."

"Yeah." She slipped on the wet grass, trying to stay on the bank rather than descend into the icy ditch water. The baby seemed to be watching her. Maybe the driver of the crashed car had already called for a lift home? But the vehicle was still warm, the tyre tracks fresh. And she could now see for herself there was a spatter of blood in the footwell.

"Look at this . . ." Steve pointed. The side of the seat was ripped, and the wing mirror was shattered. On the driver's side the windscreen was cobwebbed from impact with a tree branch, which still poked treacherously sharp ends through the glass. There were shards of glass everywhere, sparkling in their torchlight. Some were coated in blood.

CHAPTER TWO

The car key was still in the ignition. A Mickey Mouse key-chain and a furry pink pom-pom hung from the ring.

Dove scanned the interior, swinging her torch carefully across the seats and into the footwells. No bag, phone, wallet, house keys or any other obvious sign of identification.

"Let's pop the boot open while we wait for backup," Steve suggested, removing his glasses to wipe away the rain before replacing them and cursing, "This bloody weather!"

With difficulty, mainly due to the treacherously wet ground, they managed to gain access to the rear of the car. Dove's stomach clenched as the boot slowly raised, but it was empty, clean, and smelling strongly of the same kind of synthetic, flowery air freshener as the rest of the vehicle.

"More blood on the grass this side," Steve said, swinging his torch into the road again. "Some footprints, too. Heading towards the woods . . ."

A noise in the pine trees beyond the car made Dove's heart rate speed up, and she straightened slowly, before aiming her own powerful torch into the trees. Two startled bright eyes topped by magnificent antlers appeared before the stag bounded away.

She still felt jittery. Something wasn't right about this scene at all, and it wasn't just the weird doll baby. Hunching her shoulders, eyes swivelling back and forth to the woods, she felt like they were being watched.

"I don't think the baby car seat came from this vehicle. Look, no way of securing it, no indents in any of the seats to show it's been in here." Steve had two young girls of his own. "So maybe it was placed in the road to cause the accident?"

"A carjacking?" Dove asked, remembering a big case from a number of years ago, where a gang had used a baby car seat as a decoy to stop drivers and then made off with their cars. "But they left the car in this instance."

"Yeah . . . So, maybe not."

The blood trail on the driver's side went as far as the ditch, where there was flattened grass, as though someone had sat or lain down in the mud. "What if the driver was concussed and tried to go for help, but ended up going the wrong way?"

Determined not to miss a casualty, Dove slithered down into the weeds, following the trampled path. "Hey, there's a way through the hedge here. Looks like someone did come this way, and they crawled out through the nettles."

Soaked now, despite her thick trousers and jacket, Dove pushed her way through. A few years ago, there had been another scenario where the driver of a crashed car had been lying injured a hundred yards from their car. The scene, she remembered, had been very similar to this one, with lots of dense undergrowth.

The immediate area had been checked, but nobody discovered the man until it was too late. A mistake. He had died because assumptions had been made about the distance he could have been thrown from the vehicle. It was one of those cases that was often used on training courses, and it had stayed with her. Never assume, always go with the evidence.

And in this case the evidence was showing her whoever had been in the car was injured and had started to make their way from the vehicle in the opposite direction of the road and possible help and medical care.

Steve walked round to the other side of the hedge, meeting her as she emerged from the undergrowth. "If they took their phone with them, why not call 999?"

"The signal is patchy down here. I've only got one bar. The trail is that side — see?" Dove pointed at the clear route from the car. She had been careful to make her own, different path, a little to the side, giving her a chance to ensure nobody was lying injured in the weeds, but also disturbing as little evidence as she possibly could.

They both stared into the ominous shadows of the pinewoods. The blood trail from the undergrowth became a pool on the shorter grasses near the trees, as the victim maybe paused for breath or to try and get their bearings. Steve's torch picked up the dark red, already turning rust in places, coating pine needles on the forest floor.

As they both entered the tree canopy, Dove jerked to a halt. On one rough tree trunk, a bloody handprint. Not true and clear but smudged and smeared as though the victim had been grasping desperately for support.

She bent down, keeping away from the blood, trying to see in the torchlight which way the person had walked.

"No more blood this way, or any indication our driver got any further," Steve reported. He glanced at his watch. "It's going to get dark soon. Let's go back and have another look inside the car."

"Where the hell have they gone?" Dove said in frustration, her voice echoing under the whispering boughs. She looked at her phone. "No signal at all in here."

* * *

They had both been treading warily, trying, despite the twin factors of urgency and adverse weather, to keep the scene as pristine as possible, but in any given situation their first priority was always to preserve life. Anyway, there was no evidence yet, Dove thought, wiping raindrops from her eyelashes with the cuff of her jacket, that this was anything but the scene of a car accident. The rain was icy, and her lips and cheeks were numb with cold.

"And there was just one set of tyre marks on the grass verge," Steve said. "If it was anything like a carjacking, you'd think there would be evidence of another vehicle. Hey, I think the rain is easing up."

They walked carefully back to the car, avoiding the blood. The smell of death and fear seemed to hang in the evening air. From the grass verge, the baby watched, glass eyes vacant yet catching the light from their torches, giving the illusion of some sinister spirit. But there was no blood on the baby, Dove thought, turning towards the road again.

The crack of a gunshot sent them both flat on the ground, diving behind their car, seeking out the shadows as torches were abruptly snapped off.

CHAPTER THREE

Almost as soon as she hit the ground, Dove, closest to the bridge, with a sight line into the woods, could make out a figure running away, shadows mingling as he sprinted through the forest.

She could hear him gasping for breath, stumbling and crashing through lower branches. A few moments later the sound of a vehicle engine ripped through the soft spring dusk. The vehicle drove off with a screech of tyres and a roar as the driver accelerated fast, heading along the road in the opposite direction of the crash.

Breathing in damp and mud, lying shoulder to shoulder with her partner in the wet foliage, Dove felt her heart pounding against her ribcage, sweat starting under her zipped-up jacket and warm top. No sign of anyone else, but she couldn't presume there was just one assailant.

She had dropped her phone as they dived for cover. She could see it now, lying in the grass within arm's length. Stretching out her fingers, she inched forward slightly.

Beside her, she heard Steve swear softly at her movement. She turned and stared at him, eyes asking a question and he gave her a quick thumbs up with his right hand but pointed to his left shoulder and grimaced.

There was blood on his shoulder. She could see the stain even in the shadows. His jacket had a neat tear, revealing his shirt underneath. Not much blood, but more as though the bullet had struck a glancing blow as it passed, narrowly avoiding more damage.

Dove frowned in concern as he shifted a little, applying firm pressure on his injured shoulder with one hand.

Every tiny sound from the forest made her nerves jangle, and she could feel sweat forming on her back, on the nape of her neck. The excess adrenalin was still fizzing around her body, demanding an outlet. Focusing, she managed to slither forward an inch more, and her shaking, questing fingertips reached her phone.

"Urgent assistance required. Shots fired!" She followed it up with a brief update on the summary of events, their current position and Steve's injury, knowing it would trigger a Major Incident alert, with multiple emergency services becoming involved, plus a Firearms Team being deployed.

She wriggled further back to safety, leaving the line open for further updates. Eyes and ears straining, she peered underneath the vehicle and through the muddy grass, brambles and spiky hedgerow for signs of life. Just because the shooter appeared to have taken off didn't mean he was the only person in those woods with a gun.

Sharp bends to either side made it impossible to see any signs of other traffic, but the quiet made it easy to hear the pattering of droplets falling from leaves to tarmac.

"Are you okay?" Dove whispered, inching round so she could check out Steve's wound properly. It seemed to have stopped bleeding.

The circumstances had changed. This was no longer the scene of a possible accident, but a major crime scene. She could feel prickles of unease along her arms.

"I'm fine. Let's just wait it out until the circus arrives and we can get out of here." Steve pushed her hand gently away. "Honestly, it's fine. Doesn't even hurt now."

"Liar." She sank back down in the grass.

There were no more shots, and backup arrived within minutes.

The Firearms tactical commander took charge of the scene, establishing a cordon and rendezvous point, keeping the ambulances and other vehicles back for an initial sweep of the immediate area. At stage two, Steve and Dove were removed from the imminent threat of danger and the Firearms Team could widen the search area. Finally, medics would be allowed past the cordon to treat any other casualties.

Dove watched as the remainder of the team was deployed, accompanied by the excited bark of the unit dogs and the calm commands of their handlers. A swift and efficient flow of bodies moved out to search the grid-referenced area.

The Firearms commander, who had taken on duties as senior investigating officer as his team secured the area, was Detective Inspector Hattrick — his name the butt of many jokes. He was taking in the scene with quick, darting blue eyes.

As he came closer, Dove smelled cigarettes and mint chewing gum, his usual aroma. She had worked with him before, and he was widely recognized as being extremely competent and thorough. "Evening, DC Milson. You two having a bit of fun on your way home from work? If you can bring me up to speed while your partner is being sewn up, we can get cracking."

"Absolutely." She went quickly through the events of the past hour.

"The figure you saw running after the shot . . . Can you describe them?"

She hesitated. "Tall, skinny, stumbled a little as he ran, but that might be over tree roots. No torch and I didn't see a gun. My impression was that it was a man, but I'm not a hundred per cent positive. He had a long jacket with a hood pulled down."

"Assuming he hasn't ditched it in the woods we are probably looking for something small. No long barrels? Shotgun?"

She shook her head. "Not that I could see, but he took the shot while we were over here . . ." She pointed. "We didn't have any light at that point, for obvious reasons, but from my position next to the car I had a clear view into the woods." She hesitated, "He was fairly close, or I wouldn't have been able to see him at all, and to get a shot in from a handgun, he would have needed to be." Dove paused as the noise of a helicopter tore through the evening sky, coming to hover over the woods, moving slowly across a grid search pattern, brilliant white light illuminating the forest from above.

"Go on," the DI said.

"We left everything as we saw it, except this, which fell out when I rested the seat against the tree." She dragged the bag from her pocket and held it up to one of the powerful floodlights that illuminated the scene.

"A beach pebble?" He examined it through the plastic bag, holding the object up to the light. "Looks like something you'd find in a craft shop. Nothing else?"

"Not that we saw. Keys were still in the ignition, no personal effects."

"Okay, thanks . . ." Someone called urgently to him. "Sorry, got to go. Can you give your statement to PC Goss over there?"

More voices on the radio and Dove gleaned the team had found signs of the getaway vehicle she and Steve had heard. She turned towards another officer who was on his phone.

"Sorry, just a quick update. The boss wants me to take your statement?" Police Constable Goss ran a hand over red spiked hair, and Dove could see sweat on his forehead despite the coolness of the night. "Short-staffed tonight. Always happens when we get a major incident," he explained.

"Tell me about it . . . We're at breaking point, the crazy number of cases the team are handling, and I heard it's even worse over the border," Dove sympathized. She waved towards Steve, who was talking to the paramedics. "He's got a bit of a scratch where the shooter just missed him."

"Either they were a crap shot, or they weren't shooting to hit us, because we were pretty big and stationary targets," Steve called over from where he was sitting in the ambulance.

"Perhaps he was just trying to get us away from the scene? Maybe a carjacking gone wrong or something valuable still in the car?" Dove suggested, still watching her partner with concern as he pulled his jacket off and submitted to medical assistance. "But then to leave the scene . . . Weird. Hey, did you run the car registration?"

"This car is registered to Martin Cartwright. Address for him is 5 Lockdean Estate in Lymington-on-Sea. No reply to his phone number so we've sent a team over there. No previous on him, but he could be our shooter," PC Goss told them.

Having given a statement Dove was soon drawn into the well-ordered teams moving quickly to establish perimeters, secure the area, collect evidence. A few officers had stopped and exclaimed over the lifelike baby doll.

The fact Steve and Dove had been on the scene, not to mention fired at, made them valuable witnesses, and they answered the questions as best they could.

Where exactly was this shooter standing, would you say?

You said you heard a noise earlier, but it turned out to be a deer?

How long were you on the scene before the shot was fired?

Intel coming in from the radios confirmed the specialist search team had discovered a handgun thrown down among the trees, presumably as the shooter fled, and the bullet casing from the single shot fired.

"Maybe he was buying time for the injured driver to get clear. He could have been called to help them out," Dove suggested and Steve, all patched up and given the medical all-clear, nodded.

Forensic teams were carefully gathering evidence from the car, taking photographs, when there was a commotion in the woods, and more radio activity.

DI Hattrick was standing next to the footbridge to the woods, and he beckoned Steve and Dove over. "They found a bag containing a mobile phone." His mouth was set in a grim line. "And a whole load more blood. Apparently, we have a clear trail . . ." He indicated his iPad and enlarged the map. "The injured person, probably the driver, made their way up through the woods using the footpath. We're half a mile on . . . Here," he jabbed a thumb, "and the trail is still good."

"Must be someone pretty desperate to hide if they could still run with such significant injuries," Steve mused.

"Or they were just terrified," DI Hattrick said, his expression darkening.

CHAPTER FOUR

Dove pulled her phone out of her pocket as she heard the *ping* of an incoming text and shot a glance at Steve as he did the same.

"Bad timing," Steve said, and they both looked down at their screens.

Dove frowned. She and Steve were part of the area Major Crimes Team, and this was a text summoning them to a caravan half a mile away.

"*Female deceased, first responders on scene. Stab wounds, witness called 999 at 8.10 p.m.,*" Steve read out aloud. "Only five miles away?"

Dove shivered as she checked out the address and grid reference, suddenly aware of her damp and muddy clothes. She pushed the thought away, and nodded. "That's a few minutes up the road. And about an hour after we discovered the car crash. Coincidence?"

She approached DI Hattrick and explained they had been called out to a potential murder scene just up the road. "We'll stay here, of course, but check in with the boss to let him know what's happening."

He nodded, wrinkles and pouches in his face wobbling at the movement and the blue eyes narrowed. "Fucking strange. Our team is over halfway up the main drag in the woods, and the scene has been cleared as far as that. No body yet. Who's the on-call SIO for MCT?"

"DI Blackman," Dove said. "Steve's just ringing him now."

Steve was sitting in the driver's seat of their car, and she jogged quickly over to him, careful to avoid the crime scene tape that now stretched across the area. The road had been closed in both directions to allow the team to work.

"Are you sure your shoulder is okay?" Dove asked, concerned as her partner winced, adjusting his position in the seat with unusual care.

"Fine. Honestly, stop fussing!" Steve hit the call button on his phone and put their boss on speakerphone, iPad on his lap. Briefly, he updated Jon Blackman on the car crash scene, and the shooting.

"Bloody hell! It's supposed to be quiet out in the countryside. Are you sure you're fit, Steve?"

"All good, boss."

"And the vehicle you heard after the shooting? Did you say the shot and the engine noise came from the woods?"

"There's a track just round this sharp bend that goes into the woods. Firearms found recent tyre tracks, and they also recovered a handgun and cartridge from the woods. Gun is unregistered and going off to the lab. Looks like a Makarov, and one of the team was saying there's been a big jump in reactivated weapons coming in from Eastern Europe," Steve answered. "Our car driver is still missing but the dogs are currently following a blood trail through the woods in the direction of the murder victim in the caravan."

"We found the track ourselves right before the shooting, and looking at the map, it's less than half a mile cross-country to the caravan address," Dove concluded, moving two fingers across her screen to study the area, noting the grid references. "And we still don't know if our car had any passengers. I spoke to the SIO, DI Hattrick, while Steve was getting patched up."

DI Blackman, his voice sharp and decisive, agreed, "No such thing as a coincidence. Was there any sign of anyone else at all in the woods or in the car? Because the caravan victim has stab wounds, and you reported a shooter. If you had a gun and wanted to kill someone, it would make sense to use the weapon to hand."

"Who else is on call?" Steve asked.

"DS Allerton and DC Conrad, plus DI Lincoln is the night cover at the station. Dove, you stay where you are and act as liaison. Steve, you go home."

Dove knew he was thinking about cross-contamination and DNA evidence collection but also their welfare.

"I'm okay. Happy to stay with Dove," Steve said uncomfortably.

"You've just been shot! Go home and see how you feel in the morning," DI Blackman told him brusquely. "You only come in if you sign off medical clearance."

"Yes, boss," Dove replied, as Steve frowned, clearly not happy at the dismissal. Her mind was spinning. Could the shooter have run through the woods from this next scene? Was there enough time for him to have chased the car driver through the woods, murdered her and then come back to . . . to what? Check out the crashed car or just make good his escape? He must have gotten a shock when he saw them poking around at the scene. A warning shot, or someone seeking to kill or injure a police officer?

Steve caught a lift home, leaving Dove with the car, and she spent the next hour liaising between DI Hattrick at the crash scene, and her boss and MCT colleagues at the murder scene.

"Dove, you're on speakerphone." It was DS Lindsey Allerton. "I've got some info for you."

"Go ahead."

"Jess has done an initial examination, and the prelims show it appears to be a carefully arranged scene." Lindsey paused before she began reading.

Dove waited impatiently. The Crime Scene Manager was Jess, a small, blonde Northern lass who didn't take any bullshit from anyone. She was also one of the best in the area at what she did.

"Okay . . . The dead woman is lying on her back on a narrow couch on the side of the caravan. There is a significant amount of bruising across her bare left shoulder and torso. Her torn and muddy clothing suggests a struggle outside, and there are six to eight slash wounds to her abdomen. The blood has soaked the lower part of her clothing. There is also bruising to her face and wrists, and the force of one blow to her face has knocked out a tooth."

"The shoulder bruising sounds like classic car crash injuries from the airbag and seat belt," Dove suggested.

"Right, that's what Jess said," Lindsey told her. "And one more red flag linking the victim to your scene. The boss said you found a heart-shaped pebble?"

"Right. It's been sent off for processing," said Dove.

"The murder victim had a small heart-shaped pebble placed in her mouth," Lindsey said soberly.

CHAPTER FIVE

"Bloody hell." Dove found her breathing was speeding up, and she was picturing the horror, running her tongue around her teeth. "Her *mouth*? Did she choke, then?"

"Jess says no, and she thinks it was done after death. She's taken a preliminary look, but she wants to wait for the body to get down to the mortuary and get her on the table before she says any more."

Dove understood. Evidence could be lost if the Crime Scene Manager was hasty, and this sounded like a prime opportunity to potentially harvest something valuable.

"She also thinks there might be something else in the victim's throat," Lindsey said. "But that will be for the pathologist to investigate. It's too far down for Jess to poke around." She paused before continuing more slowly, reading from the notes, ". . . Cause of death is most likely to have been that the victim bled out via the femoral artery. Probably some internal bleeding, too, but if they made it from the car through the woods to this site, the fatal hit didn't occur until they were in the caravan, or it would have all been over in seconds."

Dove rubbed a hand across her face, trying to put together the sequence of events in her head, imagining her driving off the road, running from an unknown gunman, or several attackers pursing the woman. There was a lot going on in one scene. Her initial thought that it had been carefully planned seemed correct, but the stab wounds suggested a loss of control, as if whatever was driving the killing in the perpetrator's mind possibly had been overridden by emotion. "How old is the victim?"

"In her early seventies. The witness is a friend, but she wasn't quite sure of the victim's age. Says she never bothered celebrating birthdays because she just felt lucky to be alive whenever she opened her eyes in the morning."

And now she wouldn't be greeting another morning . . . Dove was finding it hugely frustrating not being present at the murder scene, seeing for herself, but she forced herself to focus. "If the victim was targeted, maybe she didn't run away through the woods, maybe she was taken that way on purpose. The perpetrator wanted her to die at her home, perhaps, kept her alive long enough to do what? Have a conversation? Get information?"

"Don't forget Jess thinks the stone heart was likely placed in her mouth *after* death," Lindsey pointed out. "The bruising and broken tooth seem to be from a blow to the face. The last note to bring you up to date is there are also numerous small cuts or slashes along both her arms from the inside of her wrists leading right up to her armpits. Jess has queried torture."

"Thanks, Lindsey." Dove pushed her tangled thoughts to the back of her mind, and quickly responded with an update from her own scene. "I just spoke to Hattrick, and he says the owner of the car, the victim's son, has now given a statement. They sent a team over, but according to his statement he has nothing useful to add. He loaned the car to his mum while hers is in the garage being repaired. No previous except a few minor driving offences, and no gun licences. I think Pete's going to take up FLO duty with him. And there's an ex-husband, too. He's getting the same treatment. Oh, sorry, I'll call you back!"

There was a shout from the crashed car, and someone was holding up a small clear plastic bag. Even at this distance Dove could see it contained brilliant white powder. Maybe Martin Cartwright wasn't quite so innocent as he had made out. Or his mum wasn't?

DI Hattrick nodded his approval. "Perhaps that's what your shooter was coming back for?" He leaned over his map again, "The dogs have confirmed the trail leads all the way to the victim's caravan, we've got the two pebbles, and a positive ID for the getaway car, although the witness can't be sure how many people were inside because the windows were tinted glass. Going to need some more bodies on this one, DC Milson, aren't we?"

She agreed. It was huge, spiderwebbing as it did across two scenes, and they were always short-staffed. Her mind drifted back to the description of the victim. The slashes on the arms, possible torture, the stone in her mouth, all rang alarm bells in her head. It had the hallmarks of a gang killing, a hit or an execution.

Now, the discovery of what seemed to be a fairly substantial quantity of cocaine hidden inside the lining of the door in the crashed car seemed to indicate Martin Cartwright had some further explaining to do.

In her previous career as a police source handler, Dove had been familiar with various organized crime gangs operating across the southeast and further afield. She couldn't recall any cases where heart-shaped pebbles had been a feature, though. The method of torture, on the hypersensitive inside of the victim's arms, however, she had seen on several occasions.

* * *

Finally released from the car crash scene, Dove climbed wearily into her car and began driving towards the police station for the briefing. It was going to be a long night.

She slowed to a stop as she passed the murder scene, peering into the darkness. The scene was still lit up with glaring floodlights so she could easily see the battered white caravan, approached by a short, rutted, potholed gravel driveway. Either side gave way to arable land, with the vast pinewoods starting around 200 metres to the rear of the property.

The remains of some sort of farm buildings were evident to the side, sheltered by a vast spreading chestnut tree. Potted plants and trees surrounded the caravan, and when Dove wound her window down, breathing in the rain-soaked air, she could hear a dog barking.

Tape had been set up around the caravan, and as the rain had intensified, Dove could see the area outside the perimeter turning rapidly to mud under booted feet and many tyres. It was an uphill climb from the woods. Alice Cartwright must have been a superwoman to get from her car to her home with the injuries she had been carrying.

Had she managed to scramble inside her caravan, turning to confront her attacker again, but just not been quick enough to lock the door and keep herself safe?

The rain had stopped completely now, and the clouds were moving swiftly away over the Downs. The busy scene held her attention for a moment longer. It felt strange to be part of this case but also not part of it.

As usual, metal plates had been laid, and she could see them winding in a careful spiral around the caravan area. After signing the log, anyone entering the scene was suited and booted in white plastic. Officers were still gathered in small groups, going methodically about their tasks. She could see the suits were splashed with mud. Jess must be cursing the weather.

Dove knew that Jess's team would also continue far into the night, while she and her other colleagues began to investigate more widely.

Dove's fiancé Quinn was a paramedic, and he often said it was so depressing to go to a shout and find a dead body. He was all about saving lives, he would add. Dove's work was all about piecing together what had happened to cause the death, about obtaining justice for the victim's family and friends, for the victim themselves. She always saw herself as working for the victim.

Dove drove onwards, wondering for a second if the perpetrator had still been on the premises when the witness arrived and discovered the body. Watching, hiding. It made for a tight timeframe, and if it was true, he hadn't killed her as well, which suggested his target had been Alice. The whole charade with the baby and the pebbles must have been carefully planned, but was the murderer trying to tell the police something, or the victim?

CHAPTER SIX

She was dancing when I first saw her, and she caught my eye immediately, but not for the reasons you might imagine. Her eyes, her hair and the almost familiar way she tilted her chin and threw her head back.

Even her low, smooth voice was just as I had imagined it would be, and I think she felt that instant connection too.

It was easy enough to engage with her and find out where she lived, what she did. Because of what I do, people trust me. They think if they can see my whole life through my profession, it must be okay. Perhaps they think we might trade secrets. But nobody really knows what's in another person's mind, do they?

It's not a clever assumption to base your trust on social media and reputation alone. Nobody knows who I really am. Perhaps I don't either . . . What's in a name? There is nobody in my professional life that I completely trust, and no possessions I couldn't leave behind in a heartbeat. I am my own self and nobody else has a claim.

We were meant to meet that night, when the music was loud, pumping through my veins. The crush of sweaty bodies was intoxicating, and dangerous. I believe in fate and here it was, showing me a way forward in the best possible way.

CHAPTER SEVEN

By 11 p.m. most of the MCT were assembled down at the police station. Dove had taken five minutes to get changed into dry clothes, re-plaited her long, wavy dark hair, and removed a smear of mud from her cheek. By the time she had splashed some cold water on her face and wiped herself down with a handful of paper towels she felt almost human again.

Lindsey turned to Dove as she walked in, her eyes bright with interest. "Getting a head start on the rest of us, you two? Steve all right?" Her short brown curls were wet, and her face was pink from the heat of the room. "Could have chosen a better night for a party."

"Yeah, that's exactly what I was thinking," Dove replied wryly, taking a much-needed gulp of hot coffee and coughing as the liquid scalded her tongue.

Thanking her lucky stars that she always kept a change of clothes at work, she joined her colleagues with her drink and her iPad.

"How's Steve doing?" DC Josh Conrad asked the same question. His black hair was still wet and he wore a towel around his neck.

"He's fine. All patched up on scene. Furious he couldn't stay." Dove knew Steve's wife would have a few words to say if she found out her husband had wanted to continue on shift after taking a bullet, even one that had missed him.

Tall and lean, DI Blackman was now surveying them through narrowed grey eyes. His shaven head was still speckled with raindrops as he waited for the others to join them before giving a quick briefing. "The 999 call came in at 8.10 p.m. and was made by Sarah Whitmore. She found the body and then drove to the end of the driveway before making the call. She said she was terrified whoever killed Alice might still be in the vicinity, but she didn't see or hear anything to indicate this." He glanced at his notes, before continuing. "She did say she heard a gunshot in the woods after she had made the call but isn't positive what time that was. She was sitting in her car at the end of the drive, off the road, and she says shortly after the gunshot a black Range Rover Discovery drove past at speed. She didn't get the number plate."

"The victim's name was Alice Cartwright. She was sixty-nine and worked part-time at Springley Garden Centre in Bear Green." Grey-haired and broad-shouldered DCI Franklin cast a beady eye across the bleary-eyed team as he took over. As usual he had a rosy complexion and gave the impression of having just been out doing something physical and muddy.

Dove always thought of him as a rugby player, especially now she knew he coached the local junior team in his spare time.

"She was returning home from work, driving her son's car as hers was being repaired at the garage," the DCI went on.

The briefing took in the pictures of the scene, before progressing backwards to the car crash. A smiling picture of a white-haired, blue-eyed woman was already up on the whiteboard — the murder board — and a route map drawn up in green marker pen showed the victim's last known movements. Timings had also been added, and it was clear, whether by accident or design, a lot had happened in what was potentially a one-hour time span between the crash and the murder.

A final photograph showed the small plastic bags filled with white powder, in situ in the door lining, which had been damaged in the crash, allowing some of the drugs to seep into the interior of the vehicle. The single bag discovered initially had turned into quite a haul. It also showed the bags of cocaine lined up, labelled and categorized, laid on plastic sheeting, before they were loaded carefully into evidence containers.

Dove stared at the photographs. There was also the weapon to consider . . . Again, the combination of drugs, torture or execution and the type of weapons used suggested links to gangland. The handgun would go to the labs, who would then liaise with NABIS to see if they could discover the origins of the weapon, but all too often this was a dead end.

She found she was tapping her pen on her notebook as she cast her mind back to the murder scene, again seeing the doll in the road as she drove round the blind corner. She had a photographic memory and had always found it easier to rewind in her head, like a film reel displaying all the key relevant points in her mind. Could the shooter have run down in time to hide in the woods near the car, before they arrived? Had he arrived to get the drugs just as she and Steve pulled up at the crash site?

"Jess and her team are processing the huge amount of evidence from both scenes," the DCI added. "Tech Support are checking traffic cam footage in the area for both our victim's car, and also our perpetrator's. There is evidence from tyre tracks and some oil leakage that a larger vehicle, probably a four-by-four, was parked up in a track about halfway between the crash site, marked as scene one, and the murder site, marked as scene two. This ties in with DS Parker and DC Milson's statements regarding our shooter." He pointed at a map now up on the lower left of the screen. "Alice left work every day at 6.15 p.m., and drove the same route home. She worked the same three days every single week, according to her son and our sig wit, Sarah."

"Her routine would have been easy to pick up on," Lindsey commented, brushing back her short curls with an impatient hand. Her brow was furrowed as she considered the information. "But as she lives alone in a caravan in the middle of nowhere, why not just kill her at home? Why go to the trouble of setting up an accident scene, which might not have worked if another vehicle came along first anyway?"

"It must be significant to the perpetrator or perpetrators," the DCI said. "It's a very bold move — a carefully planned sequence of events leading to the elaborate staging of the body, with the stone in the victim's mouth. Possibly she wasn't meant to be found until the next morning?"

DI Blackman continued, tapping Sarah Whitmore's name on the board. "More sig wit info." He pointed to the garden centre and nursery in Bear Green on the whiteboard, and then pulled up a map on screen. "Alice departed from work at 6.15 p.m. as usual but left her purse. Sarah stayed until 6.45 p.m. tidying up, and she started her drive to Alice's caravan to return her purse at around 7.20 p.m. She did try to ring Alice and left a voicemail. She didn't take the route through these country lanes, where the accident was staged, but instead took a longer route along the main road, approaching the caravan from the north on Swallows Lane." He tapped the map with the electronic pointer.

The DCI took over. "Sarah Whitmore stated she couldn't see Alice's car when she arrived, so assumed she must have stopped off on the way home for some reason. She knocked on the door, heard the dog bark from his kennel, but heard nothing else. She tried Alice's mobile again and left a message." He paused and took a mouthful of coffee, scanning the room for comments.

DC Josh Conrad, in the seat next to Dove, was scrolling through documents on his iPad and he looked up, frowning. "The friend who returned her purse was an anomaly, out of pattern, and must have shocked the perpetrator."

"Sarah didn't see anyone or another vehicle until the possible shooter's vehicle went past a few minutes after her

31

999 call at 8.10 p.m.," Dove said, scanning the statement, "yet given the timeframe we have, it's likely she just missed the perpetrator leaving Alice's caravan. Steve and I were at the car crash scene at 7.15 p.m.," she added.

DI Blackman commented, "The pathologist will be able to tell us more, but CSM is fairly confident our victim was still alive when she reached her home. There are no signs of a struggle in the caravan itself, or of any break-in. According to Jess's initial findings, it appears she may have been tortured before death, and bled out in seconds after a femoral artery was hit. Did she know her attacker?"

"No indication she suffered the fatal hit before she got inside the caravan, and no indication she was forced inside. Lots of rage in those injuries," commented DS Pete Wyndham, rubbing his moustache with a thoughtful hand. "She pissed someone off good and proper and she knew it. She must have put up one hell of a struggle initially at the crash site, so why did she stop fighting? Because she was finally incapacitated, or taken hostage up to the point of her death?"

CHAPTER EIGHT

"How was her son, Martin?" DCI Franklin asked.

"As you would expect, until the news came through that a ton of cocaine had been found hidden in the linings of his car doors." Pete grinned. "Maybe not quite literally a ton . . . He went from grieving son to *I want my solicitor* in a millisecond. My first impressions of him would be that he is genuinely devastated at his mum's death, but is now shitting himself he might have done something to cause it. He has previous for some minor possession charges dating back to 2006."

"I thought he had no previous?" Dove queried, puzzled. "I'm sure it got checked out before Firearms went down to his place."

Pete shrugged. "Hat Trick losing his grip?"

"Doubt it," Dove said coldly. Pete could be bitchy at times, his comments supposedly humorous but actually sharp. "They were pushed, so maybe someone gave him the wrong intel."

"Thanks, DS Wyndham. Right, let's get cracking," DCI Franklin said, and Dove saw thankfully he was ignoring the daggers two of his team were looking at each other, as the DIs began to assign duties. Tempers always flared at key stages, and everyone was exhausted, working, as she had told Pete, at full stretch for months due to the staffing issues. Mistakes happened. The police officers were only human, after all.

Usually priding herself on needing less sleep than an average person, even Dove was yawning by half one, the initial energy rush wearing thin. In these early stages of the investigation, information usually came in from officers on the ground pretty quickly. In this case, the search team from scene one, the crash site, had already submitted their report. Every piece of potential evidence, right down to the litter in the hedge at the roadside, had been bagged and tagged.

Scrolling through, Dove could see plenty of evidence had been sent to Forensics, and the summary was clear and concise. DI Hattrick — 'Hat Trick' — was, as she had said to Pete, extremely competent. She traced the timeline through yet again. An hour. An hour from the time Alice likely had swerved off the road to avoid the baby, made her way on foot through the woods, and was followed and attacked (and possibly tortured?) in her home.

Jess had added a note that Alice was extremely fit and muscular for her age, and Dove remembered seeing a rack of medals hanging proudly on the caravan wall in the crime scene photos that were being downloaded to the main file. She also figured that explained how the woman had managed the trek up to her caravan before finally keeling over.

Technical Support called in a possible suspect vehicle at 1 a.m., by which time Dove, on her third coffee, had the caffeine jitters. There was a buzz of excited chatter as the team in the office responded to this discovery.

The CCTV and traffic cam had been able to trace a black Range Rover Discovery from a set of traffic lights about half a mile from scene one, as the crash site was labelled. It was travelling extremely fast and had been caught on cameras near the town centre on one of the industrial estates. The last sighting was on Coast Road, the vehicle heading west out of town at 8.41 p.m.

Dove frowned, noting the last comment. The registration number was illegible to the cameras, probably deliberately blacked out with mud or paint.

By 2 a.m., as the initial findings had been sifted, the DCI called them back in and divided the teams. Dove's half would go home for a couple of hours' sleep, with instructions to be back for 6 a.m., while the night shift would continue and take the day rest. There was no nine-to-five in policing, and normally Dove loved the unpredictable hours, but she had just worked what amounted to a sixteen-hour day and she felt shattered.

Luckily, in the still hours between the last swathe of heavy darkness and the first glimmer of early morning light, the roads were quiet. She drove along the coast, seeing several homeless people camped out in the shelters on the seafront, trolleys and boxes piled up around them. The orange glow of a few cigarettes lit the darkness, and the dying flickers of a bonfire on the beach provided a yellow glow and the scent of smoky embers, which filtered in through the slightly open windows.

Dove liked to drive with plenty of ventilation, which annoyed both Steve and Quinn, the people she most shared a vehicle with. But she shrugged it off. She liked fresh air, not fuggy air conditioning, even in the winter months.

A group of men were staggering along the pavement past the pier, singing loudly and drunkenly, but they seemed happy enough. They veered alarmingly near the road, and she slowed down and gave them a wide berth.

The drive home only took twenty minutes at this time of night, and she passed the construction site, the road to the marina, noting a few kids on bikes in the shadows next to a grubby, salt-stained terrace notorious for drug dealers. The flotsam and jetsam of coastal life. Familiar landmarks.

She wondered again if Alice Cartwright had died because of her son's involvement in drugs. If so, he was going to bear a heavy burden. And prison time, too.

The small, Victorian end-of-terrace house she shared with her fiancé had no parking, so as usual Dove was forced to park near the end of the road. She didn't mind. The soft early spring darkness on the coast was salty and soothing. The waves rumbled in the near distance as she fumbled for her key.

Quaintly historical Abberley, with its pretty cobbled streets and tourist-trap ancient buildings, had long since been swallowed by brash, concrete-and-glass Lymington-on-Sea. The land between the two settlements had been covered in a rash of new housing and industrial estates, and now the uneasy alliance provided a perfect venue for partygoers and tourists from London. Those seeking the clubs and all-night entertainment headed along the road to Lymington, and those seeking peace and sunshine stayed in Abberley.

It was a great place for Dove, who, as Quinn often said, was a city girl with a beach lover's heart. She loved the proximity of the coastline, but also the gritty darkness of the city's underbelly. Both fed her psyche in different ways.

Dove sent a text to check in with Steve, before crawling into bed, accompanied by Layla, the smooth-coated, golden-eyed cat who had turned up soon after Dove moved in. Layla had made it plain she had chosen her home and Dove, initially concerned she had no time for a pet, soon realized Layla was totally independent and very vocal at feeding time.

She hugged her knees up under the duvet, wriggling into a sitting position, trying to warm up, and the cat purred approvingly. Her fiancé Quinn was still working his own night shift, but she put in a quick call and caught him on a break.

"Hi, babe, how's it going?"

"Knackered. Got to be back in at six, so I'll miss you coming home. How's your shift?"

"Yeah, not too bad. It'll be quiet for an hour or so now, until everyone starts falling out of bed at around four a.m. How's Steve? You said earlier they thought it was just a scratch?"

"I think it hurt more than he let on, but the medics said it was just a surface wound."

He was silent for a moment. "You think the shooter was watching you both from the trees the whole time?"

"Maybe . . . It's all guesswork at the moment. Maybe he killed the victim, came back down the track in the woods, saw a couple of strangers nosing around and let out a warning shot? The dog handler picked up trails in the woods so we know the route she took, but he followed her, hunted her down."

"Jesus. That poor woman."

"I know, and it was really tight, too, the whole thing was over in under an hour judging by the time our witness arrived."

"Crap, I need to clock back on. Well, see you sometime, babe, and stay safe."

"You too, Quinn."

His voice was comforting, grounding as always and she ended the call half smiling at her fiancé, and half frowning at the complexities of the new case.

She had hardly been asleep when she found herself showering, feeding the cat, and driving to the police station again. Over the years she had tried to train herself to sleep deeply for a couple of hours and come out of it fully refreshed. Sometimes it worked, but generally it didn't.

CHAPTER NINE

Dove stopped only to grab a coffee from the machine before a short briefing. No further information had emerged on the suspect vehicle, and lab results were backed up as usual, so they could be waiting on forensics for hours or even days.

DI Blackman called over to her, "Dove, can you do an intel search on those pebbles or stone hearts, and when Steve arrives, I want you to both head out to talk to our witness again, Sarah Whitmore. She called and asked if someone would go to her house. I know . . . I know," he read her expression with ease, "but she was really insistent and hell, we haven't got any other big leads at the moment apart from the shooter's getaway vehicle, so jump on it." He glanced down at his phone, which was buzzing on the table, and silenced the device with a quick tap.

"Sorry. Right, Lindsey and Josh, check out the CCTV and traffic cam and see if we can get a handle on this suspect vehicle and driver. It was dumped round the back on an industrial estate so check it out."

"On it, boss," Lindsey said briskly. She didn't look exhausted at all, Dove thought sourly as she booted up her computer, and Josh was his usual bouncy self. His team nickname was Tigger, and he didn't appear to need sleep.

Other pairs were dispersed to follow up with known contacts and check out the leads generated by the reports coming in. As there were drugs involved, the regional drugs squad would also be involved. Soon other information, from the first responders and from the uniform teams who had been conducting door-to-door searches, would start to come in. Dove yawned widely, and Lindsey slapped her on the back. "You're getting too old for this early morning stuff, aren't you, Milson?" But her eyes glinted with mischief.

"Yeah, it's all downhill from now on," Dove told her. "I need caffeine and sugar and I'll be fine."

"Great stuff! Wait until you hit forty, mate, then it really takes an effort to get out of bed." Lindsey grinned before yelling to her partner and the two were soon hunkered down at their own computers.

Dove grabbed another two coffees from the machine in the corridor and passed one to Steve, who had just arrived. "How are you feeling?"

"Fine, I'm on the painkillers, but it's all good and I've been cleared for duty. Zara is not impressed and has specifically told me not to do anything dangerous. Thanks for the coffee. Did you manage to see Quinn this morning?"

"Yeah, we spoke briefly, and he just texted to say he's going to bed now and to have a nice day!" She grinned, thinking that once again Quinn was on a run of night shifts and they were going to be passing each other briefly on shift changeovers.

"Pretty much what Zara said this morning, except she's working from home with the two monsters climbing all over her. Luckily her mum's coming over to take the kids out for a couple of hours at lunchtime." Steve smiled fondly. He had two daughters, and the youngest was only two months old. "I wonder if I'll ever get to sleep through the night again. Sometimes I think I just come to work for a rest . . . What did I miss and what are we doing?"

Dove laughed, told him and took a gulp of her coffee as she attacked her keyboard with vigour, pulling up multiple files and searches on the intelligence database. This was a vital piece of kit for the police, enabling different areas to compare crimes like for like, searching for patterns and potential perpetrators.

"It's a really standout scene, so we shouldn't have trouble with matches," Steve said, tearing open a packet of crisps, sneaking a sidelong glance at Dove.

She grinned but didn't comment on his choice of snack.

Steve continued, "The torture and stone heart elements lend themselves more to a gang hit, though. Perhaps Martin Cartwright is smarter and a bit more dangerous than we initially gave him credit for?"

"Yeah, I was thinking that too. Maybe it was a warning to Martin?"

* * *

"And we have a hit," Dove announced half an hour later.

"What is it?" Steve had just put the phone down after arranging a meet with Sarah Whitmore, the witness.

Dove jabbed the screen. "2008. Evan Houselow was discovered unconscious at his place of work, having been hit from behind with a heavy object. He had a small, roughly carved heart-shaped object placed in his mouth and was lucky he was found relatively quickly by a member of the family."

"He lived on the Seaview Estate. Not far from here, and very much not our favourite place," Steve pointed out.

The Seaview was a huge, sprawling estate further down the coast, ruled by three organized crime families, and law enforcement was never welcome.

"He was attacked at his place of work after he arrived to unlock the gates at five a.m.," Dove carried on reading. "He didn't see his attacker and claimed to have no memory of the attack."

Steve was reading over her shoulder. "In an unrelated case, Evan was later arrested and charged with child cruelty and was also involved in an investigation over the alleged death of a child. He wasn't charged on that one because there was no evidence."

Dove looked up. "He sounds like a right joy to be around. No wonder someone whacked him over the head. Looks like he came out of prison in January this year. And he has a previous for illegal firearm procession in 2005. And drugs. In this case pills and some blow in 2006 and 2007, but not enough to upgrade to a dealing charge." As usual when a connection was made, she felt a renewed rush of energy and purpose, which probably had something to do this morning with the caffeine and the second bag of fruit pastilles she was munching her way through. Occasionally a thought flitted through her head that she should be following a more sensible diet instead of relying on sugar and caffeine to get her through her working days and nights. But only occasionally.

"Shit. I wonder if he owns a black Range Rover Discovery . . . Or am I being cynical?" Steve pondered. "Did Alice get caught in the crossfire of something she was totally unaware of?"

"Could be. No known gang connections." Dove finished reading the intel on Evan Houselow. "Well, he was the victim in the stone heart case. The rest is interesting as background. DI Christie Marks. I'll try and get a number now," Dove suggested. She pulled up the details of the case and sent them to her phone, before grabbing her coat as she headed out, closely followed by Steve.

"Lots to go on, though. If you find out who was SIO investigating his attack, I'll send this lot over to the boss so he can get someone to chase up Evan." Steve glanced at his watch. "I said we'd see our sig wit in half an hour. She lives in Bear Green, near the garden centre."

Her brain was buzzing. Why the stone hearts in the mouths? It was surely too bizarre for there not to be some kind of connection between the two cases, even so many years apart. She would see if there were photographs of the stone discovered in Evan's mouth. Both stones from their current investigation were beach pebbles, carved and painted, so fairly distinctive. As Hat Trick had suggested, they looked like the kind of thing you might find in one of the little pop-up galleries and craft shops down on the seafront.

"I wonder why she wants to see us? She wouldn't say on the phone," Steve said.

"Hopefully it's something super useful, or we could have been following the lead on Evan. Or hunting down beach pebble artists." Dove, in the passenger seat, was rereading Sarah's witness statement.

Sometimes, sleep could jog the memory and reveal vital evidence after the initial shock had subsided. She hoped this would be the case. It would also be interesting to ask the woman again why she had taken a different route to her friend's home to return the purse. The purse had been found, as Sarah had stated, on the floor of the caravan where she had dropped it in shock.

"Beach pebble art?" Steve queried.

"Doesn't matter! Hey, Sarah says she checked to see if Alice was breathing, but it was obvious she was dead." Dove frowned. "It must have been a matter of minutes between her killer leaving and Sarah's arrival. You'd think Sarah might have at least tried to help her, instead of running away."

"Be fair," Steve said. "She's just seen her friend covered in blood, and with that arterial bleed there were serious spatters on the wall, the floor. It was horrific from the photos, and you've seen what these scenes are like. *And* it's a remote location in the dark. I think it's plausible she freaked out and ran for it."

"I wonder if she noticed the stone in Alice's mouth? It isn't mentioned in her statement," Dove replied thoughtfully. "She says she got close enough to see if she was breathing, before she ran for it. And she took a different route to her friend's house. Did she deliberately avoid the lane so she didn't run into the ambush?"

CHAPTER TEN

I don't often feel things, but it hurts my heart to see her like this. On the outside she's fine, but on the inside, I know something is broken and it has been for a long time. Should I tell her what I suspect? What I know must be true. Our relationship hangs by a fragile thread, and my secrets are not all her secrets.

I study my face in the mirror, inspecting my eye colour, the shape of my mouth and chin. For some reason my physical appearance has become more important in the last few months. I loop my hair back, add some hair product and smile. It looks fake. I stop smiling.

Between all of us there is a certain something, just a faint mirror of an image, like a tracing that won't quite fit over the original. It shows in the tilt of a head, the gesture of a hand, or the way we turn our bodies.

Does that make me the original, or the copy? Who was first and who was last, really?

There is a twist of white powder still left in my pocket and I lay out a couple of lines on the glass table. No more questioning today. I am happy, supremely confident in my own judgement, and I have made my decisions.

CHAPTER ELEVEN

The road leading from the crash site to the caravan was still cordoned off with blue-and-white tape, so they took the longer route along the main road.

"I still think it's worth flagging that Sarah took this route to return Alice's purse. I mean, the other way is shorter and more direct," Dove pondered, dipping into the jelly sweets in her pocket. Damn, the packet was nearly empty.

Steve overtook a tractor and outsize trailer with care and shrugged. "Maybe she just didn't think. There isn't that much in it."

Bear Green was a small village just outside Abberley, and only a couple of miles from the victim's caravan. Just a few farms, a square of red-brick new-builds and a slightly dubious-looking pub with cracked shutters and a faded sign.

Springley Garden Centre was a collection of glasshouses and straggling untidy plastic, and sprawled, an unsightly eyesore, to the west of the village. As they passed the garden centre, Dove finally managed to get the number of the DI in charge of the Evan Houselow assault and Steve parked outside Sarah Whitmore's house as Dove put the call on speakerphone.

"Christ, that's a blast from the past!" DI Christie Marks had a shrill but commanding voice.

Dove explained the similarity with their current case. "Did you ever have a suspect?"

"A list as long as your arm. He was an evil fucker, that Evan Houselow. I assume you have accessed the file, but nobody was talking on the Seaview, so we never got even within sniffing distance of an arrest for a minor assault on a known bastard."

"How unusual," Dove commented sarcastically.

DI Marks laughed. "Right. The investigation was hindered by the usual *nobody saw anything* response and it was also right before CPS took his child abuse case forward, which again as you probably already know, he was sent down for. So bottom line was, nobody really cared Houselow had been assaulted when it was known he had been abusing his kids."

"He was living with a girlfriend?" Dove had checked the file.

"Mostly. It was an on/off relationship from what we could gather. Lily, I think her name was. The pair liked to mix blow and alcohol so spent a lot of time raging round completely off their heads. There were four kids who gave evidence, as I remember. All his own kids, and it was claimed there were at least eight more, but nobody could pin them down. It was a big case."

"And the murder of a baby?"

"That was an odd one. Not my case because I was working on him as the victim, but the family couldn't seem to agree if there ever was a baby. There was a tip-off and the search teams found baby clothes in the lake behind Abel's Gym, but no body. Lily was off her head on drugs and there were no medical records to prove she had given birth within the last couple of months, so I think the general consensus seemed to be that Evan was looking like he was going down for it but in case he didn't, one of his neighbours decided to take a bit of justice into their own hands and try to frame him for murder, so it became a sure thing. Why the interest anyway?"

"We had two stone hearts at two recent scenes. One was found in the victim's mouth." Dove gave her a quick summary.

"Right." She was quiet for a moment. "In the mouth of the victim and in a baby seat?"

"Right."

"It seems odd that Evan was the victim, and now he's a suspect . . . I suppose this woman can't be the person he suspects of his own assault. Revenge?"

"Pretty harsh revenge for a whack on the head. Yeah, it doesn't make that much sense, but it's the only match we have on the intel," Dove said thoughtfully.

"He was, and I imagine is, a very arrogant man. Ego as big as the marina, and well . . . you get where I'm going with this. Right . . ." There was a sound of scuffle and shouting in the background. "Sorry, got to go, but get back in touch if I can help with anything else. Try Houselow's probation officer. See if he's been keeping his nose clean."

Dove called this information through to DI Blackman.

"DI Lincoln and DC Amin are going to bring Evan in for a chat now," he told her. "He's staying in a sheltered housing flat near the Westdean Industrial Estate, which is where the CCTV picked up our suspect vehicle last night. Even better, uniform have just found a black Range Rover Discovery in one of the derelict garages at the back of the industrial estate. See what else you can get from our witness. If she knows of a connection between Alice Cartwright and Evan Houselow that would do nicely for starters."

* * *

Sarah Whitmore was dressed in pink tracksuit trousers and a white T-shirt. Her short grey hair feathered around her face, and she had dark circles under her eyes.

"I still can't believe it. It was shocking." Sarah blinked hard. "Alice was always so full of life, and so energetic. She walked miles with the dog every day, and she always said she would never retire. She ran a marathon last year! You know, I said all of this in my statement."

"Right. But you did specifically ring the station this morning and request another visit?" Dove checked, a flash of irritation spiking her words at the thought of a wasted journey.

"I know I did, and I want to help find out who did this. I thought maybe if we could go through it one more time, I might remember something else . . ." Sarah looked miserable, her voice trailing away.

"Right. But nothing extra at the moment?" Dove prodded.

"Not really . . ."

"Had you known Alice long?" Steve asked, glancing at his watch. Dove could tell he was also frustrated.

"Oh, ages. We've been through such a lot together. Children, husbands, and then when we both retired the garden centre seemed to be perfect. A couple of days' work a week just to keep us out of trouble." Sarah brightened slightly.

"Did you work together before you retired?" Dove asked.

"Alice was a midwife." She smiled. "She always loved babies and she was such a caring person. We just knew each other from mutual friends, perhaps around the time she married Gerald . . . Forty years ago? They just had the one son, like Oscar and I. Martin has already been in touch. He's devastated, poor lad. Would you like a drink?" Sarah got up abruptly and went into her kitchen without waiting for an answer.

"We're good, thanks, but if you need a drink go ahead," Dove called after her, and exchanged glances with Steve. Sarah wasn't currently a suspect and there was no evidence from the scene to suggest she had done anything that wasn't already in her statement. "You mentioned you have a son too? Is he able to come and be with you?"

"Jack is working up in London this week. But he is due back later today and he's asked me to go and stay for a while. He lives in Abberley." Her voice trailed off and there was the sound of a tap running.

Sarah returned from the kitchen, carrying a glass of water. She had filled it a little too full and water slopped onto the carpet as she walked. "Oh!" Tears started to run down her cheeks, and Dove snatched a wad of tissues from the box on the coffee table and mopped up the mess.

47

"It's okay. It must have been a terrible shock and we understand you are grieving, but anything you can remember or tell us might help us to understand what happened to Alice," Steve said gently.

Sarah darted a glance at him, and then at Dove. She opened her mouth and hesitated before shaking her head and shoving another load of tissues into her face to mop up more tears.

"Were you in the medical profession as well, Sarah?" Dove realized her earlier question had not been answered.

"No!" It was too sharp, too loud, and she must have felt it as well because she tried to smile at them, "I was a social worker on the area child protection team, so I rarely saw Alice in a work capacity. We only saw each other as friends, not really colleagues."

"Right. I know this is hard, but did you notice anything unusual when you found her?" Dove asked, watching her carefully.

"No . . . I just . . . I don't know. It was awful of me to run away but I was terrified, it was so dark, and I just didn't think . . . I could tell she was dead." Her eyes were pleading with them to understand, "If there had been a chance that she was breathing I would have stayed and, you know, done something while I called for help. She was dead, wasn't she?"

CHAPTER TWELVE

"We will need to wait for the official report to confirm but it does look as though she probably died before you arrived." Dove leaned in and showed the woman the photograph of the stone heart on her iPad screen. "Does that mean anything to you?"

Sarah shook her head, "No, sorry, nothing springs to mind. Where did you get it? Does it belong to Alice?"

"It's a stone heart, probably a pebble from the beach, but worked on to give it more shape, and painted red. Does that have any significance to Alice that you can possibly think of?"

The woman licked her lips nervously, peering at the photograph. "Well, Alice did like art and crafty things. She went on a painting course down on the beach last year, arranged by the little gallery . . ." Sarah seemed to realize she was rambling and abruptly stopped before staring at the pebble again. "Where did you say you found this?"

"It was in Alice's mouth."

"*Oh!*" Sarah was deathly pale now, one hand creeping up to clutch at the folds of her T-shirt over her own heart as she stared at the photograph.

"Sarah?"

"I don't know anything. Sorry, I really don't. I thought I could be more helpful . . . My brain isn't working properly. If you leave a card, I can ring you if I remember anything else."

"One last thing," Dove said as they rose to leave. "Does the name Evan Houselow mean anything to you?"

If Sarah had been pale before, now her face was ghost-white and Dove put out a swift reassuring hand to touch her arm, almost fearing she would faint. "Sarah? Are you okay?"

"No, I don't know the name. Goodbye."

She hustled them out and slammed the door shut behind them.

Back in the car Steve turned to Dove. "Well, she was pretty terrified, and I wouldn't say it was of us."

"You think Alice and Sarah might have been somehow involved in Evan's child cruelty conviction?"

"Why?"

"She was a social worker in child protection and Alice was a midwife, both working with babies. Something connects them, and the perpetrator has shown us this case is all about babies, unless we're missing something. Sarah was freaking out when we mentioned Evan's name."

"But Sarah isn't the one who's dead."

"No."

They drove in silence for a while, until the DI called. Dove put him on speaker and quickly updated him.

"Makes sense. Can you get down to the mortuary next? Apparently, Dr Isiah has got something interesting to show us. He has a backlog as usual, but we managed a small queue jump because our victim is interesting." There was a note of amusement in DI Blackman's voice.

Dove wasn't keen on the mortuary and the labs, but she did find pathology fascinating. As she had promised herself that she would try for promotion at the end of the year she also felt it would be a good chance to further her knowledge. Dove had the greatest respect for Dr Isiah, who was eccentric, a law unto himself and extremely intelligent. "Sure, we can do it. Maybe twenty minutes?"

They did it in fifteen, parked up and headed to the reception for their passes. Dove inhaled deeply before the automatic doors leading to the labs opened with a smooth hiss. The corridors beyond, smelling of disinfectant and death, led directly to the state-of-the art facilities and labs. Just as he had a few years ago, around the time of the Glass Dolls case, Dr Isiah had mysteriously secured private funding to get his facilities updated a couple of years ago.

After being issued with passes, they gowned, masked and gloved up before following a member of the team into the lab.

A digital clock flicked through the seconds on the wall, a reminder in this place of time passing, Dove always thought. She nodded at her boss, CSM, Jess and another officer. Various members of the team were present at each stage of the investigation, to ensure continuity and documentation was followed through. Any inconsistencies could lose a case or result in the CPS rejecting what had previously been watertight findings.

Dr Isiah nodded at them from behind his thick, wide-rimmed glasses. As always, he moved with grace and precision as he worked.

He also always got straight to the point, with no chit-chat. "You can see her tooth was broken before the stone was inserted, probably from a blow from a fist or blunt object. We have yet to confirm. It isn't very big, and even if she had been alive, it wouldn't have been large enough to obstruct her airway entirely. Of course, if she was conscious, she would have coughed, spat it out," he added.

"Jess thought there was something else in her throat," the DI said impatiently.

A stern glance told them to wait until he was ready to share. "Yeeeess, there was something else." Very carefully, documenting the whole thing via camera and Dictaphone, the pathology team moved through their routine.

With no discernible shaking of his hands, Dr Isaiah removed a small slip of pink plastic.

"Bloody hell, this case is like a Halloween horror show," Steve muttered indistinctly from behind his mask. "What is that thing?"

The item was photographed, measured and then unfurled with tweezers.

Dr Isiah spoke for the recording, ". . . A pink hospital bracelet. It is extremely small, measuring just two inches long, suggesting its intended use might be for a baby or small child."

CHAPTER THIRTEEN

Stepping out of the harsh artificial lights and stench of disinfectant, Dove inhaled the salty city air gratefully, relieved to be back outside. An interesting find, as the DI had said. That was a bloody understatement. She was sure she hadn't imagined even Dr Isiah's eyes lighting up when he extracted the pink bracelet.

DI Blackman, who had followed them out, indicated to his car, and spoke over his shoulder as he walked towards it, "I've got to do some press now. Can you go and talk to Gemma Rogers on the Seaview? I'll send the address over. She is the last person Alice called on her mobile at 6.30 p.m. last night, so either as she walked to her car or while she was driving home. The call lasted six minutes."

"Sure." Dove pulled a face at Steve, and he grimaced. "We think Sarah knows more than she's letting on," she went on, "and she didn't really give us anything to add to her statement from last night, so we have no idea why she requested another visit. We wondered if she feels threatened, if she's somehow involved." She unlocked the car and pulled the door open as she spoke.

"Okay, sounds plausible. Does she know Evan Houselow?"

"Says not, but she looked absolutely terrified when we mentioned his name. The stone thing really freaked her out. Maybe she knows why it was in Alice's mouth?"

The DI nodded. "We're waiting on lab results for the Range Rover, but Evan is claiming someone is setting him up, and making a fuss, so unless we get a positive ID or some decent evidence, we'll have to leave him for the time being. DI Marks sent over some more stuff from the previous case, where Evan was the victim. Oh, and we are still waiting for the lab re: DNA from the scene, as previously mentioned. I wish we could afford a bloody rapid test!"

"Yeah, great, thanks, boss." Dove waved him off as he drove away, before sliding into her own vehicle. She looked at Steve, who was already in the passenger seat. "I really am not looking forward to the Seaview. Last time I was there we lost a couple of wheels, and Quinn's been to call-outs where they took all *four* wheels and left the truck balanced on piles of bricks." She sighed as she navigated through the afternoon traffic on the coast road, heading out of town.

Steve agreed, "We drew the short straw. At least we don't have to talk to Evan. I feel like I might have some trouble being objective having had a glimpse of what he did to those kids."

The rain had stopped but low clouds had rolled in from the English Channel, cloaking the Seaview Estate in a swirling grey dankness.

They drove slowly along the road, looking for number eighty-six. The roads and buildings were mainly well kept and no different from the same type of development in any other area of town. But here and there glimpses of the undercurrent showed. Burnt-out cars rammed in a kids' playground. Graffiti decorating the garage blocks, a rundown gym surrounded by a sea of plastic bags and empty bottles.

Gemma Rogers's house was on the southern edge of the estate, next to a haulage yard. The noise of lorries and a fine mist of dust rose over the wall, which was topped with razor wire.

Dove glanced at the sign next to the yard entrance. "I remember a few years ago when the Nicholls Haulage lorries were used to transport all sorts of things that weren't your normal cargo."

"I haven't heard of any trouble recently," Steve said. "In fact, I had to interview the boss, Andy, on a case right before you joined. He was really helpful and said he knew there was a past to the business, but he was going straight."

"It was two brothers who ran it," Dove remembered, turning away from the yard. "I know one died in a stabbing, and last I heard the other was away for a long stretch."

A woman was standing in the doorway of number eighty-six, chatting to a young mum with a double buggy filled with two angelic-looking toddlers, plus an older child who was jumping in puddles, shrieking with laughter as his red wellies overflowed with water.

His mum was laughing, but the blonde woman in the doorway called out, briskly telling him to get out before he got completely soaked.

As the police officers approached, both women and children fell silent and glared at them.

"Catalina, I'll see you tomorrow, darling. Go on, Jordan, your mum needs to get the babies home for dinner."

The woman with the buggy adjusted a shoulder bag and steered her family past Steve and Dove, eyes downcast, although all three children now blinked curiously at them.

"Gemma Rogers?" Steve cautiously introduced himself and Dove.

"Yeah, you can come in." She gave a quick look up and down the road before she almost shoved them through the door.

Gemma had long bleach-blonde hair extensions, sharp, suspicious green eyes fringed with long black false lashes, and a very bright red lipstick. Her long red wool dress showed off her curves and her feet were bare.

Although she was curt with the two police officers, Dove saw how her expression and tone of voice altered completely when she bent down to speak to the two children playing Lego on the floor.

They both picked up their toys and went off to another room, where other children could be heard talking and laughing. Gemma yelled at someone to put the kettle on.

"What do you want then?"

"We are making routine enquiries after the murder of Alice Cartwright," Steve explained. "Did you know her?"

Gemma sat down on the couch and stretched her feet out with a sigh. Beneath the paint and polish, she looked exhausted, Dove realized suddenly.

"Did you know Alice?"

Gemma frowned and ran a hand through her extensions, slowly, thoughtfully combing out the tangles with her fingers. "No."

Dove turned her iPad round to show Gemma a photograph of Alice. "Are you sure? Have you ever seen her around?"

Gemma stared at the photograph before shaking her head. "No. I mean, I've seen her on the news this morning, but I don't know her." The piercing green glare took in both officers. "She was a midwife at Arrowhill Hospital, wasn't she, they said on the TV?"

"Yes. She retired in 2012."

Gemma shrugged. "Lucky her." She got up and heaved a plastic basket of laundry onto the tabletop.

Steve's voice was quiet but stern. "Any idea at all why the last call she made before her death was to your mobile number?"

CHAPTER FOURTEEN

I watched him carry my sister away.

I bashed my fists on the window, shouting, screaming as he walked through the kitchen, picking his way over the debris I knew littered the floor.

But he never heard me, and the others couldn't understand what I was trying to do. They didn't understand anything. Too young or too bloody stupid. Frustration welled up, tears falling as I carried on scream-ing until he was gone. I never even saw a car, but I knew that was it.

He had done it before, and he would do it again. Always the babies, always the smile. Should I have told someone? Of course not. Nobody would believe me, just like nobody would believe me if I tried to tell them what goes on down here.

She was my real sister. A tiny, beautiful bundle of perfection. I held her gently in my arms the day she came home from hospital and fell in love. Instead of a future of screeching and stinky nappies, I saw only her delicate, petal-like features, felt her little fingers curling and uncurling in my hands. I could have made it different. I could have protected her. I should have protected her, but I let her down when I kept silent.

I wondered, for a long time afterwards, if it was my fault for doing things, or for not doing things. Either way I lost someone who was precious to me, and the only one who has ever truly touched my heart.

I wasn't supposed to hear her name, I learned that very quickly, but I kept the name in my mind, tucked close to my heart, as though by doing that I could keep her safe too.

That hot, sweltering July evening, I swore I would find her one day, and that I would find him too. We would meet on equal terms, and he would pay for what he did.

A week later the police came to drag the lake. I watched the divers and listened to the gossip. I was there when they found it, but for me it didn't change anything. I know what I saw, and nobody could take away the pictures in my head.

She was there, and then she wasn't.

CHAPTER FIFTEEN

Gemma froze, her eyes narrowing, lips pursing. Before she answered, she grabbed a blanket from a pile of laundry and started to fold it in quick, neat squares. "No . . . Now you showed me the photo I was thinking I might have met her. I mean, she looked after babies, I look after babies, but like, not in the same way."

"Did she call you last night?" Dove asked.

"I don't know, I don't remember any call. Maybe she called and it went to voicemail."

"Can we see your phone please, Gemma?"

She brushed her hair back in a dismissive gesture. "Oh, do you know what, I gave it to one of the kids this morning when they were out playing, and they bloody lost it."

"Come off it, Gemma. What did Alice say to you? The poor woman is dead, and if you know something, anything at all, it could help catch her killer. Or would you rather do this down at the station? You could be a key witness in this investigation." Steve was losing patience, and his tone was brisk.

There was silence for a minute, as Gemma weighed up her options, the internal struggle evident in her face.

"Okay, fine. I know her. My kids were born at Arrowhill, apart from bloody Lolla, who came out on the kitchen floor."

She gave a short and shaky laugh, transforming her face from hard and suspicious to approachable and amusing. The flash of character was gone in an instant. "Have you two got kids?"

Steve jumped in to answer, but the woman still looked questioningly at Dove. She winced a little, but the answer was ready. "No, I don't."

Bland, giving nothing away, she thought, but the green eyes probed for a moment and a quick nod, before Gemma took a deep breath. "It's true I've lost my phone. I did know Alice, okay? Not properly, just because I stayed in touch with her after I met her at Arrowhill. I had Archie, Lolla and then the twins, and there were complications. They were born at thirty-one weeks. She looked after me."

Dove waited, hardly daring to breathe, as Gemma continued. "She was kind, and she didn't judge. A lot of people judge if the dad isn't around, or if you live down here and have a lot of kids. It's not for them to say who's a good mother and who isn't.

"I had a couple of miscarriages after that, and I needed a D&C twice, so I was in hospital for the operations. She was there again, just coming off duty or taking a tea break, popping in to check on me. She didn't have to come and find me after a long shift, but she did. Arrowhill was like that. You felt safe and it was small, so you got to know some of the staff. If you were a new mum, you felt like they were on your side."

"So, you've known Alice for how many years?"

"Ages. We weren't, like, close friends, but maybe once a year we'd catch up. She told me her ex-husband had been diagnosed with dementia, and her son, Martin, he's a bit older than me and he went off the rails and started doing drugs for a bit . . . I think he's all right now. Grown up a bit, as Alice said!" She laughed again.

"And why did Alice call you last night?" Steve probed.

"It was just a quick chat to see if I was free for a cuppa next week. She loves seeing all the kids when she comes round. I haven't seen her for about eight months now, but I said yes. We fixed a time for next Tuesday and that was it."

"What time was this?"

"Maybe 6 p.m. Or maybe a bit later . . . I'm not really sure."

"Any reason why you denied knowing her when we first asked you?" Dove put in, carefully.

"None of your business, really. I didn't kill her and whoever did, it's nothing to do with me. I don't need any trouble, do you understand?" Her expression was hard, but her eyes were filled with grief. "She was a good person, and I can't think why anyone would want to hurt her."

"What about any other friends or work colleagues of Alice's? Did she ever talk to you about any disagreements, anyone who might have cause to hurt her?"

"No! I told you, we didn't keep in touch that often, and you must be joking. Like I said, nobody would want to hurt her. She moved to the caravan after her divorce because she wanted space and peace. Rather her than me, but I could tell she was happy."

"Do you know this woman?" Dove showed her a picture of witness Sarah Whitmore.

Gemma studied the photo. "No. She another midwife?"

"Why do you ask?"

She shrugged, and then smiled as two teenagers came in with mugs of tea. A girl and a boy, probably around thirteen. They could have passed for older, and the boy had a scar across his forehead, reaching down like a hook to one eye. They both scarpered as soon as they had dumped the mugs on the table.

"How many kids are you looking after today?" Steve asked.

Gemma smiled. "Feels like hundreds, but only six today. There's always a space at my place. I've been child-minding since I was fifteen and as soon as I got my own place it just meant I could take in more kids. Most of this side of the estate uses me to mind their kids."

"Do you know Evan Houselow?" Steve asked, glancing at his watch.

Gemma scowled and blew on her tea. "He's out again now, isn't he? He'd better not come back to the Seaview, that's all I'm saying. His family sold the scrapyard and left just after he was sent down. Poor bloody kids . . ."

"Is there anything else you can tell us?"

She sat thoughtfully for a moment. "For a while, maybe six months, when I'd just had the twins, there was this rumour of kids going missing. Some of the kids I minded claimed to have seen a man going into houses in broad daylight and taking sleeping babies. They called him the 'Smiling Man', and someone said it was Evan." The woman shrugged. "Whispers and rumours! I think it was a load of bollocks. Kids got taken by the socials sometimes, but mostly if a family was in trouble, they came to me."

"What do you mean?" Dove made a note about the 'Smiling Man'. Interesting, but she couldn't see any links to Alice's murder at present. It would be worth checking out, though, even if just to see if any children had gone missing during the time period.

"They knew they could trust me." She smiled through her cigarette smoke. "I always loved kids. You do what you have to. My eldest went to university, and my youngest has got his own garage, now." Pride in her kids shone through her tough exterior.

"If you grew up here, did you know Evan's kids?" Dove asked, drawing a quick timeline in her head. She figured they would all have been roughly the same age.

Gemma frowned and shook her head, fiddling with the neon pink hairband she wore around her wrist. "I knew of them. The scrapyard is off Pinkley Road, so about half a mile from here. Max was much older. But I used to mind Katrina when she was little. She was five years younger than Max, and then the twins, Leo and Lukas, they were only nine when Evan was sent down, brave little things."

"They gave evidence against their father at nine years old?" Dove was shaken. And impressed. As Gemma said, brave little things.

Gemma nodded. "Lots of them worried me, but you know, don't just write the parents off because they've got addiction issues, or violent partners, or whatever. They need help, most of them, not a nosy old busybody from the local authority wanting to do assessments, or put them on registers," she said fiercely.

"Unless the kids are in danger?" suggested Steve.

"But who gets to make that call? Bloody socials did nothing about Benny Milward, did they? Just let him suffer until they killed him. And although Evan got banged up, he didn't stay in long. He should have gone down for years longer after what he did!"

CHAPTER SIXTEEN

Dove stared at her. The Benny Milward case, in 1998, had been a horrific example of neglect and missed opportunities to intervene. The two-year-old eventually died as a result of injuries and neglect inflicted by his own parents.

"Don't want to talk about Benny, do you? People don't ever forget and that poor angel, even though it was twenty years ago, we'll never forget. Everyone let him down, you lot included." Gemma scowled at them, pushing her hair back and tying it up in a ponytail with the neon pink band.

"And they shouldn't forget, either. It was a terrible case," Dove agreed, catching Steve's eye. "Hopefully lessons have been learned from it."

He nodded. "Is there anything else you can tell us that might help to find Alice's killer?"

Gemma shook her head and turned away quickly, but not before Dove had seen her eyes were bright with tears. Did she care or was she acting? Without any other evidence, Dove felt it was the former.

"Okay. If you could just sign your statement, we'll be in touch if we need anything else." She thanked the woman for her time, and they exited with crossed fingers.

"We still have wheels," Dove noted in relief as they got into the car. Even as she spoke, a car screeched round the corner and as it drew level with their vehicle, someone hoisted a can of red paint over the car.

"Fuck off, pigs!" someone screamed over the music and the car screamed off towards the haulage yard.

"Let's get out of here." Dove was already pulling away. Luckily the paint wasn't on the windscreen, but totally obscured the passenger window, dripping slowly down the glass.

"Number plate was blacked out," Steve observed as they turned onto the main road. "Can you still see to drive?"

"Of course. We'll just make sure we swap cars with Lindsey when we get back," Dove said dryly. "Bloody hell, it's nearly eleven already."

"Let's see if there is anything new in from the labs." Steve was silent for a moment as he scrolled down on his phone. "That will be a big fat no, according to the updates. Shit. But they've found a match for Evan's prints on the Range Rover."

"Bingo! Gemma obviously hates him, but this rumour about him taking other peoples' kids can't be true. I mean, his neighbours would have noticed!" Dove mused as she indicated left opposite McDonald's. "And he wasn't convicted of killing Lily's baby, so we need to check that out and find out where that rumour came from. DI Marks said there were question marks about whether there ever was another child in the house."

"And there was nothing in the charges about kidnap. The kids he abused were his own and his partner's. Lily. She was an addict and a prostitute, apparently, and social services were very aware of them," Steve added.

"Yeah, but kids fall down cracks, like poor Benny. Understaffing, lack of communication, parents moving around, all the kind of thing that leads to a tragedy like that. I get what Gemma said about the estate looking after their own, but it's huge. There must be over three thousand houses. You can't tell me it's any different to the roads where you or I live. People get away with all kinds of stuff behind closed doors, it doesn't matter where they live or who they are."

Frustrated the car park was full, Dove eventually pulled in to a tiny parking space, right next to the wall on the passenger side, and Steve winced as she edged the car in. "How am I supposed to get out?"

"Breathe in," she told him. "Let's grab a burger on the way up."

"No, you go ahead, I brought something in with me. You know, it'll all catch up with you, this fat and sugar."

"Fine." Dove grinned at him. Steve was notorious for his fad diets, which without fail fell by the wayside after a few weeks. She didn't feel their job and working hours were especially conducive to a healthy diet and was aware she drank too much coffee and ate way too much unhealthy food. So far, this had been balanced out by her active lifestyle, and as she often told her sister, Ren, who expressed the same concerns as Steve, there were worse vices to have.

The scents of frying onions, bacon and mushrooms from the mobile food van in the car park made her stomach growl, and ignoring her recent musings on healthy food, she added a doughnut to her order.

While she waited, she texted her fiancé, knowing he was likely to be still asleep, but feeling like she needed to touch base. She was fine with all this baby stuff, she assured herself, breathing in the damp spring air. She was over it and had accepted her life would not involve children. Sometimes, still, it just hurt that someone else had made that decision for her.

"Ready!" the girl behind the counter yelled, waving the delicious-smelling package.

Dove shook off her demons and went inside with her meal.

DI Blackman was updating the murder board, and Dove sat down at her computer, quickly updating her and Steve's paperwork before she moved on with the searches.

Steve emerged from the tiny kitchen area with a bowl of soup.

"What are you eating?"

"Butternut squash soup with black pepper and herbs."

"Looks lovely." She swivelled her chair back and showed him a scrawled mind map. "Guess what? Alice and Sarah *were* both involved in Evan's case. They had both contributed reports flagging their worries and these were used by the prosecution team. The twins, Leo and Lukas, were in the neonatal unit for five weeks. Alice only worked on the maternity ward a couple of days from 2009, so that she could also help with cover for the community midwife." She skimmed to the bottom of her document. "Also, both previously worked over the border, Alice at Royal General and Sarah at the local authority offices. In 1998 they both moved to Abberley with their families, to take up jobs down here."

"Is that helpful?"

"Not sure. It gives a motive for Evan to kill both of them, but as there were hundreds of files and reports contributing evidence to the case, I can't see the whole prosecution case hinging on these two women. Benny Milward's case was in 1998," she added.

"We can check and see if either of them was involved in any part of his case, just in case it's relevant. And Gemma?"

"According to her statement, Gemma met Alice when she had her first baby, didn't she?" Dove tapped her pen on the desk, calculating. "So, she has known her for about as long as Alice has been living in this area. I don't buy it that her kids have lost her phone, though. Too convenient. I checked it in, and it's switched off. No recorded activity since Alice called her last night."

Steve peered at his own screen. "Just for background, Arrowhill Hospital is closed and the site is up for redevelopment." He moved the cursor over the Google Maps image.

"Which is a shame, because if for some reason there is a link between where Alice worked and our perpetrator, it's going to be fun getting files from some hellhole archive somewhere. The word digital seems to have bypassed the NHS for anything that predates 1995," Steve said sourly.

"Ouch!"

"It's true. I've had a couple of cases, before you joined us, where I needed files from old medical facilities," he told her.

"Listen up!" DI Blackman called over the chat and rattle of keyboards. "We've got a DNA match from the caravan and the stone in Alice's mouth. It belongs to Sarah Whitmore, our witness."

CHAPTER SEVENTEEN

I found it by accident and now I can't stop returning, again and again.

I need to force myself to find somewhere else, because even I can see my behaviour is a little bit odd. But I can't help it.

My partner was convinced I was having an affair. Bewildered and hurt, I suppose, by my night-time wanderings, it would turn into a proper argument with words I couldn't take back.

I couldn't tell him where I went, what I was doing, that sometimes I lay curled in the rotting beds staring at the stars, or sat at the nurses' station, just imagining, listening to the ghosts who roamed peacefully across the site.

When I saw the cribs, I just knew I had found my place. It is where it all begins and sometimes ends. There is something special about the place you are born and the place you die. I imagine I see ghosts, spirits, and sometimes I drift away with them, smoking, inhaling the dank and decay, and the minty odour of my smokes.

One night he found out. He followed me to Arrowhill, saw me park the car on the side road, slip through the fence. The only other person he saw was the security guard, who unfortunately had company that night. Very obvious and noisy company, and they were getting down to business behind some trees, right after my other half followed me in.

A girlfriend, a wife, a passing stranger or a professional, I'll never know, but that was the end of my relationship. He was furious, but I was too. How do you jump to that kind of conclusion in seconds? After the initial hurt, I just couldn't be bothered to defend myself. He always was a stubborn, arrogant bastard.

After we split for good, for a while I convinced myself I was happy. It was a relief, not having to wear a mask, not having to feel the weight of guilty secrets every time we had one of those deep conversations you have after a glass of wine.

Now I'm alone in a different flat, I only have to pretend at work, and when I get home after a shift, I can sink back into my past, let my whirling thoughts take over. Little things like not having to hide my search history, not having to be another version of myself, make me so much happier. I tell myself this every day, and sometimes I even believe it.

It's a pattern, one I have kept since childhood. I did love him, and now he's gone. It's my fault he's gone.

CHAPTER EIGHTEEN

By seven the team was beginning to flag and DI Blackman called a quick briefing. "Just to update you all, we have finally had some results back from the lab, which as you know, include a match for our sig wit, Sarah Whitmore. Josh, I think you and Lindsey spoke to her?"

Lindsey nodded. "She didn't stop crying from the moment she opened the door, but she has now changed her statement to say she went inside the caravan, touching a few things on the way, as it was dark, and the light didn't work. She wanted to check Alice was dead, so she also touched her, and saw the stone. She was horrified by the stone and went to pull it out before remembering this was a crime scene and she probably shouldn't touch it."

"Do you believe her?"

"Not sure. I can't see why she didn't just tell us in the first place. She's not stupid and she must have known we would get her prints off anything she had touched. She's going to stay with her son, Jack, who lives on the Bexley Road. He's been interviewed but he was up in London at work at the time of the murder. Big media job. Doesn't seem that interested in what his mum or his mum's friends get up to at all."

DI Lincoln took over. "Alice wasn't a big fan of social media, but she was on Facebook. She had Gemma and Sarah in her contacts on there."

"Evan Houselow says he's never heard of Alice Cartwright," DC Amin put in. "He denies knowing anyone who was involved in his trial, except his kids. Says it was too long ago to remember."

"He doesn't have an alibi for last night," Steve pointed out.

DCI Franklin joined them. "If he didn't kill her, we need to find out who did and why Evan is remotely involved. If he is. We only have the vehicle evidence so far."

Dove chewed her thumbnail as DI Blackman continued. "Alice didn't have any other children apart from Martin, and her sister moved to Canada with her husband in 2009. She says she hardly ever heard from Alice. They just kept in touch on Facebook, or the odd email. No other family and few friends. Her work colleagues, her boss, all say how kind and wonderful she was. Nobody has suggested even the smallest disagreement, and certainly no motives for murder." He looked up as his phone pinged. "Next batch of lab results coming over."

Dove and the rest of the team studied them in silence for a moment.

"No DNA evidence yet to suggest Evan Houselow was present at either scene, but he does have firearms offences on file, and our possible suspect vehicle was found in the vicinity of his current address, with his prints in it. On the night in question, he says he was going to meet a woman at 8 p.m. at the Crown in the beer garden but won't say any more except she never showed up. He isn't on the pub's CCTV." DC Amin sounded disappointed, and she checked her notes before speaking again. "That's it on him for the moment."

"He's bricking it that he's going back inside," DI George 'Vampire' Lincoln informed them. With his grey hair and skin, and general air of doom and gloom, there were rumours that this particular DI only came out for the night shift.

"We can't let this become a witch hunt with Evan as a scapegoat. He is claiming the vehicle belongs to a mate, who lets him drive it sometimes," DI Blackman informed them. "His probation officer says he's not showed any hint of trouble so far, but he's only been out for a month. He is attending regular counselling sessions and signed up for a back-to-work programme for recent offenders. A model of good behaviour, in fact."

"He's been a nasty piece of work, though, and I'm not sure I believe someone with that history could just change it up. Leopards and spots and all that." DI Lincoln sucked at a milkshake straw with relish, finishing his drink before wiping the back of his hand across his moustache.

Dove winced. She hated milkshakes and wasn't keen on the lingering line of pink that still decorated the Vampire's facial hair.

The DI continued, "I say Martin Cartwright is a better bet. Drugs history, car stuffed with powder. I think he pissed off a dealer and his mother paid the price."

"Big assumption. Can you back it up?" The DCI raised an eyebrow.

DI Lincoln smiled. "Not yet. Maybe this afternoon if my intel comes through."

"Smug bastard," muttered Lindsey to Dove.

"He's bound to be right, though," she whispered back. The Vampire had an uncanny ability to hit on the right answers, yet he didn't often seem to leave his chair and computer screen.

"Does Evan Houselow have any family left in the area?" Lindsey queried.

DCI Franklin nodded and tapped his screen. "His kids. One of his sons, Lukas, has been in trouble since he was in his teens. No history of violence, just petty shoplifting offences but he seems to have been going straight for the last few years. Steve and Dove, you dig into him and pay him a visit. Evan is claiming he has visited all his kids since he was released, *and* that he visited Lukas the day before Alice was murdered . . . Just one big happy family now."

"I'd be surprised if it's all water under the bridge after what those kids suffered," Steve said. "I suppose Evan has also found God," he added sarcastically.

"Exactly. Find out whether Evan is bullshitting and if Lukas knows where he's been and what he's been doing since he came out."

"Yes, boss."

"There is another son, Leo, who lives down in Brighton now. Both of them testified in court, via video links of course, against their father, along with the eldest, Max. Paperwork shows Max was killed in an RTC a few months after the trial. The final testimony came from his daughter, Katrina," the DCI added.

"What about the rumours of another baby, born in 2002, preceding an abduction allegation by Lily Windsor?" DI Blackman asked.

DC Conrad answered. "I did follow that up, and there seemed to be some confusion as to whether there ever was a baby. There was no record of the birth, no medical records. Acting on information from a source, the lake behind Abel's Gym was searched and an item of baby clothing was retrieved." He took a swig of his energy drink and continued, "The mother, Lily Windsor, was adamant her baby had gone missing, but nobody could verify she was ever even pregnant. Evan Houselow denied there had ever been another child at all, as did the neighbours and the other kids in the family."

* * *

Dove searched the records for the four known siblings connected to Evan Houselow, and discovered a marriage certificate for Katrina, who had subsequently changed her surname to Bentley and moved to Arthursdale in West Yorkshire.

She called across to DC Amin, "Maya? Could the baby have been born at home and never registered? What about the other kids? They must have known if their mother had another baby?"

Maya brushed her hair back from her face. "It is possible. I mean, I had both my kids at home, but for nobody to notice a pregnancy, and then for the baby to vanish? Assuming there were no medical complications, I suppose, yes, in theory it would be possible — but unlikely unless you lived in the middle of nowhere."

"So, the only person claiming the baby existed at all was Lily?"

"Right. She swore she had given birth to a baby girl but refused any medical examination which might have proved it. Eventually she was judged unreliable. She was an addict, her partner was violent with all of their kids and they were known to social services. All this happened weeks before the kids went to the police about the abuse." Maya looked back at her desk, leaned over and passed a wad of paperwork to Dove. "I printed this out because I find it easier to read a hard copy. None of the kids backed Lily up, they all said they hadn't seen a baby."

"Thanks, Maya, I'll have a quick read-through." Dove was slightly intrigued by the mysterious baby, but also sickened to her core at the thought that a baby girl might have been a victim of Evan's rage.

She speed-read the documents. According to the reports, Lily's children had all claimed to know nothing about a baby. The tip-off to drag the lake had come in along with some bloodstained baby clothing. The blood was contaminated by an oil leak from a drum dumped next to the lake and couldn't even be confirmed as human. The item of baby clothing retrieved from the lake had also had bloodstains, but these were also from an unknown source.

An anonymous witness had rung in and claimed to have seen a man carrying a baby in the early hours of the morning, walking behind the gym, before placing the child into the lake, thus triggering the multi-agency search.

Dove decided to take a quick break for some fresh air. Her brain felt like it was being fried on this case. Despite having two scenes to deal with, and extensive evidence, all documented by Jess and her team, it seemed that the perpetrator was still one step ahead. Could Evan's kids be involved in this case? Unlikely. Or had their father come out to get swift revenge on those who had helped put him behind bars? Which would surely mean his three remaining children were in a position to become possible victims. And Sarah. Was Sarah in danger?

Both Alice and Sarah, with the kind of work they'd done, must have stirred up some controversy, some ill feeling, but surely Sarah would have been far more of an obvious target. Why Alice? Dove pressed her hand to her forehead. The marks on the victim's arms were still nagging at her brain. The Vampire still seemed convinced it was drug-related . . .

Her phone rang while she was snagging yet another coffee, despite the caffeine jitters already buzzing around her body telling her she should have water instead, and she glanced at the caller ID. It was her sister, Ren.

"Hi, Ren, what's up?"

"Nothing major, just wondered if you might like to come over sometime soon. Are you still at work?" Ren sounded worried, and Dove felt her heart jump a little.

At the back of her mind was always the horror of her brother-in-law getting in touch, somehow overturning his convictions. She knew this was impossible, but she still had the nightmares. They had tried hard to move on, but the spectre of Alex and the evil he had done haunted their family.

"Yeah, probably going to sleep over on the floor by the looks of this case." Dove frowned, biting a thumbnail. "Is everything okay? I know you mentioned Elan had a bit of a cough?" Elan was her three-year-old, much-adored nephew.

"I did see that poor woman was murdered last night and I thought you'd be busy but . . ." Ren sighed down the phone. "Eden wants to talk to you. She's . . . she has concerns about one of the other parents at the nursery and doesn't know what to do."

"Hell, Ren, that's not really one for me, I wouldn't have a clue about kids," Dove told her, instantly bewildered.

"You do, and anyway you know what Eden's like once she gets anxious. I'm worried she might be heading for another episode, and she's been doing so well dropping most of her meds and everything." Ren's voice was strained.

"Okay. If she wants to call me, she can, or I can drop by on my way home tomorrow or the next day? I'm so sorry, Ren, but I haven't seen Quinn for twenty-four hours either and I might not finish until eleven tonight, depending on what comes up. I don't want to keep Elan up, either, if I'm really late . . ." She hated that her voice trailed off, having made at least three legitimate excuses, but she still felt like she was letting Eden down, letting them all down.

"That's okay, Dove, I'll tell Eden and I really appreciate it." Relief was audible in Ren's voice.

Dove ended the call and leaned her head against the cool glass of the window for a moment, feeling that familiar squirming guilt that always hit when she put work over her family, and then grabbed her coat for protection against the next rain shower that would surely arrive as soon as she stepped outside the door. She caught Steve up at the food van in the car park.

"I got you a coffee. Want another burger and chips?" he called.

"No thanks. Even my stomach can't take any more grease at the moment," Dove said. "Coffee would be great, though." She walked over to help him carry his supplies. "How much food? We aren't going on a trek!"

"I'm knackered. I think I got two hours' sleep last night," Steve replied, yawning. "I need anything I can get my hands on to keep me awake. Fuck knows when we're going to get home tonight, and health food bars are not cutting it."

The darkness had fallen properly now, and lights from the police station, the road, the industrial estates and the coastal strip of bars and trashy clubs filled the sky, turning the grey drizzle into tiny dancing stars.

The open plan office was filled with loud voices and a sense of urgency when they returned.

"What did we miss?" Dove asked quickly, setting her coffee down on her desk without taking a sip.

Josh called over his shoulder, "Sarah Whitmore has just been found dead."

CHAPTER NINETEEN

"Fuck!" Steve swore beside her, dumping his box of food and picking up his work bag.

"Let's get out there, people!" DCI Franklin was out of his office and giving orders. "Dove and Steve, you come to the scene, Lindsey and Josh too."

DI Lincoln picked up his iPad. "Jon, I'll stay here with DC Amin and the rest of my team. We'll pick up on the evidence and get everything moving this end."

"Thanks, George. Right, my team, let's move!"

Sarah Whitmore's body was lying in an alley, not far from Dove's sister Gaia's club. Like Alice, she was lying on her back, hands neatly crossed on her chest, legs together. Her face was bruised and there was a cut on her forehead, but no other obvious injuries, until the first responders pointed out the back of her head.

"Looks like she fell and hit her head on that skip," one offered, pointing at the blood trail.

Jess's van was already parked near the scene, and as usual a cordon had been set up to retain evidence, but also to protect the victim from the curious general public heading out to bars and clubs, as well as the press.

Dove noted that the alley — which was set between two high buildings — went nowhere. It was dark and obscure enough for someone to commit a murder without being seen from the main street. There were cameras on the all-night grocery store opposite, but none in the immediate vicinity.

She and the rest of the team carefully suited and booted up, cursing the light rain for yet again making the evidence harder to contain.

Dove walked on plates round to the back of the skip and found one of Jess's team carefully taking photographs of a bag of shopping, which was spilling contents across the dirty concrete. Eggs broken and a plastic bottle of milk dented. Some pasta sauce and a bag of spaghetti.

"Does she have her purse and phone?" Dove asked.

Jess was kneeling by the body. "Hallo to you too, and no, we haven't found any personal effects so far, apart from what we currently assume to be her shopping bag."

"Sorry, hallo, Jess." Dove looked grimly down at the body. She felt somehow that they had not guessed correctly, had not protected Sarah, when they'd discovered she might be a target. But that was ridiculous. No outright threats had been made, and Sarah had no connection to the drugs found in Alice's car.

"Evan Houselow has a rock-solid alibi for this one," the DI came off his phone, "He's been with his counsellor all evening."

"He has a counsellor?" Lindsey rolled her eyes.

"He might have been set up," the DI pointed out. "He's an obvious choice if anyone knows him and his history. No tunnel vision."

Dove sighed. The DI was right, she had been focusing on Evan, her mind snagged on the stone pebbles and Sarah's obvious fear at the mention of his name.

"No signs of any stab wounds, and her arms are clean." Jess was taking notes straight into her phone. She moved methodically, smoothly, avoiding the gauzes, plastic packaging and other paraphernalia from the now departed medics.

"Rigor is established, so she may have been here for at least one to two hours when she was discovered. She was last seen at 6 p.m.?"

"Correct. She left her son's house to go shopping. The son has been working online since she left, and we're checking his server and phone to confirm activity. Does she have a stone in her mouth?" DI Blackman asked quickly, his plastic suit crackling as he moved back towards the body, avoiding the photographer.

After another photograph, Jess carefully examined the mouth, with deft gloved fingers and forceps. "Yes, she does. I can't be sure if she has anything else in her throat, though. That will have to wait for the pathologist."

"I'm sure he'll be delighted to get another one to bump up the list. I doubt we'll get so lucky this time," DI Blackman remarked.

A uniformed first responder approached Steve and indicated a group of teenagers. "We've had a couple of reports of a man running away from the scene, and these girls are able to give a more detailed description. We've sent a car out to see if we can find the person they describe and we're checking cameras."

"Boss?"

"You two deal with it." DI Blackman nodded and Dove and Steve walked over to the group. Five girls, all dressed for a night out, were huddled on the side of the street. Someone had given them blankets and they were sharing them, wearing them like shawls.

Steve introduced himself and Dove. "You said to one of the officers you got a good look at a man running from this alley?"

The girls glanced at one another, before one of them spoke. "We were at the pub, the Lion, and we were moving on to Stage 32 because they've got this new DJ . . ." she rattled on before finally getting to the point. "This man came flying out of the alley and bumped into Charlotte. She dropped her purse . . ."

Another girl chipped in, ". . . We thought he was trying to mug us, so we yelled at him, but he just pushed through and kept on running down towards the seafront."

"Did you see which way he turned when he got there?"

They considered, before a pretty redhead said decisively, "He turned left. I remember because I thought, great, that's the way we're going, I hope he's not going to cause any trouble."

"And then we looked the way he had come, you know, from the alley and there was a woman lying there."

"Kerry's a student nurse," the redhead indicated one of her friends. "So we got her to do her thing while we called for an ambulance. She was going to start CPR but the woman was . . ."

"She was stiff and cold, definitely not breathing."

"We think he must have mugged her," the first girl said firmly.

"And a description?" Steve asked.

"Tall, slim, with a baseball cap pulled down. I want to say blonde hair . . . Maybe not . . ." She frowned and tapped her lips with her long nails, "Dark clothes and Adidas white trainers."

"I think he had green eyes. No, grey eyes."

"And he was wearing CK One." A girl who hadn't yet spoken chipped in and then flushed red as the others giggled. "What? He smelled nice. He did practically knock us all over, he was so close. He's also probably a smoker or has been with someone who does smoke, because I smelled that on his clothes." She smiled at Dove and Steve. "I have a few problems with my eyesight, so I do notice other things instead."

"She has a sixth sense, too," the girl called Charlotte said protectively.

Leaving the girls in the care of a uniformed officer, Dove and Steve made their way back to the body.

The alleyway stank of rotting rubbish, and Sarah's body lying in the bright glare of the floodlights looked raw and sad. Dove glanced away. Two bodies and no credible suspect yet. She wasn't convinced the man running away had been anything apart from a chancer checking the body for cash or phones.

If he was the killer, if Sarah's death wasn't an accident, why stick around for a couple of hours, perhaps even watching her die? It didn't make sense.

As they drove back to the station, they passed the group of girls off to continue their night out at the clubs along the seafront.

Steve was still trying to work through the events leading up to Sarah's death. "According to her son, she went out to get some shopping. He offered to go, but he was working, and I'm not sure how seriously he's taking the investigation anyway. Lindsey said he had zero interest in Alice's death. She and Josh are going over there now."

"So, her son let her walk out into the dark on her own, after her friend has just been murdered? And if she just popped out for shopping and was gone for two hours, maybe he would have noticed? Bloody great," Dove said, but her own feelings of guilt were still simmering. They couldn't protect everyone, she reminded herself. But Sarah's death, and the arrangement of the body, the significance of the stone heart, meant two murders linked and potentially more victims on a hit list. But why?

CHAPTER TWENTY

"You two go home now when you've filed the paperwork from tonight and be back at six. Leave it to the night shift for a couple of hours," the DI said.

"Yes, boss." Despite her exhaustion, Dove was reluctant to go, to leave the hum and buzz at the station. There would be a night shift working through after this second murder, and they would follow up everything they could. She was no good if she was making mistakes due to fatigue. There was a narrow line between working hard and working when fatigued, which could cause major mistakes.

As usual when she was feeling stressed, the memories of her time with an organized crime gang resurfaced. The subsequent investigation had cleared her of wrongdoing, but she knew — and Chris, her DI on the Informant Unit, knew — that she had been too close to the wire. Burned out from constantly changing her identity, yet addicted to the highs of playing with fire, and the results that often prevented the loss of lives.

She had been exhausted when she'd made that last phone call and hadn't noticed her CHIS, or covert human intelligence source, had seemed unusually reticent. There had been a rumour of corruption on the Unit, a worry that someone from the inside had tipped the gang off. Dove didn't believe that. It was her own fault she had ended up captive, tortured and almost fatally injured.

A harsh lesson that had almost ended her career and her life.

"You go home, DC Milson, you look like shit. I'm staying and I've got extra uniform bodies coming down to help with the door-to-door." DI Lincoln, who always seemed happier at work than home, and once again did not appear to have returned to his abode since leaving it the previous night, was settling down at his desk with a fresh box of doughnuts and a pile of paperwork.

Dove gave him a weak grin and he smiled at her. Not always a gloomy vampire. She caught a genuine hint of concern.

"You sure you're all right, George? Not going to grab a couple of hours' sleep?" DI Blackman queried.

"No chance. I'm going to keep up to date on this one," DI Lincoln said. He extended his hand and selected a pink doughnut covered in chocolate sprinkles, biting into it with relish and, speaking through a mouthful of sugar, added, "I'll catch a few hours' kip tomorrow lunchtime, or around two a.m. downstairs. Works for me."

Dove drove slowly home, her body aching. The night was clear now, with just a few wispy clouds hanging across the moon, like cobwebs on a dewy morning. Cold and quiet with the main rush of traffic having been and gone.

She sent another quick text to Quinn as she arrived home and, yawning, dragged her bag from the car. The car door slammed shut, echoing down the peaceful suburban road.

Despite her exhaustion, Dove smiled when she let herself in and discovered a bunch of spring flowers in a vase on the kitchen counter. There was a note propped against it:

Love you, even if I don't see you very often! X

A wave of emotion brough tears to her gritty, tired eyes and she brushed them away, cross with herself. It was just a vase of flowers! She was such an emotional wreck when she was in the middle of a tough case. Not at work, of course, but in the rare moments she let herself return to being just Dove. Not a police officer, just a woman in dire need of some sleep.

But instead of switching off now she was home, her mind was still churning, scrabbling around for new ideas, links in the case. Underneath all of it was the baby-related thread of emotion she had tried to stifle earlier.

She and Quinn had made their decision, but this case was getting to her. Dove took a deep breath. She knew several ways out of the panic attacks that might plague her sleep if she allowed her thoughts to really take hold.

Even as she made the decision to pop down the beach for a quick swim, her body, treacherously, suggested the sofa and a mug of soup might be a better idea. Ignoring it, she pulled on her wetsuit, tucked her keys and purse in the little dry bag she buckled around her waist and grabbed her board.

Living just a few minutes from the sea was a definite plus, she thought for the hundredth time, as she jogged over the road and across the shingle. Ten minutes and she was in the water.

The lifeguard station was in darkness, but all along the seafront, neon lights from the clubs, bars and cafés cast a dirty glow towards the moon, stifling the stars with their yellow, red and green strobes. It was low tide.

She waded out to a decent depth, before getting up on her paddleboard and picking up the oar. Surfing would always be her first love, but in conditions like this, paddle-boarding would do nicely.

The peace, the lazy rhythmic splash of her paddle and the whisper of the waves all allowed her time to process the day. She kept an eye on her watch. After half an hour, she was jogging lightly up the beach again, and within an hour she was showered, sipping at that mug of tomato soup and digging into a family-sized bag of Doritos.

It was only as she went to check her phone again, wondering why she had no contact at all from her fiancé and slightly worried, that she knocked a magazine off the coffee table and found Quinn had left his phone at home. No wonder he hadn't replied to her texts tonight.

She picked it up and was about to put it back next to her own when she noticed the texts that had popped up on the home screen:

Can't wait to see you again.
You are so hot. Xxx
Do you want another photo?

Three texts. All come in within the last half an hour, and all were from a number not listed in Quinn's contacts but were signed off by 'Malina'. One last message was a WhatsApp and there was a photo in the profile. A woman. A half-naked woman.

Dove sat staring at her fiancé's phone, almost holding her breath, feeling her heart beating way too fast, fingers tingling. She felt almost dizzy. Neither she nor Quinn knew each other's passwords. Why would they? Surely it must be some weird joke, or someone spamming him.

The home screen was a photo of her and Quinn on the beach, each with a bottle of beer in their hands, laughing. Blue sky, hair ruffled by a hot breeze. He said it was one of his favourite pictures of them together.

She carefully lined his phone up next to hers, running through her options. He would see that the texts had come in when he got home. How would he react?

Despite her fears and insecurities, deep down Dove felt she knew that if Quinn wanted to see someone else, he would just break it off with her first. He wasn't the type to hide things like that. Was he? She ran her hands through her hair and pulled on an old T-shirt.

The bathroom mirror showed large exhausted amber-brown eyes and a smear of tomato soup on her lip. She half smiled at this, and the woman in the mirror changed from someone unapproachable, shuttered and cold, to someone completely different.

She wondered about this as she cleaned her teeth. Innocent until proven guilty. In her heart she knew there would be a rational explanation. In her head, a small, pathetically vulnerable creature scrabbled for reassurance.

"Fuck off," she said quietly to her reflection. They were getting married this year, there was no way Quinn would cheat on her. He just wouldn't.

And when, early next morning, he greeted her with a kiss as they once again passed each other in the kitchen, heading in opposite directions, she only said, "You left your phone at home!"

He looked absolutely exhausted. Dark purple shadows under his green eyes, black hair spiked and messy, and deep furrows in his forehead, which he kept rubbing with one hand, as though to chase the fatigue away. "I know! What an idiot. Oh, thanks, babe, is that coffee?"

She handed him a mug and he sipped gratefully, shrugging out of his uniform jacket, slumping at the countertop as he checked his phone.

Dove watched him carefully, probing with new eyes, seeking reassurance or . . . or something. She was already dressed for work, with her hair caught up in a tight plait, and a headache throbbing behind her eyes.

Nothing.

"Sorry, I've got to go," she told him, leaning in for a kiss. "See you later, maybe?"

"Yeah. This is your last night, isn't it?"

"Thank Christ for that." He smiled at her. "Maybe you'll get a day off soon too. Good luck with the case today."

She lingered for a second, before grabbing her bag and heading out the door into the cold greyness. Why hadn't he said anything? Did he think she hadn't seen the texts? It hadn't occurred to her to check his emails, or rifle through coat pockets for suspicious receipts, but she suddenly had an urge to do just that. Wasn't that a cliché? How would she feel if her first instinct was correct and there was nothing to find? If he had suspected her of the same, accused her, even, she would have been furious. And hurt. Trust worked both ways. So did betrayal.

The rain started to fall as she reached the roundabout and indicated left to the police station. She would wait, she decided, maybe talk it over with her sisters. Although even that felt like a breach of confidence. Maybe just wait until he said something.

But the whole way to work she couldn't stop thinking about it, and for the first time in her career, when she arrived in the briefing room, she wasn't thinking about the case, about two dead women and a hit list. She was thinking that if her fiancé was having an affair, she wouldn't be able to bear it.

CHAPTER TWENTY-ONE

The lights and the music seem to intensify, creating a kaleidoscope of colour around her.

The patterns shift and reform, and I can taste the red, the blue and orange, feel it soaking into my skin. Briefly I can escape the pain and memories, return to my own world and just be normal. The little line I took before I came out tonight helped me relax.

This is what I do, and people like me all the more for it. I can give them what they crave, and in turn that gives me a feeling of peace. Peace and power.

There is no need to question their motives, and they can't see inside my head, can't begin to imagine the raw mess behind my smiling exterior. I remind myself I hate smiling, but as a new track comes on, I can't subdue a genuine flash of happiness and the corners of my mouth stretch irresistibly upwards. I tip my head back and lose myself in the dancing crowd, sweat pouring down my face, damp under my T-shirt, but I don't care. I could be anywhere.

The DJ is up on stage, a queen controlling her crowds. This is the only time I feel whole, and I can tell she feels it too. Suddenly everything I've been searching for is right here. I haven't considered how to move further forward, but as we grab drinks at the bar, shouting comments back and forth about the music and the general awesomeness of the night, I feel like I've known her all my life.

Perhaps I have.

CHAPTER TWENTY-TWO

Dove had just entered the building when her phone rang with an unknown number. She answered, balancing bag and coffee.

"Is that DC Milson?"

"Yes."

"Sorry to bother you so early, but I met you last night? I was with my friends. My name is Charlotte."

The teenagers who had been such good witnesses. "Hi, Charlotte. I'm sorry that happened to you, but I hope you had a good night in the end?"

"Yeah. I mean, we did go home early because, you know, it was a dead body and it wasn't a great start to the night. It sort of put a damper on things."

"True." Dove wondered if the girl was going to get to the point. "So, what can I do for you?"

"We went to the Thursday night session at Stage 32, and the DJ was amazing. But . . . I didn't get too close at first because he was on stage behind the decks, but I can't shake the feeling he was that man we saw running away from the alley."

"Right. What do the others think?" Dove was making mental notes. Cameras had picked up the man fleeing the scene halfway along the seafront as he jogged past Kenny's Irish bar . . . So, in the general direction of the superclub. Could he have killed Sarah, then turned up for work less than a mile away? Then there was still the far more likely option that this man was robbing the body and nothing to do with the actual killing. There had been no wallet, phone or jewellery on the dead woman.

"Oh, they aren't sure, but we were in the front row when he finished his set and came off. He jumped down and went towards the VIP area, and we were close to him. Beth agrees with me. He wasn't wearing a baseball cap and he just had a vest on, but . . ."

"Do you know his name?" Dove made it to her computer, dumped her bag and coffee and was googling the club's session list.

"Not his real name. He's DJ Darkness."

"How original," Dove muttered under her breath. "Okay, thanks. Are you okay if I need to call you back? On this number?"

"Yes, of course." She sounded relieved. "Sorry, I haven't slept much thinking about it, and I didn't want to waste your time."

"No, you've been really helpful," Dove told her and ended the call.

DJ Darkness played a couple of regular gigs along the south coast, including a club in Brighton. He had also been living and working in Spain for eighteen months previously. Benidorm. She found his social media, full of cool shots of his partying with presumably cool people. Possibly even famous people, but she wouldn't have recognized them. And the music? Who didn't love clubbing as a teenager? She smiled to herself. Now she was a secret jazz girl when it came to music.

* * *

"Prelim results on Sarah Whitmore indicate she died of a head injury sustained while falling backwards or having been pushed

92

backwards onto the skip. The bruising on her face was from the fall due to placement and angle. Some bruising on her upper arms consistent with having been grabbed and held. It could be that her attacker followed her from her son's house and chose the moment when she was away from a street cam, on a fairly quiet street," DCI Franklin concluded the morning briefing. "Similarity to the murder of Alice Cartwright is the stone heart placed in the victim's mouth after death."

Dove jumped as Steve nudged her. "Hey, you're miles away today. What's up?"

"Nothing. Just lack of sleep," she told him briskly, pushing all thoughts of Quinn's texts to the back of her mind.

"But we don't know what she was doing in an alleyway, at least a hundred metres from the Co-op where she was shopping. Cameras show she left the shop with a bag of shopping approximately five minutes before she was potentially attacked. Bag of shopping was found behind the skip, but phone and wallet are still missing."

She waited until the briefing was over before approaching the DI and rapidly summarizing her call from the teenager, Charlotte.

"Find out who he is. Go to the club and see if they know his real name," he told her. "I agree it seems far more likely he was a chancer who just found the body, but he might still have her phone . . ."

* * *

Stage 32 was a huge glass-and-chrome building, hung like a Christmas tree with lights, colourful banners promoting club nights and resident DJs and, near the queueing area, framed posters of high-profile visitors. At night, with flashing neon and strobe lighting, it looked amazing. But like many of the commercial premises that came alive at night, in daylight it was litter-strewn, deserted, and empty.

"DS Parker and DC Milson. Major Crimes Team. Can we speak to the manager?"

"Guess you found him." The man scowled down at them.

Six foot five of solid muscle, Dove reckoned, but as she looked more closely at his face she grinned. "Hallo, Buzz. Don't you recognize me?"

He stared at her for a long moment before his face creased into a smile. "Gaia's sister! Sorry, darling, I didn't recognize you. All I saw was the badge and it said trouble."

"Thanks. I didn't realize this was where you'd gone." Dove turned to Steve. "Buzz was at California Dreams when it first opened."

Steve nodded, still eyeing the man warily.

"I didn't want to leave Gaia, but this one was a managerial job, so I went for it. What can I do for you?"

"We're actually looking for one of your DJs," Dove explained, "DJ Darkness?"

"I hope he's not involved in anything he shouldn't be. I have a no-trouble policy in the club so if any of them are in trouble I'll kick their skinny arses out of here," Buzz said, a hint of menace returning to his square face.

"We just need to speak to him. He might have some valuable information relating to an ongoing investigation," she fudged slightly. "Do you have any contact details for him?"

Buzz stared at her, dark eyes narrowing, accusing. "Alice Cartwright. Murdered up near Bear Green. Stabbing on the beach on Sunday night, and a jumper at the station this morning. And some woman was killed last night two blocks down, wasn't she? I heard it was a mugging that went wrong. Does this kid have anything to do with any of those?"

"Ongoing investigations," Dove told him, but she smiled, remembering Gaia had said nothing got past Buzz. He knew every local, every incident and every bit of gossip in town and along the coast.

The man nodded, as though she had confirmed something. "Yeah, his name's Leo something . . . Hang on, I'll find out." He yelled across at a woman polishing glasses on one of the bars, "Hey, Lisa, be an angel and go and find out the contact details for Leo — DJ Darkness?"

The woman gave him a thumbs up and disappeared through a door behind the bar. She reappeared five minutes later and walked over with a neatly written name and address.

"Thanks, love." Buzz squinted at the paper. "Leo Windsor. Nice kid but plenty of attitude. Lots of talent, though, so I hope he hasn't screwed up."

"So do I," Dove told him. "I'll let you know."

As they walked outside, Steve said, "Leo Windsor? As in Evan and Lily's kid who testified against his dad and helped send him down?"

Dove screwed up her eyes against the brightness and inhaled the scents of the town. Salt, dirt, candyfloss and cigarette smoke. The roadworks on the roundabout had resulted in a traffic jam reaching all the way up North Street, and the exhaust fumes lingered on the air, adding to the city stench. Frustrated drivers were hooting, and eighties dance music was blaring from a red van. Dove forced herself to focus. "Yes, but why in hell's name would he be hanging around Sarah's body, or did he see who killed her?"

"He lives in Brighton. Swanky area, too. Are we going to drive over there? Let's check in first. If there's the slightest chance that he might be going to point a gun at us, I'd rather it wasn't just us pitching up on his doorstep," Steve said, massaging his healing shoulder.

CHAPTER TWENTY-THREE

Dove drove them back to the station, and Steve hunted down DI Blackman while Dove looked up contact details for the other Windsor/Houselow siblings and tried without success to get hold of Leo on the phone. He had two mobile numbers, and one was switched off, while the other went straight to voicemail.

"No joy from Leo's phone, but I got an address for Lukas and his phone number. He works for a security firm, and is on shift now," Dove announced, forcing her mind back onto the job in hand as she felt herself drifting again. Exhaustion was getting the better of her.

She and Quinn had planned a honeymoon in Cornwall, and just now the wedding couldn't come fast enough, even if she was thinking more about the two-week break and a Cornish surfing holiday than actually saying her vows at the present moment . . . Oh God, would she even get to say her vows? The horror of the text messages kicked her in the gut, making her feel nauseous.

". . . and as a result the DI is calling in a few favours and persuading our colleagues further down the coast to go and check in on Leo Windsor's apartment. Hey, did you see Leo and Lukas are twins? Gemma said she had twins. Maybe it's something in the water at the Seaview?" Steve nudged her, but she barely felt it. "Hallo? I'll even get you fresh coffee on the way if we stop at that amazing café I've heard about. You know, the one opposite Boots," he added as she still didn't react. "*Dove?*"

His voice seemed to be coming from a long way away. Even though she could hear his words perfectly she felt disconnected from reality, as though she were listening to a podcast in the shower.

"Come on, Milson, wake up!" Concern edged into his voice and she forced herself to snap back to the present.

"Sorry, yeah, funny, it's a good one. Eden should be on the early shift this morning, but she swaps around a lot because she's doing a couple of college courses too."

"Is that still okay for her? Working with her mum, I mean? Especially with the baby?" Steve was still giving her a slightly odd look, but she couldn't cope with any sympathy, or even a lecture on how there was probably a rational explanation. She just needed the balls to ask for that explanation herself.

"Seems to be, and she's got Elan into nursery now, so she gets more time to work and plan her life." Dove considered her niece. "She's pretty tough, really."

"Guess she's had to be, with everything that's happened to her," Steve said soberly.

"Yeah." As soon as they parked up, Dove dashed in for coffees and cake to take away, but her sister took one look at her face and pulled her into the back.

"What's wrong. Is it Quinn?"

"Bloody hell, Ren, are you a psychic now or what?" Dove blinked at her. Ren had always been the best of them all at reading people, but Dove thought she had herself well under control. Clearly not. "I don't have time to talk, we're off to do an interview."

"Tell me quickly then." Her sister stood with her arms folded, dark curls pulled back with a red flowered headscarf and scarlet lips pursed.

"Okay. I found some texts on Quinn's phone from another woman, and a WhatsApp message. Her profile picture is her with her boobs out." Dove bit her lip, pushing down the emotion as it rose in her chest. Her words seemed to echo around the room, repeating again and again until she had to fight the urge to put her hands over her ears. *You've got this. Whatever happens, you'll be okay* . . . It had been a long time since she had needed to use her mantras.

Ren studied her in silence for a moment, while Dove watched her own amber eyes mirrored in her sister's, waiting. "Have you talked to him about it?"

"No! I haven't had a chance, and what if he is having an affair?" Because it was Ren, she allowed herself to say it out loud.

"You don't really think that?" Her sister sounded so certain. "Come on, Dove, Quinn adores you. Probably just some weird spam. It's easy for anyone to get hold of your number these days."

"I'm sure you're right . . . Well, actually I just don't know . . . I just feel like shit." She glanced down as her phone pinged. "And I need to go now!"

"Talk to him," her sister called after her as she hurried out the door and into the car. "Don't let it fester, Dove!"

* * *

Steve drove to one of the new housing estates to the west of Lymington-on-Sea and, even at a distance, they could see Lukas sitting in the small box-shaped office near the gate to the development. The roar of machinery and the shouts of the workers came from a block of half-built flats, and as they arrived a cement mixer pulled in and was waved through the barriers.

DI Blackman called as they edged into the side of the road and switched the ignition off. His voice came loud and sharp over speakerphone. "Message from Brighton. Leo Windsor isn't at home, and nobody has seen him since yesterday evening. No flatmates, but the landlord let them in, and his flat looks like he hardly lives there. No more stuff than you'd keep in a hotel room, apparently."

"And no wallet or phone belonging to Sarah Whitmore?"

"Right," the DI agreed. "I touched base with Interpol and Leo had a few near misses with drugs offences while he was working in Spain. They're sending a report over."

"Noted, boss." Steve ended the call and pushed his phone into his pocket. "All set?"

Lukas seemed eager for any distractions and Dove could imagine how boring the job was when there were no intruders to deal with. He was a tall, good-looking boy in his late twenties, with a small scar on his chin, shoulder-length blonde hair, and dimples when he smiled. Having studied pictures of Evan and Lily on file, Dove supposed Lukas and Leo took after their mother.

"Are you allowed to come outside? It's stopped raining. Or if you like we can talk to your boss and get you out on a break?" Steve asked after the introductions were made.

"Nah, we can talk in here, it's fine. The boss on this site has gone into town for a meeting. Said he wouldn't be back until four." Lukas shrugged, his skinny shoulders expressive. His thin red cotton uniform shirt was emblazoned with a black SECURITY logo, and his ID hung around his neck.

"Lukas, where were you last night between 6 p.m. and 9 p.m.?" Steve asked, shifting uncomfortably in the confined space.

"I was at home last night. I live with a couple of mates, and they were out, but I had an early shift, so I just went straight to sleep after a few beers and a Netflix movie," he told them, grey eyes widening as he spoke, flickering between the two of them. "What's going on?"

"We are investigating the deaths of two women in the area and it's possible your brother has some information that might help us."

Lukas considered this, fiddling with his ID pass, turning it over and over in his hands. He had very long black lashes,

Dove noticed, which made him look boyish and vulnerable. "Can we ask you about your brother, Leo?"

He looked surprised, then resigned. "You can."

"Do you know where he was last night?"

Lukas drummed his fingers on the console that operated the barriers, and dropped the ID, now fidgeting with his phone, which was on the small desk area in front of him. "Yeah, he was sleeping at my place last night."

"You didn't mention it just now," Steve replied.

"I forgot. We often sleep over at each other's places. He was still asleep when I left."

Dove stepped outside to relay this information to the DI and then returned to find Lukas looking defensive.

"Is Leo in any trouble?"

"Not that we know of, but as we said, we are investigating two deaths. A woman was attacked in an alley off Northern Road last night, and a man resembling you or your brother was spotted leaving the scene."

"Are you arresting me? Or Leo?" His voice was sharp with fear now, the lazy charm slipping away.

"No. We think Leo, if it was him, might have valuable information. He might have seen something that would help us explain what happened to the victim."

"The woman you found . . . She's dead?"

"Yes."

"Shit." He studied their faces. "I honestly can't see Leo attacking a woman, and of course that goes for me too. Can't prove anything, but we were at the flat and if you want me to say anything else, I need a solicitor, don't I?"

"You can sign a statement with us right here, or we can make this a formal interview down at the station if you prefer?" Steve suggested.

Lukas considered this, his annoyance apparently subsiding. "Nah. I haven't got anything to hide and neither has Leo. I think we should go outside. I need a smoke, and like you said, the rain's stopped."

CHAPTER TWENTY-FOUR

"How about Evan, your dad? Have you seen him since he got out?" Dove asked.

"No," he scowled. "He wouldn't come near me after what he did to us. He should have stayed behind bars, the bastard." His words were suddenly edged with stone and the brightness went out of his face. "Evan enjoyed everything he did back then, hurting people, controlling them, and I can't imagine his tastes have changed since he was inside."

"Are you in touch with your sister, Katrina?"

He was silent for a moment, eyes wary, but he answered clearly enough. "Yeah, she moved back down here after Lily died. She was coming back anyway because she's got a boyfriend down this way now. I haven't seen her much in years, so I'm glad she's back." He seemed to feel like this needed an explanation. "We weren't really a close family, but when you've been through hell together you have this bond. Ever since the court case, we might have lived in different countries, but we have like this sixth sense, this bond that goes way beyond normal . . ." His face reddened, voice trailing away, like he felt he had exposed too much.

Dove showed him the photos of Alice Cartwright and Sarah Whitmore on her iPad. "Do you know either of these women?"

He studied the pictures then shook his head slowly before jabbing a finger at Sarah's photo. "I don't think so, but she looks familiar. I don't know where I've seen her, though . . . I need another ciggie. Do you want one?" He chucked his partially smoked cigarette down in the grass and stamped on it with a large boot, before quickly lighting another one. His hand shook slightly.

"Sarah was a social worker and part of the local authority child protection team."

"Was she involved in our case?" Lukas took a long drag on his cigarette, before exhaling into the damp air.

"Yes," Steve informed him.

"I wouldn't remember her from back then. It was years ago. Ancient history." Lukas stared at them both for a moment, as if debating whether to share something. Eventually he said, "You think Evan came out and killed these women because he wanted to get back at them for putting him away? That's crazy!"

"Is it?" Dove asked. "We aren't assuming anything, we're working on the evidence we have, and I don't think we suggested Evan was responsible for the deaths of either of these two women."

He stared at them, scowling again. "You don't understand what it was like. When me, Leo, Katrina and Max decided to grass Evan up we had to speak to so many people, so many police, socials, counsellors. I fucking lost track, and in the end, I would speak like it was just a story that had happened to someone else. Then I'd see the shock on their faces and realize all over again how bad our lives had been."

"I'm sorry, Lukas," Steve said gently.

But the young man was staring out at the road now, lighting another cigarette, almost talking to himself, "All about how my mum would disappear for a couple of days after a bad row with Evan, and how we used to get locked in the cars to keep us out the way."

"What made you decide to tell the police about Evan?"

He shook his head slowly as he spoke, almost as though he was swirling memories around, sifting through the horrors of his past. "Katrina had moved out for a couple of weeks, even though she was only fourteen then, and Evan decided me and Leo had been staying out late too much and not doing his rounds for him." He gave a half-laugh. "We had to go out on our bikes and deliver drugs like takeaway pizzas by the time we were six."

"Go on." Dove's phone buzzed but she ignored it.

"He was hitting Leo with his fists and Leo was trying to fight back. I tried to stop him . . . He seemed to calm down a bit and we thought maybe the worst was over. But when Katrina got home, he beat on her with a length of industrial hose. He half killed her, and he was yelling she was a whore and all that. She was *fourteen*, for fuck's sake, and she wouldn't have been with some boy anyway!" Once again Lukas's eyes were far away. "That was it, and that was the moment we knew we had to do something to stop him."

"Where had Katrina been?"

"If things got really bad, we used to go and stay at Gemma Rogers's mum's place. She was a childminder, and Gemma took over from her when she passed away. She even lives in the same house still." He smiled. "Gemma's a proper princess. There's nothing she won't do for those kids, any kids, and her mum was the same."

"Gemma can't have been much older than you and Leo?" Steve checked.

Lukas nodded. "He'd had two kids of her own by then and taken the business over from her mum when she was poorly. Gemma didn't get on so well with Evan, I don't think. I heard Lily arguing with Evan about her just before Katrina got home that time."

"What did he say?"

"Not much that I remember, just hearing her name mentioned in anger. Then Evan beat Lily up and shoved her in with us for the night. We were always locked in the cars at night, sometimes in the day, too. You must have read the reports. It wasn't so bad unless you got taken into one of the vans, but that was the girls mostly." Lukas was silent again, staring into the distance this time, as though picturing the scene. "Lily never said a word to us that night, just cried herself to sleep holding this pink baby blanket. I think it was Katrina's old blanket. She was sentimental like that."

"You must miss her," Dove said.

"Lily? Yeah . . . You know she took an overdose last year? It was Christmas Eve . . ." He was silent, eyes dark with the emotion, his mouth set in a hard line, almost as though he were willing himself not to cry.

He looked up quickly as a group of teenagers roared past in a battered green BMW, pulling a U-turn in one of the site entrances. "Just gotta keep an eye out, not that I think they'd pull anything in daylight, but my job is on the line if they do," he explained.

"Do you get break-ins on the site?" Dove asked, trying to put him at ease. When he spoke about the past, his eyes were dull and haunted, but as soon as he came back to the present he brightened up. A heavy burden. Well, she knew a little about that.

CHAPTER TWENTY-FIVE

One night, he appeared in the car park after I finished work, wrapped up in a thick black puffa jacket, his face familiar, but older, sagging at the edges.

I don't know why I expected him to look different. The man had been in prison, not to a plastic surgeon. His sharp, chiselled features that had once pulled so many women were still there, and his thin, muscled body was still evident in the skinny jeans and white branded trainers.

"All right? Long time, no see."

I'd heard he was out, and if I'm honest part of me was expecting him to show up. Almost everyone else had gone, and he would need money or something . . . I'm not hard to find. Even so, the sight of him made my gut clench. I've chosen my own version of the past for so long now I've got comfortable with which parts I allow myself to remember and which parts I keep locked away.

Even though my heart was skipping beats and my palms were sweaty, I scowled at him. I had my dignity. I was an adult now. "I heard you were out," I said.

"I heard Lily died in December. Makes me really sad that she just ended it."

"Bullshit it makes you sad. Whose fault is it she finally couldn't cope? It was true, wasn't it, what Gemma said?" I threw this in without much hope, but he had needled me.

Lily had only been dead four months and here he was crying crocodile tears as though he had nothing to do with it. The old anger was rising in my chest, kindling sparks from my grief. The pain was making my fingers tingle. I shifted my bag to the other arm and straightened up, shoulders back, chin up, before I repeated my question. "Go on, was it true, Evan? Going to let it out after all these years?"

He ignored this, the one question I wanted him to answer, and just another thing he had denied any involvement in. A bit like when he said he never hit me, like I got the bruises and broken bones all on my own. "Can I walk with you? I need to talk to you."

"Fuck off, I don't have any money. Or any drugs." I looked around for security. There were still a few people around, too, even at this hour, so I felt safe enough. Evan could have a weapon, though. He had always liked guns and knives, and that puffa jacket was bulky enough to be hiding anything.

"Okay, okay." Surprisingly, he raised both hands and backed off as though I had threatened him, "I've served my time. I know I can't make good what I was like back then, but I've changed. I've got a proper job now, and a place to live."

"Of course you have."

I tried not to sneer, adjusting my bag securely across my shoulders, and started to walk. "Goodbye. Don't ever come near me again, and don't even think of fucking following me or I'll call the police."

"Wait! Okay, I'm sorry. It . . . it wasn't true. I should have told you before, properly, instead of just leaving it. Didn't you believe the police reports, the newspapers? She's not dead."

The words I had waited to hear. I kept on walking, but more slowly now. Of course, I hadn't believed anything, and he had never sat us down and told us why Lily had been so crazy or what had really happened that weekend, or why we were threatened to within an inch of our lives never to talk about it.

"Why didn't you answer my messages?"

"I couldn't . . . I wasn't thinking straight in there. Sorry."

I was still walking. Two sorrys in a matter of minutes. Not a word Evan had ever been familiar with. He'd be telling me next he was sorry for making all our lives a misery.

The thud of my footsteps on the tarmac matched the slow beating of my heart. I was almost holding my breath, still pretending to walk away from him. I knew what I'd seen.

But I couldn't tell anyone. Not even after we blew the whistle on Evan's abuse and our miserable lives, told them every single thing that happened to us, even down to what they did in the vans Evan rented out, right at the back of the scrapyard. At the back where nobody could hear the screams.

Most of them, the kids, pretended nothing had ever happened. It's what we all did to start with. Katrina might have carried on pretending if we hadn't persuaded her to go to the police.

I can still see her, with blood soaking through her top, one eye half closed and already bruising. She listened to us, and then she spat into the dust, stared at the spot where her saliva had landed. We all looked down as one of her teeth lay white on the dirt, surrounded by a foamy mouthful of blood.

"I'll do it. Let's go now," she said, raising her chin slightly, shoulders back. Even her white trainers were splashed with blood. She swayed suddenly, and she would have fallen if we hadn't supported her to the car.

Lots of reasons not to stop and talk to this man following me across the car park.

"I want to talk about Cara."

I froze, one foot off the ground, unable to hide my instinctive reaction to her name. Was fate finally throwing me a double six? It seemed like, this past couple of months, everyone wanted to talk about Cara.

CHAPTER TWENTY-SIX

As they drove back from their chat with Lukas, Dove took the road leading uphill past the church to the Arrowhill Hospital site. Steve made no comment as she parked next to a line of dirt-encrusted recycling bins. The rain had stopped and although the sky was still full of drifting clouds, a few rays of sunshine made the wet tarmac glitter.

"Let's take a look at this place," Dove said. "It's a common factor and something is bugging me about it, but I can't quite get what yet."

"Gut feeling?" Steve rolled his eyes. "Like we don't have anything better to do."

"Maybe. It won't take long." Dove glanced down at her watch.

The bored security guard at the gate was eager to accompany them, clearly desperate for a distraction. He jangled his bunch of keys importantly and took on the role of tour guide.

"So why do you want a look, then? Kids have been causing trouble again recently. Lots of graffiti and they get inside and take videos for those kind of YouTube channels about derelict buildings. Have you seen them?"

"I've seen a few," Steve replied. "Can you identify the kids from these videos?"

"No chance!" the man scoffed. "They're a pain in the arse but they aren't stupid. Never show their faces, so I don't know anything about them except they're bloody fast. Although there's one of them, a girl, and even she doesn't exactly show her face because she wears a mask, you know, like a Halloween Scream mask." He paused to examine a hole in the wire fencing. "She fell off the roof and twisted her ankle a few months ago and I found her just crying in pain. Still had her mask on and she managed to scarper when she saw me coming . . ."

He gave them a sidelong glance, "Of course, I had to let her go. She's not one of them doing the graffiti, she just does videos. I've watched her stuff myself and she's pretty good at arranging rooms and all the equipment."

"But if the person wears a mask, it might not be a girl, then?" Dove suggested reasonably.

"Course it is." The guard made a gesture with his hands, outlining what was clearly supposed to be a female figure. In case they were slow on the uptake, he added, "Great boobs on her."

Right. Dove managed not to roll her eyes and made a mental note to follow this up. Someone who was taking a particular interest in the old hospital, someone who posted their interest on YouTube.

The old A&E entrance was overgrown with weeds, and a small sapling sprouted from the roof. Broken windows, colourful graffiti and mouldering piles of rubbish gave the air a sour smell. Huge *Keep Out* signs were nailed against the broken window frames.

"Is it safe to go inside?" Dove glanced at her watch.

"Only some parts. I can let you in the side door next to the maternity ward. The basement is out of bounds and there's a lot of water damage, but most of the hospital was built on one level. The oncology ward was the only one on the first floor, and that's structurally unsound. I expect it'll come down in the next storm." He pointed to the far end of the building, where a double storey had been added, now perched precariously amid loose panels and a half-broken metal chimney.

"Let's have a quick look, then," Steve said. "If you could just let us in, we'll sign out on our way back. Don't want to take up any more of your time."

The guard opened his mouth to argue, his face disgruntled at the dismissal, until Dove said, "Actually, could you do us a favour and send me the links to those YouTube channels you were talking about? Especially the one with the girl you mentioned, the one who hurt her ankle?"

"Yeah, yeah, I can do that." Good humour restored, he beamed at her. "You got your email address? Or your phone number in case I remember anything else about any of the kids."

She passed him a card and waited until he'd trotted off before she and Steve pushed the heavy door cautiously open.

"I hope you realize you are never going to get rid of him now that he's got your contact details," Steve told her.

She turned and smiled sweetly. "That's why I gave him yours."

Steve's curses were muffled by the dense air of the derelict building.

"Same security firm as the one Lukas Windsor is employed by," Dove added, having clocked the distinctive red logo on the security guard's ID pass.

"I wonder if Lukas ever does shifts up here at the hospital, and if he is as diligent about not letting intruders in as he is down on the new development?" Steve mused.

The building felt like it could have been made of concrete bunkers, utterly closed in and more reminiscent of a prison than a medical facility. Moss grew in lighter corners, where water ran down the walls, dropping through rotted floors to a dank below-stairs prison. Dove peered down a set of stairs marked *Mortuary*, but seeing the gap-toothed stairs and the hole in the wall where the lift shaft lay open to the elements, disappearing far below in a terrifying tunnel of darkness and coiled wires, she changed her mind.

"Bet those kids go down there," Steve said, shining a torch down into the depths.

"The YouTubers? Yeah, but I quite like having working limbs, so I'll pass for now," Dove retorted, moving on.

CHAPTER TWENTY-SEVEN

The maternity ward, optimistically named Daffodil Ward according to the battered sign on the main doors, was partially open to the sky, but the shell remained intact. Various furniture, beds, a desk and nurse's station, all dank and mouldering, lent a sinister air to the place.

The hospital wasn't big, and the maternity ward looked like it could have held a maximum of fifteen beds. Small enough to get to know all your patients, Dove thought dryly. It gave her an odd feeling, almost like the ghosts of crying babies were still inhabiting the site, the echoes of past tragedies and triumphs still lining the half-derelict walls. A wave of sadness was unexpected and almost winded her in its violence.

"Would you tell your children if they had been adopted?" she asked Steve suddenly.

He had been struggling with desk drawers, but now turned in surprise. "I think we would, yes, I'm sure we would. Why?"

"Jess says she'll tell her twins when they are old enough to understand," Dove said thoughtfully.

Steve waited, hands on hips. "You want to share something?"

She bit her thumbnail, dithering, before she answered. "This case is getting to me a bit, that's all. It's just the baby thing and the choices people make. I don't know . . ." She didn't want to bring up the texts from Malina just now. There was only so far she would go at work, and she felt disloyal to her fiancé even thinking he might be cheating on her. It wasn't something she could put into words yet.

There was sympathy in Steve's eyes. "I'm sorry, mate, it can't be easy. If you want to talk about it at all . . ."

Dove smiled at him, relieved he had attributed her distraction to other causes. "Thanks, I think I just have to deal with it, but instead of keeping it all locked away, I thought I'd try letting people know when things aren't okay. That's progress, right?"

He winked at her. "It's brave, and you are awesome. Now come on, partner, let's finish up and get out of here!"

As they walked the length of the ward, Steve added, "Evan Houselow. I can't see why he would have come out and started killing people. I'm not sure Lukas was telling us the whole truth, but we don't have any evidence to link him to our victims yet."

She appreciated the subject change, pulling her mind back onto the case, away from their surroundings. "We need to find bloody Disappearing DJ and find out if he happened to be in an alley with Sarah Whitmore last night. And something else I've been thinking about: the date Sarah and Alice moved to this area wasn't long after the Benny Milward case."

"Do you think they were involved?" Steve considered. "Even if they were, it doesn't mean it has any significance in this case. The Benny Milward case was a multi-agency failure, and there were hundreds of people involved."

"I wonder if there is any truth in the claims that Evan killed a baby?"

"Someone else would have known if Lily was pregnant, had a baby . . . And for the kids to deny it as well. They had a thousand good reasons to add murder to Evan's list of violence."

"I know one thing, Evan had better stay clear of the Seaview or someone will get him. Gemma was very clear on that," Dove remarked, as she picked her way carefully across the floor to some peeling wallpaper. It hung just above the last bed in the row, opposite the gappy window that looked out across the weed-strewn site. She paused. Something had caught her eye.

The last bed on the row had clearly been arranged for one of the YouTube photographs or videos. It was half made with a hospital blanket and pillow, none of which could possibly be originals, given the cleanliness of the bedding. A small, shabby teddy bear sat at the head of the bed, watching with glass eyes, reminding Dove of the doll from the car crash site.

There was a chair next to the bed and, bizarrely, a row of old surgical instruments laid neatly on the floor.

"It's like a horror show, and those rusty things look like they would predate the hospital, even," Steve said, bending down to get a better look as Dove snapped a photo of the forceps, scalpels and other instruments.

"Well, we can check out the YouTube videos and see who set all this up, I guess," she suggested, relieved the wave of emotion had passed.

The wallpaper must have originally been a cheery pattern of yellow ducks on a blue background — now faded by the elements, it hung sadly, limply. Gently Dove pulled it back.

There was writing on the wall.

Hush little baby don't you cry,
Mama's going to sing you a lullaby.

Underneath in different, much more recent lettering, in small round capitals, was the name *CARA*.

CHAPTER TWENTY-EIGHT

.

"Who the hell is Cara?" Steve said as Dove drove them back into the town centre. He was scrolling through the photos he had taken at the site, pausing on the image of the writing on the wall.

"No idea. Probably not relevant at all. It's like people who scribble their names on the back of toilet doors, or on bus stop seats," Dove suggested. "Might be one of those YouTubers?"

Arriving back at the police station, it was a struggle to fight their way through the press. A high-profile story was always a draw, but they remained stony-faced, waiting until the security barriers had been raised and they could leave the crowd of reporters behind.

"You two tracked down DJ Darkness yet?" Josh asked as soon as they came in.

"No. Brighton sent someone over to his place, but he's gone AWOL. His brother reckons they were together at his place last night, but who knows?" Dove was nursing a bacon sandwich and felt the brown sauce she had liberally applied start to ooze out onto her fingers.

"I've seen him play at a couple of clubs. He's pretty good," Josh admitted.

"He might well be, but he's also bloody hard to find," Steve said sourly.

Dove shifted her iPad and took a huge bite of her sandwich before licking her fingers.

"That is truly disgusting," Steve told her.

"You're just pissed off because you didn't get one too," Dove mumbled with her mouth full.

"I think the finger-licking thing is hot," Josh said, dark eyes gleaming with mischief. "Did you know it's a fetish? Google it."

Dove looked down at the remains of her sandwich, her appetite fading fast. "Thanks, Josh."

"Sorry, Dove, couldn't help it. Look, time to go in." Grinning, he scarpered towards the briefing room.

DI Lincoln came out of his office and raised his voice so they could all hear: "We have another match from the lab, this time from the crash site, and the woods with partial prints and DNA from a hair sample, both of which belong to Evan Houselow. Martin Cartwright is also going to be interviewed under caution. The drugs discovered in his car have been traced back to the garage his mum's car was being repaired at, Benson and Sons on Ironworks Road."

"How super surprising Jay and Kevin Benson might be involved in some kind of drug dealing," Lindsey said sarcastically.

Dove knew Lindsey had been on the area drugs squad before she joined the MCT. "Old friends?"

"How could you tell?" Lindsey grinned maliciously. "Can't wait to see what they have to say for themselves this time."

DI Lincoln listened intently to their conversation, his expression blank, and when they had finished, he cleared his throat and went on, "We'll be bringing Evan in for a formal interview, and potentially holding him pending further evidence. We can place him at the scene of the crash, and that's enough for his solicitor at the moment."

"Bloody hell," Josh said, leaning back in his chair and letting out a whistle. "Suspects and solid evidence. Oh, do we know yet if Sarah had a hospital bracelet in her throat?"

"No, the autopsy is scheduled for tomorrow morning. Even Dr Isiah couldn't get it moved up this time. We need to get a handle on this case, or we'll be dealing with front-page stories nationwide well into next week, so well done, everyone, let's keep at it." The DI was clearly under pressure. He shuffled a few files on his desk.

After trawling through reams of documents and three more fruitless calls trying to track down the elusive DJ Darkness, aka Leo Windsor, Dove grabbed two cups of coffee from the machine in the corridor and handed one to Steve.

"I'm going back to look at the YouTube videos for Arrowhill."

She began to trawl through, fast-forwarding in places. Lots of teenagers, a few older blokes interested in the history. All there illegally. She found a couple of girls, but none wearing Scream masks.

Steve's email pinged as she leaned over the computer.

"Hey, it's our friendly security guard from Arrowhill," her partner said sarcastically. "He starts it, *Hi, gorgeous . . .*" Steve spluttered into his drink. "I don't think I can cope."

"Shut up! Forward it to me if you can't handle the heat. Anyway, maybe he means you: the email address starts with *steve@*, doesn't it?"

"Done." But he was still laughing, and she couldn't help grinning back.

"Idiot."

There were five links, four of them directly to the masked girl's channel. She had over 300,000 followers and Dove felt a flash of respect. The girl didn't speak much but allowed her photography and videos to do the talking. Her set-ups were great — eerie and emotive — and she certainly got around.

"Are you on the Arrowhill one yet?" Steve asked. "Maybe her name is Cara? The writing for the lullaby was old, but the name looked recent."

"It doesn't say. She's UrbEXGirl in her profile. Just checking out a couple of others she's made. Wait a minute. What's that?"

"Background on the Arrowhill site, seeing as we're taking an interest." Steve brought up Google Maps, moving over so he could see her screen, "Abberley General had two new wings built and the multistorey car park, so I guess it was more modern and they didn't need both. Nothing has been built on the old Arrowhill site yet, it's just flagged for housing. But the initial searches from the local authority turned up some kind of contamination in the soil that was deemed unsafe for human habitation. Look . . ." He tapped at her keyboard and opened a document.

Dove was still staring at the derelict site via the satellite pictures, flipping back to her YouTube videos, trying to locate the maternity ward among the jumbled mess of weeds and crumbling buildings. "What a waste of time. Although . . . this contamination. I wonder if it affected any of the hospital patients?"

"Don't think it could, it was buried underneath the soil. Doesn't matter anyway, does it? Look, it was a rubbish tip in the fifties and the gases, etcetera, could cause harm if disturbed."

"Anyway, look at all these videos. Apparently, the place is a magnet for the kind of people who break in and take photos and videos in derelict buildings." She leaned over and showed him the list of titles. "Total clickbait!"

Arrowhill Revisited.
Shit Scary Hospital Ghosts.
Midnight at Arrowhill.

She played the first few seconds on a couple of clips, but they were all very similar, mostly teenagers or younger adults from their voices and stature. Their faces were all either hidden by masks or scarves pulled up, hoodies pulled down, or the camera just showed the hospital site, never the intruder.

"Totally staged. Why do people leave their shit when they move out?" Dove wondered, staring at photographs of hospital beds, old equipment, wooden desks with drawers of files open and rotting. "I'm hoping they took all the medical records before they jumped ship."

"That's why you can never find any. It's all left in their abandoned sites," Steve suggested dryly.

"She's very professional, the girl the security guard has a crush on, and I guess she makes some money from this channel." Dove scrolled down to the Arrowhill video and studied it. Like the others, the set-ups were great, but particular attention was paid to Daffodil Ward. The last bed in the row had the chair and teddy bear, Dove noted, and she checked out the date on the video. Three months ago. As the camera panned, she tried to see if the surgical instruments were laid out on the floor, but the angle was wrong. In one frame, the girl gently moved the frond of rotting wallpaper and gave a close-up of the written lullaby. Infuriatingly, she didn't pan far enough downwards for Dove to see if the name had already been added.

"Anything?"

"No. Not anything new, anyway. So, she likes old buildings, and she's done three videos of Arrowhill, which might suggest she especially likes the site, or just that she's local. But she's also done four in Ashford, over in Kent. She does spend a lot of time in the maternity ward, and she's got the lullaby in shot, but I can't see the name."

Dove scrolled down again, checking out another video. There were a couple of lads, probably in their late twenties, and she watched them breaking and entering, creeping into the old hospital site. Their commentary was amusing, and she held her breath as they entered the maternity ward. The date the video was showing as 19 January.

The teddy bear wasn't there, and the boys seemed to be concentrating on finding ghosts. But there was a set-up at the nurses' station that made her rewind and freeze the video, going through it frame by frame.

"Steve?"

He was chomping on a health food bar, with obvious distaste, and clearly grateful for the distraction.

"Watch this . . ." She played it again, waiting for his reaction.

"I can't see anything."

"Look!" She paused the video in exactly the right place and jabbed the screen with a finger. "On the nurses' desk there's an arrangement of stuff, and put there for photos I'm sure, but look at the object next to the teacup."

"A biscuit?"

She rolled her eyes with impatience. "It's a stone heart!"

"Shit . . . I don't know, though," Steve said doubtfully. "Do you think? The picture's really grainy."

"It definitely wasn't there when we visited," Dove told him, scrolling down to the photos they had taken on Daffodil Ward.

"Okay . . . Maybe it is a stone heart. Send the link down to Cybercrimes and see if they can find out who these two clowns are."

"I'll see if Josh can do anything with the clarity right now. He used to work in Cybercrimes, and he might be a pain in the arse but he's also a tech whizz," Dove said as the officer in question passed by her chair.

"I heard that, but I'll ignore it because I know how much you love me really," Josh called over his shoulder. "Go on, what do you want?"

Dove explained quickly and waited while Josh studied the video and sent the link to his phone. She also sent it down to the lab and tech teams. Her heart was racing. Steve might not be convinced but she was sure it was another roughly shaped pebble, just like the ones left in the mouths of Evan Houselow, Alice Cartwright, and Sarah Whitmore. And tucked next to the doll baby.

Four stone hearts.

CHAPTER TWENTY-NINE

Lots of bad things happened in the cars after we were locked in for the night. I hunkered down in the front seat, right on the floor in the footwell sometimes.

If you were in the wrong car, you were subjected to crude comments, to those little videos, and then it got worse if you were in two battered old white camper vans at the back of the yard.

The pretty ones were always targeted, and it only stopped when we grew too old and too strong to be manhandled into the car. But before that, for one long, boiling-hot summer, they had things their way. Once I realized it was only the pretty, cute-looking kids who were forced to take part, I took action.

I cut my hair with some scissors from school, so it was really short, with a hideous jagged fringe. I scribbled on my cheeks with permanent marker pen and cut my arms with the end of a compass. It worked. For me now, it was mostly a slap round the head or the occasional fist in the gut. Nothing I wasn't already used to.

They pretended I wasn't there, and I pretended the same for them. Down the end of our road, on the way to school, when we bothered to go, and that was just for the free food and drink, was the beach. I would sit on the pebbles, watching the sea and the sky, running my fingers over the sand, the stones, feeling the shapes and textures. Some pebbles were perfect, and I would slip them in my bag for later, to distract me during the long nights.

If you sat with your back against the seawall, nobody could see you were there at all. You could vanish for a whole day, and at that point in my life, that was exactly what I wanted, to lose myself and to blend in with the background.

CHAPTER THIRTY

DI Blackman came out of his office, phone between shoulder and chin, a pile of papers in one hand, a mug of tea in the other. He paused his phone conversation. "Dove, you and Steve go over and talk to Gerald Cartwright, please."

"Alice's ex-husband?" Dove asked. "Lindsey said he didn't seem to quite process that Alice was dead when they broke the news. She said he insisted it was a mistake."

"His carer has said he's becoming very agitated and wants to talk to the police. She called the main desk half an hour ago," DI Blackman told them. "She also said he won't leave his home because he'll find it too stressful, so we need to talk to him there. It's possible he knows something useful. Alice called him twice the day before she died, which, from her call history, is unusual. Her son also confirmed that, in the nine years since they divorced, his parents didn't see each other or communicate much."

Steve rang the number for Gerald's carer, while Dove opened an email from the tech team. She scanned it quickly. The IP address had been hard to pinpoint, but there was some information. None of it linked back to Lukas or Leo Windsor, though. She opened another file and pulled up a driver's licence photo of Katrina, the fourth sibling.

"Half an hour." Steve came off his phone. "She doesn't look like her brothers, does she?"

"No. I can't get it out of my mind what Lukas said, they all went through hell together and that bonded them. It's just . . . Kids shouldn't have to go through that. Hell, nobody should have to suffer like that." She gave herself a mental shake. "They are all back in this area, and their mother Lily passed away before Evan got out."

"So what?"

"I don't know yet." She shrugged. "I'm certainly not thinking they'd team up with Evan to murder Alice and Sarah. It's just something is bugging me . . ."

"It usually is," he told her. "Come on, let's find out what Alice's ex-husband wants. Oh, I just heard they raided Benson and Sons . . . Lots of blow and some pills. Looks like it wasn't just Martin's car doors that were being used to transport the drugs."

"I missed that."

"It's not on the file yet. Lindsey's still got mates on the squad and they let her know what happened."

"So was Alice's son involved or not?"

"Apparently, he's not the sharpest tool in the box, and they think the garage has been using customer cars without their owners' knowledge. Martin Cartwright designed their website for them, thought they were his mates, but I guess he's feeling a little stupid right now. They copy the keys while they're in for a service, and attach a GPS tracker, and result: unsuspecting, free drugs couriers."

"How would they know where the car was going, though? What if someone took their car over to France for a holiday, and they took the drugs with them?"

Steve grinned at her. "No idea, mate, not my scam, but they've been busted anyway. Oh, but this bit is good. The owners admitted Evan Houselow has been doing a few hours at the garage for cash in hand since he came out. He's on the security cameras from the next building working at the garage all last week."

"Do you think he's in on it?"

"Straight out of prison and straight back in if he was, and it's not looking good for him at the moment anyway," Steve said, looking in the glove compartment of the car. "Hey, did you eat my energy bar from yesterday?"

"Nope. You ate it yourself. I had chips and you had your bar," Dove reminded him. She drove fast, but carefully, sending a flock of seagulls squawking noisily up into the grey skies as she took a right turn on the seafront, heading out of the town into the rolling green of the Downs. She glanced at Steve. "I wonder what Evan will say about the drugs, though?"

Steve grinned. "I'm quite sure the DI is grilling him as we speak."

* * *

Gerald Cartwright, Alice's ex-husband, lived in the middle cottage of a rundown trio of what would have historically been farmworkers' cottages. Now they stood in a riot of nettles, brambles and early bluebells.

"Nice," said Dove appreciatively. "Sometimes I think I'd like to move out into the countryside a bit more."

"You'd hate it," Steve told her. "No chippie four doors down, and no beach across the road. You're a city girl with a surf obsession, and the fields wouldn't cut it."

"Good point." Dove pushed her way past an overgrown rosemary bush, releasing the heady tang from the fragrant leaves. She knocked on the door.

There was no answer, but she could hear someone moving around inside.

"Hallo?" Steve called loudly, making several crows squawk in alarm and take flight.

The movements stopped and slow, cautious footsteps could be heard inside.

"Who is it?"

"DC Milson and DS Parker from the Major Crimes Team. You wanted to talk to us. We would like to ask you a couple of questions if that's still okay?"

The door opened and an elderly giant of a man peered round. His face was crumpled with fear and his faded blue eyes were red-veined and half sunken into folds of weathered wrinkles.

"I was waiting for you to come."

"You were?" Dove glanced at Steve as they followed the old man inside.

"Yes." His voice was trembling, and he caught hold of the door jamb as they passed, hooking shaking fingers onto the ledge, almost as though he felt he needed support. "Yes, but you didn't so I had to get Connie to ring you. Because I'm next, you see. They'll kill me next."

CHAPTER THIRTY-ONE

The living space was cramped but comfortable, with beautiful glossy houseplants on every surface. It was a bit like taking tea in a jungle, Dove thought. She smiled at Gerald's carer, who introduced herself as Connie. Dove wondered for a second if she seemed familiar. Connie was a tall, athletic young woman with numerous glittering piercings and plaited brown hair with tints of pink. She carefully carried a tray of huge mugs of 'builder's brew' from his tiny kitchen area, then offered to leave the room.

"Yes, Carrie, thank you, please leave me with the officers," Gerald said, with dignity. He took a sip of his tea, and beamed at her, all worries apparently vanishing. "Thank you, Carrie."

She smiled fondly at him, with a touch of concern wrinkling her forehead and puckering the edges of her mouth. "If you need me, I'll be in the conservatory. And Gerald?"

"Yes, Connie?"

"It's okay. Everything is as it should be."

He nodded and repeated her words a couple of times as she addressed the officers. "Gerald sometimes forgets where he is or what is happening, but we have our mantra, and we know we are safe. *Everything is as it should be.*"

Dove felt this had been said more for Gerald's benefit, but she nodded in agreement. Quinn's stepdad had early-onset dementia and she had witnessed first-hand the terror and frustration he experienced with this cruel disease.

"You worked at Arrowhill Hospital with your ex-wife until it closed?" Steve started, but Gerald shot him a look, worry returning to his eyes.

"You don't need to soften me up. You know I did, and you know I worked with them, or you wouldn't be here. We thought we were doing the right thing . . ." Unexpectedly his eyes were wet with tears, and he dashed them away with a gnarled, battered hand.

"Go on. What did you do?" Dove asked gently, slightly alarmed by his genuine distress. She hoped he wasn't about to confess to murder.

"It started with the Benny Milward case. You remember?"

Both officers nodded. Dove made a note. Gemma Rogers had also mentioned Benny's case several times.

"It happened time and time again. But social services were understaffed, child protection was a two-person office with case files bursting out the filing cabinets, medical records weren't kept, there was always an excuse as to why these children weren't saved." Gerald took a sip of his tea and paused, as though looking for the right words, sifting through memories. "I have gaps, you know, in my memory, but I still feel . . . everything. Times when I can't remember where I am or even who Carrie is. Or Carla . . . No, *Connie*!"

Dove bit her thumbnail, listening to his words, wincing as the emotion flowed off him in waves. She exchanged a glance with Steve. They both knew specially trained officers had been to visit Gerald and taken a statement the day after Alice's murder, but he hadn't mentioned his ex-wife's demise today.

"We called them the lost children, you know. They just slipped off the radar, always someone else's problem." His eyes were unfocused now and with his left hand he kept pulling at his jumper, fidgeting with the neck and rubbing his shoulder. "They all died. All the lost children die in the end." He was mumbling now.

"What do you mean they died?" Dove felt herself freeze at his words, and Steve raised his eyebrows at her.

"They all died, I tell you, all of them!" Gerald raised his voice angrily now. He thumped a fist down onto the coffee table, sloshing his drink everywhere and decimating a small cactus in a pottery dish.

"Gerald, who died?" Steve asked calmly.

Connie was already coming into the room, and she spoke gently to Gerald, reassuring him that everything was as it should be.

"I want to talk to these people. It helps to talk." He turned crossly to his carer, but his anger seemed to have dissipated. "I've told you before I need to get rid of my memories so I can have peace again. They hurt me . . ." He touched his head and looked pleadingly at Dove. He was such a big man, but with such pain in his eyes that she felt herself getting slightly emotional.

"Gerald, what children died?" she asked softly.

Again, he ignored the question, continuing to ramble on, occasionally gesticulating to give emphasis to his words. "It was Alice's idea. She and I were always on the ward, although I was really behind the scenes. Nobody really notices porters and we go everywhere." He gave a short bark of laughter. "We're part of the scenery, but we get to know people."

"Go on," Steve told him, rescuing the cactus and replacing it back into the pottery dish.

"It wasn't a big hospital, and the maternity ward was just the other side of A&E. It was more like what they used to call a cottage hospital. Not like Abberley General."

Gerald took a gulp of the new cup of tea Connie had just placed before him. "I worked at the Royal General, and I know we could have saved Benny. He was abused since he was a baby. Came back in at five days old with bruising, the report said. We were there! Why did nobody follow through, check the reports? Did you know he had forty-two separate injuries when he died? Even his tongue was bruised . . ."

"Did Alice work at the Royal General hospital while Benny was there?" Dove asked, pushing down a rising nausea at the thought of the poor child's suffering.

"Yes, we both did. I told you already! She was on duty when he was born, and she filed a report after the birth, flagged the parents for help. They were very rough with the baby, she said, and left him crying while they went outside for a smoke, just left him on the ward for a couple of hours while they were on their phones outside."

"How did you meet Sarah?" Steve prodded carefully.

"Sarah?"

"Sarah Whitmore, Alice's friend. She was a social worker, wasn't she?"

His gaze slid sideways, almost as though he felt he had been caught out or said something he shouldn't have. "No. Never heard of her. We had to pick them very carefully, you see. It meant some could be saved but many more died. And how do you choose between children?"

"Gerald, what do you mean about picking the children? Do you mean you or Alice were involved with child protection when they removed at-risk children?" Steve asked.

"We took the ones who needed it most." He gulped down his tea as though he was desperately thirsty, and then rubbed his chest. "Connie, do you have any more of those indigestion tablets, please?"

"Of course. I'll just get them from the kitchen." Connie vanished with the empty mugs and came back with two white tablets on a saucer and a glass of water.

Despite their best efforts, Steve and Dove were unable to get Gerald back onto the topic of the lost children.

As the man sucked on an indigestion tablet, Dove let out a long breath. "Do you know Gemma Rogers?"

He shook his head after careful thought. "No, I don't. The name wasn't mentioned as far as I remember."

Steve was tapping his pen on his notebook. "And you think someone is coming after you because of what you all did . . . um, saving the lost children?"

"I know it." He reached into a drawer in the desk behind him and pulled out a heart-shaped pebble, offering it to Dove on the palm of his hand. "I got this yesterday, and I knew. Alice knows too. And David does. I don't know David, though."

"Gerald, did this arrive in the mail or was it hand-delivered?" Dove was up from her seat and whipping a pair of gloves from her pocket.

"In the mail, of course. Padded parcel, I wondered what it was, but then I knew. Alice knows too, but she knows everything. We had to do something, because we couldn't let it happen again, you see . . ." He put the heart in his pocket.

There was an awkward silence, before Connie said, "Gerald, Alice has passed away, hasn't she, love?"

He shook his head. "Don't be ridiculous. Alice is dead? I spoke to her this morning. You two police officers can call Alice. She knows all about the lost children. It was her idea, I tell you. She had death threats after Benny's case, you know."

"Gerald, are you saying you and Alice took babies from their parents?" Steve asked, still incredulous.

"Too many . . . One year there were nineteen deaths. We saved two. Just two . . ." He shrugged, and got up, beckoning them to the window. "For all the babies who went to sleep and never woke up, I planted a tree. See the pink blossom over there? A cherry for the girls and magnolia for the boys." He turned back from the window and smiled his wide uncomplicated smile and Dove for a second flashed back to Gemma's voice, *They called him the Smiling Man and they said he took babies from people's houses.*

Gerald spoke again. "A cherry for the girls and magnolia for the boys. Everything is as it should be, isn't it, Connie?"

CHAPTER THIRTY-TWO

Gerald remained in front of his window, staring out at the garden, and didn't move even as Dove thanked him for his time. She could see a tear rolling down his cheek and she didn't want to embarrass him.

In the hallway, Connie spoke quietly. "He is suffering, poor man. Whatever he said to you could be completely true, or it could be his way of trying to patch together and make sense of his memories. His emotional memory is currently far stronger than his factual memory."

"How does that relate to his recall of past events?" Steve queried.

Connie considered. "Well, the best way to explain it might be that he remembers how he felt, but not where he was, or who he might have been talking to at the time. Dates, names and places may be missing or in the wrong order, or not feature at all."

"Has he mentioned children dying before? Or even he and his ex-wife 'saving' children?" Dove asked.

"No, but I've only been working with him since December. It was when your colleagues came round and told him about Alice that he started talking to me about the missing children. The lost children, he kept saying, too." She frowned. "It breaks my heart to think of children suffering, and I think it weighs on his mind. In fact, no, I'm wrong . . . He had a visitor, a friend — Sarah, I think — a few months ago and he's been very down since then."

Steve brought up Sarah Whitmore's photograph and flipped the screen so Connie could see. "Was this Gerald's visitor?"

"Yes, it was!"

"Who else has visited recently?"

"Alice." She twisted a strand of hair in her fingers, thinking. "That was unusual. He told me he hadn't seen her since Christmas. His son, Martin, comes once a week, and he sometimes comes at the weekend to help out in the garden. Actually, the last few times he came they've been clearing out the loft and the shed. Gerald's a bit of a hoarder and he had loads of old newspapers and magazines, Martin said. They burned most of them over there," she indicated out of the narrow hallway windows to a recent bonfire site in the front garden, to the east side of the house.

Visible through the kitchen windows, the cherry and magnolia trees swayed gently in the spring breeze. How old were the trees? Dove wondered. Ten, twenty years? She turned back to Connie. "Did he mention the stone heart that was sent to him?"

"No, sorry, and normally we go through his mail together. You can check with his night carer, Donald, just to make sure. I've got his mobile number."

Dove went back into the room in some trepidation, hoping her request wouldn't upset the poor man even more. He was still standing where they had left him, but he turned his head as she spoke. "Gerald, can we borrow the heart, please?"

He nodded, expression once more serene, and removed the object from his pocket. Dove slipped on a fresh pair of plastic gloves and popped the heart into an evidence bag. She carried numerous items in her work bag, and even though the chances of any prints were slim, it was always worth a shot.

Steve was giving Connie his card and thanking her as Dove walked slowly back into the hallway. Somehow, the business card dropped, and Connie bent quickly to retrieve it from the floor.

As she moved, Dove suddenly knew why she had seemed vaguely familiar. The quick, athletic drop had mirrored a jump made in the YouTube video she had been studying. The figure was the same, the hair . . . Maybe . . .

"We were at the old Arrowhill site this morning, where Gerald and Alice worked," she told Connie conversationally.

The younger woman's gaze didn't shift. "Were you?"

"Have you ever been there?"

"I . . . No, I haven't. I heard it was going to be redeveloped," she said, moving towards the door and opening it for them.

"What's your full name, Connie?"

She looked flustered. "Connie Batchelor. Why?"

"It's just that Gerald called you a few other names: Carrie, Cara . . ." She substituted Carla for Cara, just to see if there was any reaction.

"He gets confused." She didn't respond to the names in the way Dove had hoped, but stood anxiously, one hand tapping the door frame, almost as though she hoped she could urge them out of the house through sheer willpower.

"Okay, thanks for your time." Dove smiled at her. "If you want to talk to either of us, just call, okay? If anything bothers you, or you remember something?"

There was no traffic and soon they were leaving the countryside behind for the bustle of the town centre, where they instantly encountered a tailback on the one-way system round Abberley.

"What do you think?" Steve asked, popping gum into his mouth as he drove.

Dove considered. She had already told him she thought she recognized Connie as the YouTuber with the Scream mask: UrbEXGirl. "Anything he says will never stand up in court, and it could just be that these are part memories

134

and part regret. The Benny Milward case clearly affected him hugely and if Alice then received death threats . . . As for his tree planting and talk about taking children, I don't know . . ." She thoughtfully emptied the rest of her sweets straight from the packet into her mouth, relishing the sugar hit.

"I wonder if he really doesn't remember Sarah or if he was trying to make sure she wasn't implicated in what he was telling us. He was a little less direct when we asked if he knew her."

"But what *was* he telling us? That child protection agencies have failed in the past to protect vulnerable children, so they took at-risk babies from their parents *illegally*? That he and Alice were somehow *involved* in the cases where there were deaths? Or that we're going in the wrong direction with the investigation, and we should be focusing on Benny Milward and his connections?"

Steve shook his head. "To answer your second question, I don't even know how that would be possible. Imagine the legal red tape, and what happens then? You take a baby, and nobody notices? What do you with it?"

* * *

Exhausted from trying to form solid conclusions from information that seemed to currently be a mass of tangled threads, Dove decided to take a quick break.

She was walking down to the car park from the office, deliberating between a bacon sandwich and a sausage roll, when her sister rang.

"Did you talk to Quinn about those texts?" Ren asked sternly.

Dove found herself shaking her head, even though her sister couldn't see her. "Not yet."

"Dove!"

"We've hardly seen each other, and, you know I trust him . . ."

"If the situation was reversed, would you mind him saying 'Hey, I saw these weird texts on your phone the other night . . .'?"

"I don't want it to sound like I'm accusing him of anything because that would piss me off," Dove explained.

"Right, but you are letting it eat away at you, and with this tough case as well, you need to give yourself a break," her sister said firmly.

"I will! Oh, Ren, while you're on — didn't you have a friend who sells beach art and stuff down in those pop-up shops on the seafront?"

"Becca? She's still down there. Why the interest?"

"I'm looking for someone, an artist maybe, who might work with the stones from the beach. Paint them, carve them or something. Can I have Becca's number?"

"Sure, I'll share her contact details with you."

"Thanks, Ren."

"No worries. And Dove?"

She knew by the tone of her sister's voice what was coming. "I know, I know . . . I'll ask him!"

CHAPTER THIRTY-THREE

"Listen up, people! Can we do an update for those who have managed to get back here in time?" DI Blackman was already heading for the briefing room, threading his way through the open-plan office, avoiding bags and bodies and exuding energy and confidence.

"How is he still awake and walking, let alone enthusiastic?" Steve said, smothering a yawn, as he got up to follow.

"It's the running," Dove told him. "He runs at least ten miles every day and he's told me it gives him the energy to push through."

"Isn't that contradicting nature? Surely physical exercise makes you tired?" Steve patted his stomach. "Which is why I don't have a gym membership at the moment."

Once the team was assembled, the DI kicked off. "We have established that Evan Houselow is working a couple of days a week cash-in-hand for Benson and Sons. The garage has been on the radar before for drugs, and it seems they haven't changed their approach to business. According to his statement, Evan knows them from way back, and when they were the only ones to offer him a job after his release, he jumped at it."

"Seems like everyone's friendly neighbourhood garage," Lindsey commented. "Martin Cartwright thought they were his best mates, and then they give a job to Evan. Proper community service," she added.

The DI nodded. "Most of you have read the report. The facts listed in it are relevant to our investigation. Evan was helping to wash cars and clean up the workshops according to him. According to the owners he was helping to pack drugs into the door linings of customers' cars." He clicked the mouse and looked up.

The wall-mounted screen showed the photographic evidence from the crash site, followed by pictures from the drugs raid at the garage. "Evan claims he had no idea drugs were in the cars, but he was sent to retrieve Martin's car, when the GPS tracker showed it was stopped in the middle of nowhere. The garage owners kept a track on all the cars containing gear, so this was a red flag to them. They sent Evan to investigate and see if a rival had got their hands on the goods."

"And he pitched up with a gun," Steve said, dryly.

"Right. Evan says he arrived, saw the car, the baby in the road, but nobody in the car. He reckons this was around 6.40 p.m. He was a bit freaked out by the baby but left everything as it was and pulled into a forestry track a little way up the road." The DI changed the screen to photos from the car crash. "Evan was convinced by now something was going on. As far as he knew the car was being driven by an old lady. Taking the handgun — which he says was given to him by Jay Benson, along with a wad of cash to go and check out the car — he went into the woods."

"That timing is super tight," Dove observed. "Steve and I arrived thirty-five minutes later."

"Right, so it does lend credence to his story that he nosed around, had a quick look in the car to see if the driver was there, and was just about to start searching the vehicle to see if the drugs were still safe when you two arrived."

Dove recalled the feeling someone had been watching them. She had put it down to the shadows and the baby, but Evan could have killed one or both of them at any time.

"So, he hid in the woods the whole time?" She heard Steve say "Shit" under his breath and knew he was thinking the same thing.

"You two poked around a bit and then went back and started examining the car. Evan panicked, realized he needed to get the hell out of there and shot at you. He does say he aimed to one side, not at either of you." DI Blackman smiled wryly at Steve. "So I guess he's just a bad shot."

Steve nodded and massaged his healing shoulder. "Yeah, really crap. Wait, so Evan never saw Alice at all?"

"He says not. He says he doesn't know her and wasn't aware Alice and Sarah even worked on his case. The evidence we currently have supports his statement." He looked towards his colleague and DI Lincoln took over.

"The significant objects left at the scenes include the pink hospital bracelet, the baby doll, and the stone heart keepsakes."

DI Lincoln was looking at the whiteboard, at the smiling photos of both victims. "Clearly these have some kind of significance to the perpetrator." He zoomed in on the baby bracelet on screen, followed by the stone hearts and the baby doll left at the car crash scene. "We have confirmed the baby is a 'Living Doll' baby and was purchased from an online company between 2010 and 2017. They sell thousands of these dolls every week. The bracelet is widely available on eBay, Etsy and Amazon . . ." He glanced at his notes. "This particular batch number indicates it was manufactured in China within the last twelve months, so probably not an old keepsake, but something purchased specifically for this."

DI Blackman had glanced down as his email pinged, and Dove noticed the intense expression on his face. It was that fire she recognized from a good lead.

"Just before we head off, we've had some results back and the autopsy report for Sarah Whitmore. She also had a pink hospital bracelet inserted into her throat."

"Bloody hell," Josh said. "If Evan is off the hook for Alice, I guess that probably means he wasn't responsible for

Sarah's death either." Towering above the rest of the team as usual, he took long strides towards the murder board and studied it intently.

"And double-check the timeline on her way home. Bear Green is a tiny place, but it does have a one-platform station," DI Blackman added. "It's a very slim chance Alice might have picked up a passenger between leaving work and crashing her car. We have some unidentified partial prints in the car still. Did she take her killer home?"

"Anything from you, Pete?" DS Wyndham, as designated family liaison officer for Alice's son, Martin, and Sarah's son, Jack, was currently juggling a load of paperwork, but he shook his head. "Nothing useful. Martin is still shitting himself about the drugs bust, and all Jack cares about is his posh job up in London. He's a bit of a wanker."

"I don't need personal opinions of witnesses and suspects, I need evidence. Let's crack down on the phone records and emails. I'm going to call the lab again. This kind of wait is ridiculous and it's holding up the investigation. We could easily be missing something vital that would halve our time spent on this case." DCI Franklin spoke firmly, frowning at a totally unabashed DS Wyndham, as he gathered up a pile of paperwork and walked briskly towards his office.

Having received their instructions, the team rapidly dispersed, with Steve and Dove hitting their computers to dig up the phone records, even though these had already been meticulously covered.

Retrieving Becca's number from Ren's message, Dove called her quickly. She was keen to help, bubbly and enthusiastic about all thing arts and crafts.

"There *is* some pebble art, but mostly things like driftwood mirrors, canvases, recycled jewellery . . . I can send you a link to the Etsy store of one artist who might be a fit?"

"Thanks, Becca, that would be great."

Dove moved more documents around on her screen while she waited for the link, thinking. Gemma Rogers was still claiming her mobile phone was lost and it hadn't been used since the night Alice died. Then there was Gerald's carer, Connie. It might be worth digging into her background a little more. She reached for her phone, pulling up the name and details of the agency Connie worked for.

"Connie Batchelor? Yes, she's been with us for eighteen months now. She worked for another agency before us. She has excellent references." The woman's voice changed. "She isn't in any trouble, is she?"

"No, not at all. We just have to carry out background checks on everyone involved in our current investigation."

"That's a relief. She really is devoted to her patients. Looks after them like they were her own family. Oh, I do know she doesn't have any family of her own. She told me she had been through the care system when she was younger . . . That's not betraying a confidence, it's on her file, because she went back to one of her foster families for work experience."

Dove shoved the phone between ear and chin and made a note of the names and dates. She ended the call and then picked up the Etsy link from Becca. A few moments' scrolling told her this artist was not the person crafting the stone hearts. The pebbles and stones she used were larger, flatter, perfect for creating mini canvases for cheerful sunny beach scenes.

As she walked over to DI Blackman's office to relay her find, she was mulling over the information she had gleaned from the carer agency. Connie must be around the same age as Evan's kids. Was there a chance she could have known them? Or could Alice, Gerald and Sarah have been involved with her professionally?

DI Blackman added Dove's findings to his next email for the team, along with the other incoming information. It was vital everyone was kept updated and aware of what the other team members and the wider community were doing, and that potential leads weren't missed.

"What about Gerald's claims of dead babies and of potentially snatching babies?"

The DI's tone suggested he wasn't keen on that lead, and Dove could see why. It could open a whole can of worms if it was true, and if it wasn't anything to do with the murders, just create a huge amount of extra work. Especially paperwork.

The office was already buzzing with extra bodies borrowed from other departments and their usual team had doubled in size due to the complexity of this investigation. Each additional person assigned to the case, every hour logged, would be costing them money, and the upper management gave the DCIs a hard time when it came to costings. Hence DCI Franklin's permanently worried look whenever he was dealing with his toppling mound of paperwork.

She jumped as her phone rang, listened intently to the caller and then called over to DI Blackman. "Boss, I've just had a call from Buzz, the manager at Stage 32. Leo Windsor is in the club now. He walked in ten minutes ago and told Buzz he wanted to do a soundcheck, which Buzz says will take him an hour or so. He's got a gig there tomorrow night."

She turned back to the call. "Is that usual? I mean, to turn up twenty-four hours early?"

"Yeah . . . Well, no, but we always offer a soundcheck, and he's a big deal now. I'm surprised his crew isn't doing it for him," Buzz said slightly sarcastically.

"I'll send a couple of cars to pick him up and get him interviewed," DI Blackman said. "Could your witnesses from the other night pick him out in a line-up, do you think?"

Dove wrinkled her nose, considering. "I can ask, but I'm not sure. It makes it much harder on the ID front that Lukas Windsor is an absolute double of his brother. They really are identical twins, especially if you saw them on a dark night, running away down the street."

CHAPTER THIRTY-FOUR

I could see as I turned the corner and started to jog that he was just standing there, looking after me. He looked like a sad old man, and I felt a jolt of satisfaction.

The bastard who had bullied us, abused us, might be out and free, but he looked like shit, and I wasn't sure the grey skin was just prison pallor. Maybe he has terminal cancer or something and feels like he's on some kind of redemption mission. But then I've seen a lot of old addicts, the ones that mix their pleasures. It eats away at them, giving their skin that death tinge.

The last time I ever saw Lily her lips were almost blue, and her eyes said she had given up. Whatever she'd been putting in her body for all those years was finally killing her from the inside out. But Lily tried so hard to get better. Evan, on the other hand, can fucking die as soon as possible, and in as much pain as possible, for all I care.

He even said sorry! I gave a snort of laughter as I ran up the steps to my flat. Not fucking likely. The man was evil as they come back in the day, and I don't believe he's changed. No, there was another reason he was dragging me along with him, and soon I would find out what games he was playing and beat him at them.

I grabbed a bottle from the fridge and sank into my sofa, leaning back and closing my eyes. Too many memories were flooding my brain. I could hear the questions again. Constant, probing questions from everyone.

The reports suggest the abuse was more widespread than the four of you? That potentially Evan might have been involved in a child sex ring?

No way. *I can still feel the squirming rush of fear, the colour in my cheeks as I shook my head, my hair falling forward to hide my burning face, but I answered the question. I always answered the bloody questions.*

That was in the vans, and I know Evan owned the scrapyard, but he just let them do what they wanted as long as they paid good money for the vans. I never saw Evan with the girls or anything and he wasn't into all that. With him, it was the control, and he liked hitting us. Like, he actually enjoyed it. When he wasn't beating us, he would be online, gaming, or shouting at the teenagers working in the scrapyard, strutting around with his chest out, the wanker. He often said he wanted to do to us what he was doing online, all the torture and that, the killing. He loved it. Especially the death bit.

They tried to do it well, to make sure we knew we were protected, but it was tough. I remember faces leaning towards me, eyes examining, judging, concluding. I felt like a lab rat, and I felt like my whole self, my soul and my body, was on display for everyone to draw their own conclusions. And all the time, I knew there was one secret I had to keep.

What about the children who didn't testify? The others involved in the abuse. Do you know if any of them are still around?

Who else was aware of what was going on?

Why didn't you tell someone earlier? A teacher? Another parent?

I'm not the only one with a secret, but who is going to tell first? Or do I keep it all to myself, enjoying the knowledge that finally I have all my answers and everything I ever needed?

CHAPTER THIRTY-FIVE

"Hi, Dove. Guess what? We found DJ Darkness." It was Lindsey. "You want to come over?"

"What the hell? Where are you?" Dove blinked in confusion and stared around the office. Steve was downstairs talking to DI Hattrick about the car crash scene. DI Blackman had disappeared into the DCI's office and closed the door. "I thought he was at the club? The DI just sent a car to pick him up."

"Okaaaaay . . . Not according to my eyes. We're at the cement works, near the old quarry. He's on his trials bike with some mates and they're hammering it round the circuit." Lindsey sounded confused. "We called in for backup once we realized we had the bike registration."

The cement works had been derelict for over twenty years now, and they were a favourite hang-out for the local teenagers. The old quarry, which curved adjacent to the property, made a great track for bikes and boards and attracted a crowd in the summer months. The security guards tended to turn a blind eye to activity in the quarry but spent a lot of time throwing trespassers out of the structurally unsound cement works buildings.

"I'll come over." Steve wasn't answering his mobile, presumably still tied up with Hat Trick, and she was desperate for some kind of evidence the case was moving forward. Dove drove fast, heading away from the coast and further inland to the secluded spot. She parked a little distance away from the main entrance, jogging quickly over to the police car parked next to the barrier. Three marked cars now blocked the other exits.

"We put a call out for his bike registration plate and got a hit from traffic about twenty minutes ago." Lindsey looked smug. "Why do you think he's in the club?"

"Nice one. Interesting he seems to have gone to ground after Sarah's death. I got a call from the manager at Stage 32 saying Leo has just pitched up to do a soundcheck. So this might be Lukas borrowing his brother's bike?"

"Or Lukas borrowing his brother's equipment and doing a soundcheck? We'll soon find out. How identical are they? You've met them both, so could you tell them apart?" Lindsey asked.

"I haven't met Leo yet, but Lukas has a tiny scar under his chin." Dove tapped her own chin to indicate where the injury was.

The noise of the bikes meant she now had to shout to make herself heard. "We'll soon find out anyway, because there's a car on the way to pick up Leo at the club right now."

They waited a couple of minutes, and the roar of engines lessened. The bikers seemed to be finishing up. They gathered in one of the dips left by the historic quarry excavations, laughing and passing round energy drinks.

"At least he doesn't drink and drive," Lindsey remarked dryly.

Dove was checking out the bikes. A proper selection. Leo's bike was a BMW, an F-850-GS, so good for off-road and on-road. Her dad used to ride a Harley Davidson when she was a kid in California, and Dove had actually passed her bike license before her car license. It was a long time since she had ridden one, though.

The bikers seemed to be in good spirits, laughing, exchanging high fives. Only as they tried to leave did the group notice all exits were blocked by police cars. There was some shouting and an air of bewilderment and anger. Officers approached the group and three of the riders took off their helmets and were soon engaged in animated conversation.

With a revving of engines, two of them, including the rider on the bike registered to Leo Windsor, tried to make a quick escape by driving through the wire fence, but the fence was strong, and it didn't break, leaving both riders in a tangled heap.

With the other bikers still talking to officers, Dove walked with Lindsey towards the blonde man who was just emerging from his crashed bike pile, chucking his helmet onto the ground in apparent disgust.

"Hallo, DJ Darkness," Lindsey greeted him cheerfully. "We've been looking for you. Want a free ride down to the station?"

The man scowled at the two women officers and said nothing.

* * *

The other four bikers were soon heading off in various different directions. All, according to their talks with the officers, had been surprised at the ambush, but happy to cooperate. No charges would be brought regarding illegal riding. The old security guard at the gate had just shrugged when he was questioned.

"They aren't doing any harm. I chase them out of the buildings, but the council is just letting this place rot. If they want to have some fun in the quarry and make use of it, good luck to them." He grinned at Dove. "I've got a Harley myself. My pride and joy."

"Do you know Leo Windsor?"

He didn't, and she drew a blank with Lukas Windsor too, despite spotting the now familiar logo on the guard's ID pass.

"This is my patch. I always put my name down for shifts here. It's quiet and everyone knows I've got the balance right. I know when to call you lot, and when to leave well alone. The council bought this land twenty years ago now. Have they done any redevelopment? No chance. It's gone back to nature, and that's the way it should be," he finished fiercely, then looked slightly sheepish. "I've got buzzards nesting in two of the old chimneys. Got some great shots of them raising their young last year."

Dove understood. This place was his place, and she agreed there was a kind of beauty in the towering derelict structures smothered in flowering weeds and tall grasses. Behind the quarry, the huge, rounded shapes of the hills on the Downs spread as far as the horizon. Sheep-nibbled turf and a haze of wildflowers.

* * *

"I haven't done anything wrong." The young man looked at his solicitor for help. "Can't you do something?"

His solicitor shook her head. "We discussed this. You are not under arrest, Leo, you just need to answer the questions."

It was slightly eerie talking to identical twins, Dove thought. She almost felt she could hear echoes of her chat with Lukas the other day. But the personalities seemed very different, even if they both had the same striking physical features. Whereas Lukas had been friendly, open and interested, Leo was closed off, sulky and suspicious. She supposed the situations were different, but this twin, on first impression, certainly appeared less likely to give them any information.

Lindsey kicked off with the formalities, introductions for the tape and the formal legal jargon, before turning to Leo. "Why did you try and run away when we asked you to talk to us at the quarry?"

"You jumped me while I was having a laugh with some mates. We weren't doing anything wrong! Anyway, I didn't run away," he said sulkily.

"No?" Lindsey raised a sceptical brow.

"I was riding my bike so I couldn't *run*, could I?" He stared at her rudely. "Why are your eyes different colours?"

Lindsey ignored his question. "Technically, no, you didn't *run*, but for the purposes of this interview, stop wasting my time. We have two people dead, Leo. If you may be able to shed any light on this investigation, step up and tell us what's going on. Where were you the night of the sixth of April between six and eight p.m.?"

"Dunno."

His solicitor leaned close to him and whispered something. Dove hoped it was along the lines of 'stop being such a brat and answer the questions like a grown-up.'

"And while you're telling us that, you can also think where you were the previous night, when the murder of Alice Cartwright occurred," Lindsey said pleasantly.

"Okay, I was working." The sulks were still there but he seemed to realize he had no chance against Lindsey's brisk approach. "At Stage 32. I had a set between 9 and 10 so I got there early and saw some mates, had a few drinks . . ."

"Did you know your brother is also currently in the station, probably in a room very similar to this one?"

"Why would you bring him in?" Anger, unmistakable and burning in his eyes. "He hasn't done anything!"

"He went into Stage 32 to do a soundcheck and showed ID in the name of Leo Windsor. The manager recognized him as you."

CHAPTER THIRTY-SIX

Anger died and genuine confusion seemed to cross his face. He folded his arms and surveyed them through narrowed eyes.

"I don't understand what you would want with either of us. We haven't done anything wrong. I . . . think I might have asked Lukas to do the soundcheck for me because I fancied an afternoon off. Lukas told me about the old quarry, and we go up there a lot. I didn't realize he was going up to the club this early though."

"Do you know any of these people?" Dove pushed her iPad towards him and flicked through the photos of Alice, Sarah and Gerald.

He hardly glanced at them before shaking his head. "No."

"Where were you the night of the sixth of March between six and eight p.m.?' Lindsey repeated.

"I don't know. Um . . . at my brother's place, probably."

"Because, you see, we have footage of you getting a bit of shopping from Aldi, walked down towards the coast, past the alley between the pawn shop and the betting shop, just before the incident," Dove suggested.

Leo looked at his solicitor, who frowned at Dove. "You don't have to answer that, Leo."

Lindsey changed tack. "Have you seen any of your siblings in the last few days?"

"I . . . Yeah, I see Lukas, of course. I haven't seen Kat for ages."

"Your dad, Evan?"

"No . . ."

"Have you seen him since he got out of prison?"

"Yeah . . ." He seemed to be considering leaving it at a one-word answer, but the ferocity of Lindsey's stare made him continue. "I saw him about a week ago. He knows I don't want to see him, but he wanted to, you know, just see me. I don't owe him anything, but I was . . . curious, I guess. I haven't forgotten what he did, either." He thought for a moment and then said with satisfaction, "He looks like shit."

"Leo, we aren't accusing you of anything, and we appreciate you don't want to talk about your dad, but two women are dead. Anything that might be relevant to the current case is useful," Dove told him. When he finally looked up at her, his eyes bright with dislike, she added, "Sometimes things buried in the past can be a motive for a crime today."

"No comment."

"All right, let's take a ten-minute break."

They paused the interview and stomped back upstairs.

"Little shit with an attitude," Lindsey observed, thumping the drinks machine in an abortive effort to get it to spit out a cup of tea. "And this bloody thing needs fixing again. I'll get Maya to bring her toolkit in. She fixed it last time."

Dove tapped her card and bought a packet of crisps. "He knows what's going on. Wouldn't surprise me if he was the man the girls saw running from Sarah's body, but if we give them a line-up, it could just as easily have been Lukas."

"Although from what you and Steve said, not in attitude," Lindsey suggested, carefully extracting her teabag and adding four sugars.

"Right. Lukas was far more open and willing to help. A bit cagey about his brother, but no more than Leo is about letting his sibling do a soundcheck and passing himself off as his twin. Let's see what's happening with his phone records," Dove said.

Leo had very unwillingly submitted his phone when he was booked in, and Dove was quickly able to locate recent messages from all three of his siblings, plus a contact listed as Mae, who had rung him almost every day for two weeks and then gone silent.

They returned to the interview room.

He shrugged. "I don't know why she calls me all the time. She's just a friend. She's at uni in Brighton and she comes down here sometimes."

"You've only called her twice, once on the evening Alice was murdered and once the night Sarah died," Lindsey said. "No communication at all between the two of you since then. Did you break up or something?"

"So what? I'm sure lots of other things happened on both those nights too." He was scowling now, and his shoulders were hunched over in a defensive position, hands palmdown on the table in front of him.

"You do know we can send this down to our forensics team and they can check out all your deleted texts too?" Lindsey asked him.

Leo straightened, looked uncertainly at his solicitor.

"Anything you want to share?"

"No."

Interview terminated, Dove followed Lindsey back upstairs, where they scrolled through Leo's social media, curious about Mae. Lots of calls, but he had only rung her twice. She found the girl's Instagram feed and bingo, there they were, arm in arm at Stage 32. Mae was extremely attractive, with long dark curls and blue eyes. She and Leo made a striking couple, if that's what they were.

Dove made a priority note to get in touch with Mae, to see if she could shed any light on Leo's movements within the last week.

"We've got no motive for any attack on Sarah or Alice from Leo or Lukas, though. The only thing we do have is a possible sighting of one or the other of them via the street cams, and your witness statement, which, not to knock it, could describe any blonde twenty-something around here." Lindsey yawned.

DI Blackman and Steve came back from interviewing Lukas Windsor and the two women officers looked up expectantly.

The DI shook his head. "Lukas says they often pass themselves off as each other and have done since they were kids. He says he fills in for Leo if his brother asks him to and today Leo fancied an afternoon out on the bike and Lukas wanted to play DJ. How did you get on with the brother?"

"Sorry, boss." Lindsey shook her head. "No joy there either."

The frustrating thing was, and Leo's solicitor had laid this out — as was his job, Dove appreciated, but it was still bloody annoying — the evidence was all circumstantial. A phone call to Charlotte had confirmed the girls didn't think they would be able to pick Leo out of a line-up but would be happy to participate.

The DCI was setting one up for tomorrow, but Dove wasn't holding out much hope.

Was it really possible someone completely different, and so far unconnected to the case, had murdered Alice close to where Evan had been hiding in the woods, and she and Steve had been checking out a suspected RTC?

Joining the dots was always hard work, but this time, she couldn't even guess which direction they went in. The paper was blank.

CHAPTER THIRTY-SEVEN

I had a lot of doubts about going anywhere with Evan, because, you know, I'm not stupid. But my secret was hanging over me, and since Lily's death I haven't been able to get it out of my head.

The pink baby blanket she had that night, that she had bought specially for Kat, that she said she was going to use for the next baby.

It was in her box of things we cleared out after her death. There wasn't much in the box. She was living in a shelter by then. Periodically she would try another rehab programme, but she never could stick it out. People don't understand how hard it is to kick addiction. It's like a disease, and it never leaves you. I doubt she would have had the strength to stay clean even if she managed to finish rehab.

She looked older, greyer, each time I saw her. Her blonde hair was greasy, thin and hung over her shoulders. Her eyes were grey like ours, and once they had been clear, like seawater washing over the pebbles on the beach. Now they were threaded with red, sunken and dried out.

But the shape of her face and her smile were all Kat's. The eye and hair colour different by a mile, but that familiarity was spooky, and also comforting. My mother had been beautiful. I could see glimpses of it, hidden under the abuse. But I had never seen her like that. She had been beautiful long before Max, Kat, me and Leo were born. When we came along, she was already sinking, scrabbling to stay afloat as the life raft floated away. That image always comes back to me when I think of Lily.

Lily smelled of death the last time I saw her, and although I didn't know what she was going to do, I still think, with hindsight, I should have known. She had been searching for a way out all her life, but she never found it. We should have hated her for her false promises, for raising our hopes, and for a while I really did, especially when I saw how we were able to get help when we finally asked. It's out there, but to take it you need to be determined.

She tried, but she was too weak to take the steps she needed. Evan had beaten the sparks from her, but to be completely honest, I think it was more than that.

Once she crossed the line she just couldn't come back. Not even for us. It helps to understand what she was fighting. I can understand she felt she needed artificial substances to live her everyday life. Drugs can be fun, they can be a hobby, and they can also be a killer.

* * *

Evan asked all the right questions the next time I saw him. It was at the garage where he'd landed a job.

The men didn't seem to know who he was, what he'd done, because they didn't beat him up or anything. Which raised another question. These couldn't be locals, and certainly not from the Seaview, or Evan wouldn't even have dared go into the shabby, rundown property.

One of the men told us about a bloke called Ray, the Collector, and how we should go and talk to him about Evan getting another part-time job, how he could always use a hand in his business.

Like an idiot, I asked what Ray collected, and they laughed like I was the funniest show in town and said he collected girls.

I felt like I was going to throw up right there. Instead, thankfully, we were off, scrambling back through the wire of the gate back onto the deserted road. These men were rank, and they thought they were kings, sitting in their derelict building, hiding out and scrabbling for work among the others of their kind. My disdain for these people seems to hang around me in a cloud, and I can see Evan wants to say something, to tell me how I need to respect these people. But he can't, because *he needs me, and because he must finally be able to see that despite everything, I've made it, and he hasn't.*

Evan tried to look disapproving back there, but I could tell he was hungry for his old life. It was true he never tried anything with the girls in the vans, or the boys either, come to that. It wasn't sex he wanted, but the hunger burning in his eyes said he wanted to be back, to have his status, his power to throw his weight around.

Like a wounded and aged animal still hanging with the younger wolves, he was clinging on by a thread. I decided I would be happy to let him dig in deeper, to watch as he destroyed what little he had left of his life.

I knew what he wanted now. My life. I had money, drugs and power, and it was eating him up he couldn't get a part of it. Out of everyone, he had approached me, because he knew. Or perhaps because of our secret, he thought he had leverage. I want to laugh in his face, and I will. But not yet. I have things I need to finish.

And of course, there is Cara.

CHAPTER THIRTY-EIGHT

Dove was yawning by the time she turned into her road, but she stopped to grab some chips and chicken from the takeaway on the corner and waited up for Quinn.

His shift was due to finish at ten, so she put the food in the oven to stay warm and poured herself a large glass of red wine. Wandering barefoot into the cramped office, accompanied by Layla, she settled down at the computer. It was certainly an odd case, and now this weird lead from Gerald had come to light — even if it was a little unreliable, it left the door wide open for potential perpetrators.

She found it hard to believe, but everything he'd said suggested that somehow he and Alice, probably Sarah too, may have taken babies or children illegally from their natural parents. And the name David? They had been unable to track down anyone in Alice's contacts, or Sarah's contacts, by that name.

Dove was vague about how abducting babies would be achieved without a massive police investigation. How would the parents not say anything? Blackmail? Did they tell the parents they were taking the kids? But that would surely be so risky. Things could easily turn nasty.

When a child had to be removed for safety reasons, one person didn't just pitch up waving a certificate. There was police involvement, multiple services, and everything was documented.

She sighed, feeling she was getting nowhere. Downloading the file that she had requested from social services, she began trawling through, noting any patterns. How would such a thing be achieved? False papers, false names and new lives.

And the children who had died were supposedly remembered by the tree planting? Had they been children who died from abuse and neglect, or had what the trio had experienced with the Benny Milward case driven them to do things that they might never have done previously? From guilt, from fear that it would happen again, perhaps they thought they could prevent it by bypassing all the paperwork, all the legal certificates and requests.

She drew doodles with a blue biro, circling over and over again until she realized she was drawing a heart and chucked the pen down.

Six girls and eight boys over an approximate fifteen-year stretch, according to the trees in his back garden. There were a lot of children under five who were considered at risk and were being monitored by child protection during that time span.

Figures and tables and graphs blurred in front of her tired eyes. Dove switched to death certificates and discovered only five in the area in fifteen years. She removed the cat from the keyboard, pulled on a soft hoodie and snuggled into it before she padded back into the kitchen to top up her glass. The printed paperwork was still in one hand. She laid it on the countertop and studied it as she sipped her wine.

The lists included children who were considered at risk by children's services, but not recorded by the police as a criminal offence. She glanced at the wording: *Where a child is suffering, or is likely to suffer, significant harm, the local authority shall carry out an assessment to see if it needs to take steps to safeguard and promote the welfare of the child.*

She considered Gerald objectively. He was clearly confused but at times completely lucid and intelligence had shone through his kind, pale blue eyes. Dementia was cruel, and as he said, had robbed him of his good memories. Could he possibly be telling the truth? But the fact remained: where were the children now?

Leaning on the kitchen countertop, long dark hair falling across her shoulders, Dove looked at the last sheet that had been sent over. More statistics. In the last month, there had been over 70,000 assessments done by local-authority child safeguarding where physical abuse was identified as a factor at the end of the assessment. Physical deaths over the period she was looking for numbered twenty-eight.

Appalled and sickened to her stomach by the numbers, she took a break and checked her phone. She sent another quick text. Nothing from Quinn. Sometimes there was a last-minute emergency call, and the crew would always respond.

Dove had finished her own meal and poured another glass of wine before Quinn came in at eleven. "Sorry babe, we had a last-minute shout, a cardiac arrest up on Knob Hill, and he didn't make it."

She kissed him, but her gaze sharpened. "I was up there today. What was the name of your patient?"

"Gerald Cartwright, eighty-six. Lived just past Summer Farm." He studied her expectantly.

She stared at him, heart racing, hand to her mouth. "Shit and double shit. Any suspicious circumstances?"

He was looking at her curiously. "No, not that I'm aware of. Someone called 999 as the patient was having chest pains. His carer, maybe? History of angina and he had a valve replacement about eight years ago. Nobody else was on scene when we arrived, though. He was unconscious but breathing when we got there but deteriorated very quickly. Why are you interested in him?"

"Poor man! He said to us today he thought he was next on some kind of hit list. We took a statement from him about seven hours ago. He suffered from dementia but seemed perfectly healthy when we left." She frowned, remembering Connie's solicitous care of her charge. "His carer was still with him then. She gave him indigestion tablets."

"Bloody hell. Well, you'll have to wait for the coroner's report, but it doesn't seem suspicious. If he felt he had indigestion, it may well have been his heart. It's a common symptom, and equally common for the patient to wrongly identify the cause of discomfort as indigestion." Quinn was pulling off his uniform shirt, chucking it on the floor near the washing basket. "I need a shower. Can I smell takeaway?"

"You can." She was shaken. The memory of the man putting his hand to his chest, the discomfort . . . When had Connie left and why hadn't she been concerned? She must have known his history.

Still pondering, she poured Quinn a glass of wine, and he took it, his green eyes fixed on her. "Dove, whatever he told you or whatever you are thinking, on the face of it this looks like a cardiac arrest, nature, fate or whatever. He was an elderly man, not in the best of health. There is no indication there was any foul play, and this was *not* your fault. Did he seem agitated when you left?"

Quinn could always see right through her. She shook her head, but her voice was uncertain. "No. Not really. He was scared of someone coming to kill him. It was stressful for him that we were there, asking questions and bringing up his past."

"Which isn't your fault. You just do your job."

She leaned back against the countertop as Layla wound her furry body in and out of her legs, the soft grey fur tickling her bare skin, the cat's thunderous purring a source of comfort. "Quinn, did you see a hospital tag, a pink baby one, at all?"

He paused, halfway to the stairs now with a refilled glass. "No. There was nothing out of the ordinary. The only red flag was the person who called 999 stated he was having severe chest pains and then hung up after giving the address, leaving the door unlocked for us. They used the call box two miles down the road. Who uses call boxes these days? Everyone has a mobile phone."

Dove stared after him as he climbed the stairs, but her mind was replaying the conversation with Gerald. *Cherry trees for the girls, magnolia trees for the boys.* The thought almost knocked the wind out of her. Gerald. His passion and regrets . . . She hoped, whatever he had done or thought he had done, he was also now at peace.

She explained this to Quinn after he came downstairs, now wearing just his pyjama bottoms, towelling his hair dry.

He shook his head. "That's a huge bunch of loose ends to tie off. If you're thinking of the children taken by Gerald and the rest, I would think it's highly likely the adoptive parents have no idea where the kids came from. Private adoption and sealed papers, maybe? But realistically, I thought that kind of thing only went on in movies."

"But they would have needed to be super organized to take a child, and somehow make sure the parents didn't go to the police . . . I suppose they might have posed as some kind of official child protection team. But then the legal paperwork, the birth certificates!" A thought struck her. "Do you think they made money out of it?"

He shrugged. "Who knows. I guess I wouldn't be surprised if money did change hands higher up the food chain. Someone would have had to file some adoption papers, and how did they manage that, with a child with no history? That's falsifying legal documents, it could end a career and result in criminal charges, couldn't it?"

"But if they thought they were doing the right thing?"

"Babe, I don't know, but it's certainly not legal, is it? You also have to consider that what one person thinks is the right thing, their neighbour might consider quite the opposite. The official process is complex and there are hundreds of assessments to go through. For a good reason. They need to be sure a child is at risk. It's a massive deal to remove a kid from their home, isn't it?" He considered the problem for a moment, then shook his head, yawning. "Sorry, right now I need to dig into some chicken and a mountain of chips before I keel over myself."

After he had eaten Dove found her eyes constantly returning to Quinn's phone, lying on the coffee table, pretty much where he had left it two nights ago.

When he came back with a glass of wine and another bottle, he was watching her with a serious expression. "Dove, I need to talk to you about something."

Her heart raced and she could hardly breathe. She poured herself another drink with shaky hands, trying to stay calm. "Yes?"

"I've been having some trouble . . . I . . ." he winced at the words, "Dove, I think I've got a stalker."

CHAPTER THIRTY-NINE

This was the last thing she had been expecting, but she took a gulp of wine, swallowed, coughed as it went down the wrong way, and managed a fairly cool, "Go on."

"Last month when I went out for a drink with Kevin and a few others from work . . . We went down to Tommy's Bar on End Street, do you remember? You were working."

She nodded and took another gulp of her drink. Layla, purring with satisfaction, kneading the blanket with her paws, turned green-and-gold eyes up towards them, following their conversational ebb and flow with apparent interest.

"Well, we went on to the pub and there were a group of women, very drunk. Kevin was with one of the women, and one of the others, well, we talked. Kevin texted me a photo and I assume she must have got my number from his phone, because now she won't leave me alone," he half laughed. "It's ridiculous, isn't it? But she . . . Malina, turned up at the Make Ready station two weeks ago looking for me. She knows where I work, she's called 999 trying to talk to me, and even though I blocked her number, she keeps getting a new number of her own. Look!"

Quinn unlocked his phone and passed it over. Dove took it in trembling hands. Over a hundred messages, suggestive photos, heart emojis. She took a long breath and let it out slowly. Her fiancé was watching her anxiously.

"Why didn't you tell me earlier?"

"When I told her to leave me alone, she said she would find out where I lived and tell my fiancée I slept with her that night," Quinn said, green eyes staring into hers.

He looked so stressed she couldn't believe she had missed it. They had been so busy with work, just passing in the doorway. No time to talk and he had been dealing with all this, while she thought he'd been having an affair!

"Quinn, you are such a fucking idiot! You should have just told me. I saw a few texts . . ." she admitted.

"But you didn't say anything?"

"I thought it might be some weird spam or something," she hedged, reluctant to admit the extent of her worries, treading carefully. "I wanted you to tell me without me having to ask." She leaned closer, meeting his gaze full on, "And I asked myself how I would feel if you accused me of something that I was innocent of, and of what it would do to our relationship, our trust."

"Shit, Dove!" He pulled her towards him and kissed her, very gently, and she responded, before laying her head on his shoulder, feeling his heartbeat and warmth. Reassuring herself it had just been a nightmare.

Eventually she sat up. "The first thing you need to do is report it. Go to the station tomorrow, and get it logged as stalking," she told him firmly.

"Come on, Dove, I'm a *bloke* being hassled by a *woman*. They'll laugh at me. Even the dispatcher at work keeps calling her my stalker. They have every 999 call she made logged, and some of them were pretty abusive, apparently."

"So at least it's logged at work." She caught his expression. "Quinn! Grow up, of course they won't laugh at you. You don't know anything about this woman. She could be mentally ill, she could have just crashed out of an abusive relationship, or she could just be obsessed by the idea of a cute man in uniform." She grinned at him, confidence restored and heart whole again, before turning serious. "But she could be a danger to herself or to you. Or even to me. Put a stop to it before it gets out of hand. Over a hundred messages isn't a joke."

"Yes, boss," he finally grinned back. "Can we go to bed now?"

"I guess so." She laughed at him, relief making her giddy.

* * *

She woke early, in the chill of the 4 a.m. predawn light. For a moment she lay still, unable to process what had woken her. A sound.

Slipping on the worn, soft T-shirt she liked to wear in bed, she padded downstairs, her long dark plait hanging over one shoulder.

Nothing. She moved from room to room, checking doors and windows. Layla, assuming it must be an early morning wake-up call, jumped down off the sofa with noise-less velvet paws, rubbing her soft furry head around Dove's bare legs.

Dove cursed herself for having an overactive imagi-nation. Malina did not know where Quinn lived, and she would see he went down to the station in the morning.

Standing in the shadows, watching a tiny glimmer of dawn steal across the sky outside, she shivered, thinking again of the information gleaned from Gerald, the good intentions that seemed to have had far-reaching consequences. *Everything is as it should be.*

She needed to check out Connie Batchelor again, just to be sure.

Secrets. Secrets had a way of coming out, even if it was years later when you thought everything was done and buried.

Now three of them were dead, which, with Evan cur-rently eliminated from the murder enquiry, all pointed towards one thing . . . Someone else knew what they had done.

CHAPTER FORTY

"Sarah Whitmore's husband was a solicitor before he died. He worked on a freelance basis, but his main client was an adoption agency." Dove, Steve and DI Blackman were gathered around the computer screen as she scrolled down, pleased with this morning's progress. Masters, Clarke and Genfold was a small boutique agency in the West Midlands, specializing in adoption and divorce.

"The current and past partners are all listed here, but we found contact details in Alice's address book for Sarah's husband — obviously she would have his details — but also David Weston, who was a partner in the firm from 1995 until his retirement in 2010." She pulled up the relevant documents and a photograph of a smart, unsmiling man with a grey fringe cut right across his eyes in a neat line. "He passed away in 2012. He could easily be the 'David' Gerald has mentioned."

"We need to see if the missing babies thing is all a bit of a wild goose chase, based on the statement from a very confused man. It does sound like pure fantasy, and at the moment this doesn't bring us any closer to our killer. Or does it?" DI Blackman remarked, studying the photograph intently. "Does David Weston have any family?"

"Yes, a wife and two daughters." Dove opened a second document, revealing a photograph of a group shot: a pretty woman smiling as she held a toddler in her arms, while a teenage girl with wild curly hair leaned her head on her mother's shoulder, also beaming at the camera. "The wife lives in Portugal now."

"Set up a call with her. It's a wild card but let's see if she can shed any light on this thing," DI Blackman said. "And then go and talk to Gemma Rogers again. I'm still not convinced that her phone call with Alice was as innocent as she makes out. She was in a good position to keep an eye on the children in her care. What if she and Alice were such good friends that she passed on her concerns about a few children?"

"She seemed pretty firm that the nosy socials should keep out of it actually, boss, but then she gave us a mouthful about not protecting Benny Milward, so who knows which way she'd swing. Based on what we've seen, she's exceptional with the kids she was looking after, and they seemed happy and well looked after."

The Zoom call was set up in the conference room, and Marie Weston appeared simply curious at having the police call her.

Steve summarized the reason for the call, and hit her with a soft starter: "It's just a question of following leads, and your husband's name came up in connection with a current case."

There was a pause, but Dove thought the woman looked more intrigued than concerned, and she didn't ask anything about the current case Steve had just mentioned.

"He passed away, as I'm sure you'll know," Marie said, "but if I can help, I will, of course."

"Did you know Alice Cartwright?"

"I don't think so . . . Sorry, did you say Cartwright? My internet connection is rubbish over here. I should be used to it by now. We moved out here when the kids were younger. Dave used to commute back to the UK."

"Yes, Alice Cartwright."

"No."

"Sarah Whitmore or Gerald Cartwright?"

She was quicker this time. "No, sorry, no bells ringing at all. Were they clients? If so, you could try the firm and see if they have any records of them?"

"Thanks, we will." Dove decided not to mention the admin support team had already put in an official request for information to Masters, Clarke and Genfold.

"Did your husband ever do any criminal cases?"

"No, the firm was adoption, divorce and family matters. They didn't have any criminal specialists."

"One more name for you . . . Evan Houselow?"

Marie pulled a face, screwing up her freckled nose. "Sorry but no. I'm not being very helpful, am I?"

"The weather looks lovely over there," Dove said conversationally, and the other woman picked up on her tone, clearly relieved at having an easy topic to talk about.

"Oh, yes. We thought about moving back when the girls left home, but we decided against it, and now I have such a lovely life out here. Home is here in Portugal now."

"You have two daughters?"

"Both working in London now, but they are quick to jump on a plane when they need some sunshine!" she laughed. "My youngest is twenty-two, and my eldest is thirty-six now. How time flies."

Dove smiled.

"You're thinking there is a bit of an age gap between them? We adopted Chloe as a baby. I wanted another one so much, but it just never happened. It was lucky Dave was in the business, so to speak. Not that he could have handled our own case, but I think it was fate that brought Chloe to us."

She was rambling now, slightly embarrassed maybe at not being able to answer any questions, Dove thought.

After a couple more general questions, Steve thanked Marie for her time and ended the call.

"Bloody hell, do you think Chloe was one of the children Gerald was talking about?" Dove was frantically scribbling on her pad, drawing up a timeline. "The dates could fit, and that might be why David began risking his career to help the vigilante group."

"That's a *big* stretch." Steve was peering at the timeline. "But she could be? But hell, I'm still leaning towards it all being bit of a pipe dream on their part. You can't just grab a kid and find them another home without any comeback at all." He pushed his glasses further up his nose and ran a hand through his hair, making it stick up in mousy peaks.

"*If* Marie was hiding any secrets, she was very good at it. Conversely, if she had something to hide, surely she would never have volunteered the information," Dove agreed. She checked her watch. The ID line-up for Leo and Lukas Windsor was due to start in ten minutes.

"I'm just going downstairs to see if any of those girls pick Leo out in the line-up," she said to Steve.

"Go for it. I wonder if we should talk to Katrina, the fourth sibling?" Steve frowned in frustration as he scrolled through some documents, and muttered, "Why can't people just update their DVLA records so I can find them when I need to!"

* * *

A parade of similar-looking men were just filing into the corridor-shaped ID room when Dove arrived.

The girls, already in position behind the tinted glass, were nervous. "Don't worry, they can't see you," Dove told them.

The men held up cards in front of their chests and the girls looked slowly from person to person. Leo was number four, Lukas number one.

"I'm really sorry, I don't recognize him," Charlotte said, clearly disappointed. "It was so dark and so quick, I really only got a glimpse."

The other girls nodded, murmuring assent. Only one still stared at the men. "I can't be absolutely sure, but I do think it's number one, not number four. It's just an impression I have. His hood slipped a little as he ran past us, and he pulled it back over his face."

"Thank you," Dove said. She wasn't optimistic. It had been a long shot and it had failed.

Annoyed with herself, Dove returned to her desk and allowed her brain to mull over another aspect of the case that was bothering her. The murder of Alice, if Evan was indeed going to be eliminated as a potential suspect, remained unsolved, and the press were loving it.

It was lucky nobody had yet leaked the story of Gerald's death and his own stone heart. "Lindsey, how far up the food chain do you think Kevin and Jay Benson are, with their dealing?"

Lindsey considered. "Low-level, but consistent. They were, and looks like they still are from the reports, still paygrade. No way did they come up with the finer details of using unsuspecting customers to carry drugs for them."

"Who were their contacts further up?" Dove screwed up her eyes as a sudden ray of spring sunshine filtered in through the dirty windows of their open-plan office.

"Mark Callo . . . Possibly Joey Nicholls five years ago. What are you getting at?"

"The marks on Alice's arms. Was it possible a rival found out what the Bensons were up to and thought she knew something?"

Lindsey studied the photographs on the whiteboard. "They wouldn't have done the staging, though, would they? They would have just gone straight to her place and asked questions while she died."

CHAPTER FORTY-ONE

"Gemma Rogers lives on the doorstep of the Nicholls's place," Dove commented.

Steve looked up from his computer, "And guess what? Kevin Benson is the father of Gemma's twins, and her daughter, Lolla."

"Keeping good company? Alice's last call was to Gemma. What if Gemma was involved in setting the whole thing up? She would have access to Alice's route home, to have been able to find out she was driving Martin's car and to have passed information to Joey Nicholls." Lindsey swivelled her chair round to face them both.

"*If* she knew about the drugs," Dove said doubtfully. "And also, you're forgetting Gemma genuinely cared about Alice, I could tell. She wasn't bullshitting about that."

"But she is lying about something. What if someone got to Gemma and threatened her kids, Kevin's kids, she might have no choice?" Steve suggested. "I think we should visit her, not bring her in to the station, just in case Joey is involved. But if she doesn't cooperate, she needs a formal interview, because she's currently looking like the main link in the case, and if she didn't have an alibi for both deaths I would have her down here right now!"

"Joey Nicholls got out of prison a month before Evan Houselow," Lindsey said thoughtfully, chewing a biro as she checked her phone. "Shall I see what he's been up to since he came out?"

"Thanks, Lindsey, we'll head over to Gemma's now." He picked up his bag and Dove followed, chucking her rain jacket over her shoulders. The promised sun clearly wasn't going to make an appearance and rain was drumming at the windows.

* * *

Gemma Rogers greeted them with annoyance. "Why are you back here? The neighbours are going to think I've got something going on with the cops now, aren't they?"

"Sorry to bother you, but we have a few more questions," Steve said pleasantly.

"Fine, whatever. But you need to hurry up, I've got triplets and another three under six at the moment and they need keeping an eye on." Gemma led them inside.

She yelled at someone, "Look out for the babies while I talk to these people. Won't be long, love."

"Gemma, we are concerned you might know something that might make you a target for violence."

"Right, you said on the phone. That's crazy but also so what? Nobody can get at me. I'm not old or stupid and when Terry stays over, which is most of the time because he's between jobs, I've got double the protection. He's a weight-lifter," she added proudly.

"We have another name for you. David Weston."

"He a dealer?"

"Not that we know of, and he's been dead a few years."

Gemma frowned and then shook her head, "Nope, then, I don't know him."

"Gemma, in the course of our investigation it has come to light that these four . . ." Dove laid out photos of Alice, Sarah, Gerald and David, "that these four might have been involved in the illegal adoption of some babies in this area."

"So? Mine aren't adopted, if that's what you're asking." But her face changed imperceptibly. There was a stress behind her eyes and her voice rose. "Alice was a midwife, for fuck's sake, not an adoption agency."

"Any babies or young children who were removed for safeguarding reasons in the area?" Steve suggested.

Dove kept quiet. They had already, laboriously, painstakingly been through the files. There were no discrepancies, no reports of any kidnappings during the period under review. Perhaps it was just all a fantasy, and Gerald's way of coping had been to invent a memory where he had saved some of the children.

"No."

"And the baby Lily and Evan might have had?"

At the mention of Evan's name, she lowered her voice. "That bastard again. I don't know what you're on about with adoption and agencies. This is old news, why are you chasing on it? There never was a baby, don't you understand!"

"Can you think of anything else that might be relevant? Have you seen Joey Nicholls since he came out?"

She pursed her red, glossy lips, picking at the nail polish on her fingers. "I dunno. Why would I see him?"

"We found drugs in the car Alice was driving." Steve was watching her closely.

"So what? You suggesting *Alice* was into drugs?" Gemma laughed derisively, but Dove noted her eyes were scared and her apparent amusement seemed forced. "You really are shit at your jobs, you two. You're like cartoon coppers!"

"We're not suggesting that at all. You had a relationship with Kevin Benson."

"Yeah, so fucking what?" She was angry now, "Do you know what, take me down the bloody police station right now and I'll get myself a solicitor. All this is crap."

"Gemma, we are trying to find out who killed Alice, so if you know something, why don't you tell us? We could have sent a car to take you down to the station for a formal interview, but we didn't want to make you a target round here," Steve told her reasonably. His calmness and general demeanour often fooled people into thinking he was a cliché, slightly overweight bumbling cop. In reality, Steve was one of the best at getting under people's skin and extracting the evidence when their guard was down.

Gemma was silent for a few moments, as though weighing up her choices. She shrugged. "I don't know anything about any drugs, and Kevin pissed off years ago. He doesn't pay anything towards the kids. They're mine, not his."

"Why do you think Alice was murdered?" Dove asked, preparing herself for a sarcastic comment.

"I don't know. I've seen the news, and it makes me sick, and her friend too. The only thing I can think of is Benny Milward. Alice told me she and Sarah and her ex-husband were all involved at some point. Maybe someone wanting to get back at them for that?" Her heavily mascaraed green eyes met Dove's. "Or Evan? Alice loved kids and she was seen around here doing her visits. Evan is a bastard, and he gets these things into his head."

"We don't have any evidence Evan was responsible for Alice's murder."

"Going back to the idea that some children were taken by some kind of illegal adoption agency, can you think of any cases of young children or babies going missing that might not have ever been reported?" Steve asked.

"A few were taken in, like the Jones's poor little boy, who was found locked in the kitchen while they went out partying. He was six, and they kept doing it. There's a whole process, you know, you can't just take a kid. You should know that!" Then her gaze sharpened. "But you really are talking about something dodgy again, aren't you, not an adoption agency at all? Fuck, don't tell me the Smiling Man is for real?"

CHAPTER FORTY-TWO

Once I had all the facts it was easy to put it together. For so many years I wondered, and the memories haunted me. Now I know and although I have had to do things I might have preferred not to, it's turned out well.

She's not what I expected, and she doesn't seem to understand, but I think we can get past that. She just needs time.

Our history brought us together. I knew as soon as I saw her, the mirror image of Kat, that she was my sister. Even her voice was similar. For once I'm not thinking about tomorrow, I'm focused on tonight. I pull out a bag of powder, turn up the music and shut the curtains.

It's going to be a good one. Just me and her.

CHAPTER FORTY-THREE

"We are exploring all lines of enquiry at the moment," Dove told Gemma. "But there is a slim chance some children might have been removed illegally."

"Fuck me . . ." She fidgeted with the hem of her pink top. From the next room, there was the sound of singing and giggling. "I think that's crazy. You're way off and Alice would never have been involved in anything like that. She was a straight-up angel and she helped people, not screwed them over."

"Gemma, did you tell the police you saw Evan carrying a baby by the lake after Lily reported her baby had disappeared?"

Gemma drew in a sharp breath. "No! Of course not. I told you, there never was a baby. Go and find out who killed Alice and this other woman! Go and arrest Evan."

"I mentioned previously, we have no evidence that Evan Houselow was involved in Alice's murder."

"But you said . . . I thought—" She looked away and Dove could tell she was rapidly reassessing the situation. Why had she been so sure Evan was guilty of the murder?

"Is it possible Lily Windsor was having a relationship with someone else?" Dove asked carefully, noting Gemma's previous outburst.

"No idea. She was terrified of Evan, but she was weak. Too weak to leave him. I wouldn't have put up with that, but give her some credit, he was smart, and he worked her like a puppet. Total guilt trip. He was always saying she'd lose her kids." Gemma tapped her long nails on the table, her eyes darting from one face to the other. Her colour had risen in both cheeks and for some reason she looked terrified.

"Maybe someone on the estate?" Steve suggested.

"What?" She cast a worried glance out of the window. "Why would she be? No idea, I told you . . ." she said loudly. There was some rustling in the kitchen, a shout and a teenage girl wandered in carrying a baby under each arm.

"Little buggers were going out the cat flap," she told Gemma, grinning.

"Take them all out in the garden. It's okay by the sand-pit now Terry fixed the fence," Gemma told her. "These two are just going."

The teenager disappeared and the sound of coats and boots going on covered Gemma's quick whisper. "Andy Nicholls. Lily was sleeping with Andy."

"You know him well?"

"No, but everyone knows what's happening with the Nichollses. Go and talk to him about Lily if you want to know any more, because I can't answer for her. He might, though." She held up crossed fingers. "They were like that for a bit when Lily and Evan were going through one of their rough patches. Surprised she had the guts to do that, to be honest, and we all thought she'd leave Evan."

"Interesting. Thanks, Gemma."

She nodded. "Andy's a good bloke and it's all legit now he's taken over. Joey's still around but . . . you know . . ."

There was another shout from the garden and Gemma hustled them out of the house. "I don't know any more, and stop coming round."

"Thanks for your time. Sorry to take up your day," Steve said loudly in the hallway as he and Dove exited, being careful to look out for red paint.

"You ready to make a run for it?" Dove asked. The road appeared empty, but she could see inquisitive faces at windows, and a man walking a dog had just turned the corner.

"Let's go. Should we pop into the Nicholls's and see if Andy's around?" Steve suggested.

"I assume you're joking?" Dove ideally wouldn't have set foot in the haulage yard without a fair amount of backup.

"I know Joey's out, but I told you, Andy's fine. I've spoken to him before. Come on, we can just have a quick look?"

"Absolutely no way. Sorry, Steve, I know you already know Andy and he might be the salt of the earth now, and the business totally legitimate and collecting for charities at weekends," she paused as he grinned, "but I walked right into something I should never have gone near when I was with the Unit, as you know, and I get the same vibes from this place."

His face changed. "Sorry, mate, I totally get it and you're right. Another day."

Dove hesitated, thankful that her phone rang, and she answered quickly, putting DI Blackman on speakerphone. "Yes, boss."

"The drugs discovered in Alice's car — well, Martin's car — are suspected to be part of a larger haul that was intercepted at the docks earlier this year. For some reason the goods are being moved undiluted from Benson and Sons, via the vehicles. The cocaine tested at seventy-five per cent purity."

"Shit," Dove said softly. By the time the drugs had been resold, twenty per cent was a roughly acceptable street dilution rate for most street sellers, though it varied depending on the area. "Straight from the source, then?"

"As you say. The shipment, from which they suspect 122 kilo bags were missing, originated in South America. I'm just about to get back on the phone to Community Investigations, and the DCI is already talking to the NCA."

"Guessing it's not a good idea to drop in on Andy Nicholls now?" Steve said soberly.

The DI was adamant. "If you need to talk to Andy, wait for backup. I know the yard hasn't had any trouble for a while, but there's serious history so don't risk it. No evidence yet to connect Joey, but I don't suppose a major deal has gone under the radar without him being at the very least aware of it."

"Yes, boss."

As Steve turned around and drove back towards the station, Dove saw Gemma watching them from her downstairs window.

CHAPTER FORTY-FOUR

They drove down towards the town, Steve consuming yet another protein bar without much enthusiasm as he drove, Dove checking in with the updated files. "If the case is going to be drug-related, how does it tie up with the baby thing?"

Steve shook his head, indicating to overtake some particularly slow and wobbly cyclists, who were riding four abreast, seemingly oblivious of the traffic building up behind them. "What we seem to have are children who were brought up by other parents, with no idea they had been taken from their birth parents illegally. I mean, shit, this is horrific."

"That's about the size of it. And it leaves the field wide open when it comes to suspects. The more I think on it, this thing could be huge. It gives a motive for someone to murder Alice and Sarah, if the perpetrator believes they took their baby away, or if one of these kids, now an adult, has somehow discovered what happened." Dove's mind was spinning, blown away by the drugs aspect that had now come to light, still clinging onto the evidence that had previously presented itself. "And Sarah's death, or murder, wasn't drug-related. She has no connections to drugs and neither has her family."

"Don't forget, I know Evan is currently off the hook for Alice's murder, but there's nothing to say he isn't pissed someone also tried to frame him for killing a baby. I still reckon that someone was Gemma. She hates him, and more, she's terrified of him."

* * *

Paperwork finally submitted, leaving an office buzzing with drug news and dealer names, Dove drove slowly home. It was still light at 8 p.m. now, and knowing the days were getting lighter gave her a sense of relief, like she had more time to accomplish everything.

It was purely a cause-and-effect thing, she knew, but she couldn't help feeling more energetic in spring and summer. Even though her workload was through the roof at the moment.

Quinn was watching a film on Netflix, with a jumbo-sized bag of Doritos and several dips open next to him on the sofa. "Hi, babe!"

She kissed him and had a moment of regret she was going straight out again. "How was your day?"

"I had a lie-in, did some study for the exams and then took a board over to Claw Beach with Sara and Will." He yawned and stretched. "Now, as you can see, I'm eating healthily and resting."

She laughed. "You look better already." And he did. The wash of exhaustion had lifted from his face, and his green eyes sparkled again. "Any contact from your stalker?"

"I'm pleased to say no. I wasn't expecting anything to happen quickly, but it seems like a visit from the police might have been just what she needed to calm down. Are you still going over to Ren's?"

She sighed, and then instantly felt bad. "Yes. I want to have a shower and then watch a movie with you, but on the off chance you'll still be there in an hour, I'll make it a quick visit. I promised her I'd go over days ago."

He waved the packet of crisps. "Can't guarantee there will be any snacks left, but I think there is an excellent chance I'll be right here when you get back."

"I'll bring more snacks back." She hauled off her work clothes and pulled on joggers and a top, adding a hoody and trainers. "See you later."

"Bye, babe."

* * *

Eden was playing with three-year-old Elan when Dove arrived at Ren's house. It was only a fifteen-minute walk from her own road but, lost in thought, Dove had walked right past the gate before her niece called out.

"Are you coming to see us, or carrying on into town?"

Dove dragged her mind from the case and smiled at Eden. The girl had pulled her hair back into a long, shiny dark ponytail, and her bare arms showed some new artwork. The last of the daylight was boosted by two lanterns hung on the porch.

"When did you get those new tattoos done?" Dove asked, bending down to hug her little nephew. He was busy pushing a toy lorry in and out of the birdbath and paid little attention to her, beyond giving her a grin.

"Last week. I got the rose and dove, and then this one is a symbol of strength," she pointed with her other hand. "The girl in the tattoo place is amazing!"

Dove inspected the intricate details and had to agree. They suited Eden, and strength was certainly something her niece possessed in spades. Eden had survived kidnapping and incarceration, escaped with her son and made a new life for herself.

"Ren said you wanted to talk to me about someone at the nursery?"

"Yeah . . ." Eden picked at a bit of tree bark, eyes cast down, frowning. "The thing is, I would never normally get involved. I think people need to be able to sort their own stuff out. But this girl, she's my age, and she's on her own with two kids under four. No family, no partner."

Still slightly at a loss, Dove nodded encouragingly. "That must be hard."

"We've met up for coffee and to take the kids to play in the park . . . She just . . ." Eden met Dove's eyes suddenly. "She leaves the kids on their own while she goes out at night."

Dove cupped her mug of coffee and studied her niece's face. "Do you know why she leaves them?"

"What do you mean?"

"I don't mean it's right, I just wondered if you knew why she leaves them? Does she have a night shift job? Or is she out partying?"

"She's got a job, she says, and she never said outright she leaves them, it's just she's let things drop."

"Does she have any family or friends who might be looking after the kids while she works? I'm not saying you're wrong, Eden, I'm just saying it's really easy to jump to conclusions because you're worried."

Her niece smiled uneasily. "I know, and I hate to think she would know it was me. It's just, she says she's been really down since the baby was born and sometimes, she is just a bit weird with her. Like, she ignores her when she's crying or . . . I don't know. I just think she might need help," Eden said stubbornly.

"Perhaps she just needs a friend?" Dove suggested, seeing Eden start to pick at the already ragged hem of her jumper — a sure sign she was getting anxious. "I can give you the number to report any concerns to. It's anonymous so she will never know it was you."

"What would you do?"

"I don't know. Honestly, I would probably try to talk to her more and even offer to babysit if she needs to work. Just to see what she says. See if she opens up. She might be struggling with the rent, or . . . I don't know. I love that you worry about everyone, but you still need to concentrate on yourself and Elan." She smiled as the little boy raced around the garden with a large truck, making *brrrrrrmmmm* noises, lost in his own world.

"Okay." Eden took the piece of paper with the number written on it and slid it into her picket. "I really miss Delta."

"Oh, love, I do too. Does she email you a lot?"

"Yeah, and I follow her Instagram every day," she smiled. "She looks like she's definitely living her best life."

"Are you?" Dove asked gently, worried something else might be concerning her eldest niece. "Is there anything else worrying you, Eden?"

She shook her head. "No, I love working in the café with Mum, and Elan wears me out but he's gorgeous. I get a bit freaked out about what I'm going to tell him about his . . . his dad, when he's older."

Dove's heart gave a little wrench. She put her mug down and hugged her niece. "You'll figure it out, and you can always just go with 'He's dead,' which is true. Elan is happy and healthy and you're both safe. That's all that matters."

"Yeah, yeah, you're right. Mum said you're staying for dinner?"

"Love to, but as Quinn is actually home at the moment, I have a date on the sofa with a pile of snacks, my fiancé and a boxset. I must just say hi to Ren, though." Relieved the crisis seemed to be over, she followed Eden and Elan into the house, where she was further soothed by the smell of Ren's stew and homemade cherry pie. It was a shame she couldn't stay.

She smiled to herself as she arrived home again, having stopped as promised for more crisps and a bag of sweets. She really must be getting old when a good night was staying in with her fiancé and Netflix. *Netflix and chill.* Delta would think it was hilarious. She must email her younger niece tomorrow, just to check in on her.

* * *

The red digital clock said 3 a.m. when Dove opened her eyes, her brain fuzzy with sleep. She really wished she could stop waking in the early hours of the morning. It just meant she felt like shit by the time she got back to sleep and her alarm went off.

Maybe she should be like DI 'Vampire' Lincoln and just admit she was meant to be in the office at weird hours, at odds with the rest of the human race. She'd be keeping tropical fish and eating doughnuts by the box soon, she thought, rolling her eyes and turning over, trying to switch her thoughts off.

But a noise from downstairs made her jerk from semi-consciousness once again. It was outside, not in the house. She sat up slowly, carefully, so as not to wake Quinn, and listened.

The smash of breaking glass and the whoosh that followed it had her leaping out of bed. She could smell fuel and smoke instantly. "*Quinn*!"

CHAPTER FORTY-FIVE

He was already rolling out of bed, hauling on joggers and grabbing Layla, who was yowling, her fur standing on end, tail like a bottlebrush. "Fuck!"

Dove was on her phone, calling 999 for the fire service as she and Quinn began to inch their way towards the stairs.

Quinn went first with the cat, and Dove, still giving information over the phone, stepped carefully after him, feeling the heat, the stench filling her nostrils as they descended.

Luckily the kitchen door had been left closed. They often did this at night, to keep the smells of cooking from drifting into the rest of the house. But behind it an eerie orange glow and the roar of fire indicated they needed to get out fast.

Dove came off the phone. "You got the back door keys?"

"No, mine are in the kitchen. Fuck, what the hell has happened?"

"My keys are here." Dove grabbed them from the coffee table and struggled with the lock before opening the back door, letting them escape into the small back garden. The smell of burning was strong, and drifts of smoke wafted across the sky. More intense black smoke could be seen emerging from under the kitchen door.

Quinn firmly shut the back door and Layla, released to safety, sprinted up a tall oak, while Dove and Quinn retreated to the rear of the garden, watching in horror as a red-gold glow filled the night air.

"Is there anything else we can do? What about Mary next door?" Dove suggested. "We could climb over the fence and get her out."

"The kitchen is on the opposite side, but yes, let's make sure she's safe. I'll go over to hers — why don't you go wait for the fire service." Quinn vaulted over the wall, and she followed, jumping lightly down onto the cold, wet grass.

By running swiftly along the length of the row of terraces she was able to get back to the road in time to see two fire engines pulling up. Her neighbours were spilling out onto the streets in their nightclothes, their faces raw with shock and bathed in flashing blue lights.

Dove stood back to let the fire officers do their job, watching the glow and flash of flames through the window, tracking the progress of the fire as it licked the ceiling inside the kitchen. Above was their bedroom, and she crossed her fingers that it wouldn't spread too far.

Her lovely home, which had become her and Quinn's home, could become ashes and blackened shards of wood in minutes if the flames spread. She realized she had tears on her face and wiped them quickly away. Forcing herself to think rationally, she was convinced the breaking glass must have been a homemade firebomb thrown in at the window. Molotov cocktail. They were easy to make and very effective. She had seen the results before.

She shivered. When she had been working for the Unit, she had met up with a CHIS for a routine chat. While they were talking the building had been a target and she could still remember the panic and confusion of the fire.

She and her CHIS had escaped, but it was only after she discovered they had not been the intended targets and that her cover had not been blown that she found out there had been five members of a rival gang locked in a room off the kitchen. They had perished in the flames, triggering retribution from their families.

And so it went on.

She shivered, teeth chattering, considering her own fire. There hadn't been enough time between the sound of glass breaking and the signs of fire for someone to have climbed in and set the place alight. No, this was a hit-and-run, probably someone with a car.

Someone with a grudge against the emergency services? The neighbours knew what she and Quinn did. It wasn't a job they could hide or would want to hide.

"Morning, DC Milson." It was PC Jack Goss. "That your house?"

"Unfortunately, yes, it is." She tore her eyes away, registering that Quinn was coming down the path of Mary's house, with their neighbour walking next to him, carrying a small bag.

She noticed then that PC Goss was looking at her like he'd never seen her before, blinking and looking away, and the male fire officer was looking at her in exactly the same way.

She was suddenly aware of the cold air against her body and realized she had escaped the fire wearing a pair of lacy knickers and her bedtime T-shirt. Fuck it, let them look. At least she had hauled on a pair of trainers, so her feet weren't hurting.

Quinn walked over, looking frankly appreciative at her lack of clothing. "Hey, did you know . . ."

"Yes, I did, and no funny comments required. At least you're wearing trousers," she informed him. "I don't even know if I have any trousers left now. Or anything else for that matter." Again, she surveyed the smoking mess of their little house.

"It's all right, my dear, the fire is subsiding, and it doesn't look to me like it has spread." Mary, slender, elderly and strong, slipped an arm around her shoulders and gave her a hug. "Look, I brought some of these picnic blankets in my bag, in case anyone was standing outside in their nightwear and was cold." She delved around and handed Dove a soft pink woollen throw.

"Thanks, Mary, you're the best." Dove draped the throw over her shoulders, and it fell in merciful folds down to her knees.

PC Goss was talking to Quinn now, and Dove listened to their conversation, pulling the throw close around her body. Not because she was cold now, but for comfort.

As soon as statements had been taken, she called her sister Gaia.

"Dove? What the fuck is wrong with you? It's five a.m. and I'd just got to bed. Shouldn't you be going to work right now?" Gaia's furious voice blasted Dove's eardrums. Her sister was fiercely protective of her sleep. As a teenager she had been known to lock all the doors and windows so nobody could wake her up if she didn't want them to.

Luckily their nomadic and very different childhood in the commune in California hadn't required anyone to get up for school . . . Gaia was now a tough businesswoman, who balanced just on the right side of the law. She owned three successful upmarket strip clubs along the coast and had shares in various other commercial properties. She was harsh, abrasive and didn't take shit from anyone.

"Yeah, sorry to wake you, but someone tried to burn our house down a couple of hours ago and I wondered if you still had that empty property down by the marina?" Dove, well used to her sister, had also detected a sharp note of concern among the scolding.

"I'm sorry, I thought you just said someone tried to burn your house down. Fuck me. Are you both okay? What about Layla?" Gaia had a soft spot for cats. Probably the only soft spot in her armoured personality, Ren had often said with amusement.

"Pretty much what we said, and yes, we're all fine, thanks. Layla is up a tree in the back garden at the moment. Doesn't look as bad as it sounds," Dove said, forcing a note of optimism.

"Who started the fire?" her sister snapped out.

"Well, I could be wrong, but Quinn had some trouble with a stalker recently. One of our neighbours saw a car driving off at high speed just after the fire-starter chucked the ignition through our kitchen window. The car is registered to Quinn's stalker."

"He has a stalker? Don't you two ever just live like normal people?"

That made Dove smile. "Like you do, you mean? Anyway, right at this moment, I'm standing on the street in my knickers and it's bloody cold, so can we stay at one of your properties, please?"

Her sister was quiet for a moment and Dove could hear rapid tapping on a keyboard. Finally, Gaia said, "The marina apartment is the only one in Abberley that's empty just now, so that'll have to do. It's clean and I'll ring ahead to the building and get the water and electrics switched on."

"Thanks, Gaia."

"Sending you the address and passcode now." More rapid tapping and Dove's phone pinged with a text. Thank God for Gaia's efficiency.

"You can come to my apartment now and pick up the keys . . . You'll need a shower and I guess your place isn't habitable at all?"

Dove put a quick question to the fire commander, and he shook his head. "Damage won't be too bad, but you can't go in yet. It needs to cool off and we need to clear the scene. You know the drill. Your place will stink of smoke, too. Everything in the house. Sorry."

Quinn put an arm round her as she spoke quickly to her sister. "I've got to work but Quinn has a couple of days off, so if it's okay, we'll swing by your apartment, and Quinn will stay and get the keys and stuff while I have a shower and go to the station."

"I'm putting the coffee on now," her sister responded. "What about Layla? She can come too if you like, but I'm not sure she'll like being without a garden."

190

"It's okay, my neighbour Mary has already offered to have her while we get the house sorted out. Fingers crossed it won't take too long," Dove said, surveying the dripping shell of the kitchen. At least there didn't seem to be as much damage anywhere else. Keeping the door shut had probably saved the rest of their house, she thought.

"I'm just glad you're all right," Gaia responded. "Oh, and Dove?"

"What?"

"Don't forget to put some trousers on if you're going to work. You can borrow anything of mine."

Dove ended the call and sighed. Gaia's wardrobe was mostly designer and featured a lot of tailored business suits and an equal amount of black leather. At least they were the same size and both tall and rangy, but she could just imagine the rest of the MCT pissing themselves laughing if she pitched up in leather trousers.

"You going to call Ren?" Quinn asked, his arm still wrapped around her, holding her close. She leaned into him, feeling the steady, unhurried beat of his heart.

She shook her head. "No, there's nothing she can do, and her place is far too small for us to stay. At least Gaia has some space we can borrow for today, and the marina apartment will be great while we get the house back to normal."

PC Goss was approaching. "You logged a complaint against Malina Evans this morning, you said?"

"Right."

"She has history for violent and obsessive behaviour, and she set fire to her ex-boyfriend's car in 2016. You already heard we have a witness who saw her car drive away from your house right after the fire started?"

"I guess she finally figured out you weren't going to give her what she wanted," Dove told her fiancé.

He said nothing, but gently pulled her tighter into his arms.

CHAPTER FORTY-SIX

It was the right thing to do, but it hasn't brought me any closer to my sister, apart from physically. She isn't like me. She doesn't understand, and why would she? The things I had to deal with, to live through, while she was miles away, oblivious to my struggles.

I can tell she finds me odd. When I talk to her, try to explain, sometimes it's like I'm talking to thin air. Is she really here after all these years, or am I going mad?

This thought frightens me more than any other. Losing control is something that happens to other people, not to me.

Lily's death hit us hard. I was fine in Spain, travelling to Ibiza, to Dubai, finally making a name for myself in a tough industry. But after Lily's funeral, Lukas and I got talking. My old feelings, my old loyalties began to fight my new life. I lost the Benidorm gig, and soon after that I split up with my boyfriend. I always told myself it was casual, and I've known him a long time.

Friends with benefits. Except it wasn't.

I went back to the hospital, to my secrets and to my art. It's become a perfect place to hide away. The others don't bother me, because I've found a place near the back they don't care about. Two burnt-out cars sheltering under a rusted roof. Not Insta-worthy so not worth a look. I do still visit the hospital buildings, Daffodil Ward and the mortuary, and sometimes I leave a piece of art, just to see what they'll do with it, if they'll even notice it.

Every night we got locked up in the cars, I would take a pebble I was working on, or sometimes a bit of driftwood, and my sandpaper and slowly fashion the shapes. Hearts, always hearts.

While I was working on my art, I couldn't hear the laughter and the screams, the pleading and the horrible sound of flesh on flesh. I blocked it out and focused on the smoothness and the roughness of the pebbles, the way they felt in my fingers, and their solid, comforting weight as they sat in my small palms.

Lots of people came out and said how cruel Evan was, how he treated his kids like shit, and how my mum just stood by and did nothing because she was scared of him.

She was, but she was also a junkie. That was her choice, but I know she was going to change when my sister was born. In the weeks leading up to Cara's birth she was more a mum to me, Kat and my brothers than she had ever been.

It did occur to me she didn't look very pregnant, but she wore long floaty dresses and sloppy tracksuits so you couldn't really tell. She was off the drugs and getting the help she needed. We made plans to kick Evan out. It was me, Lukas, Kat and our baby sister against the world.

Something went wrong that evening, and I just knew that everyone was crying, shouting. Lily was shouting.

Did I even hold my sister in my arms for those few precious seconds? It is a memory I can't shake, but I can't be sure it happened. Not really. Evan beat her up, he beat me up, and he told us Cara wasn't real, that Lily had lied to us all because she was crazy.

But I saw a man taking her away, I really did. My life would have been different if I had never seen him take her, never wondered what happened to her.

Instead, I have spent most of my life searching for my sister, the key to my happiness. And now I have found her, I realize she isn't the key to anything.

Now that I have found her, I need her to go away.

I need Evan to go away too, but I think he should meet Cara before he does. After all, in the end she found us, didn't she?

CHAPTER FORTY-SEVEN

Dove arrived at work two hours late to find Steve had gone out with DI Blackman to follow up on the fourth Houselow/Windsor sibling, Katrina, hoping she might be able to shed some light on her brothers' recent movements.

"You don't look your usual sunny self," Lindsey pushed her chair back from the computer, "and you're never late. Which normally is extremely annoying, but today suggests you've had trouble."

"Very perceptive." Dove felt like she'd already drunk a gallon of coffee at Gaia's smart designer apartment this morning, but out of habit she entered the office gripping the standard paper cup filled from the machine. She'd also added a share-size pack of jelly sweets to get her through the day.

"Shit! The most exciting thing I did this morning was make a bacon sandwich," Lindsey told her, after listening to the story of Dove's firebug.

"Believe me, I would have preferred a bacon sandwich. What did I miss?"

"Well, since the drugs circus has moved in it's all pretty organized on that front. But there is still no evidence to suggest who killed Alice or who made the hit on her car, complete with baby, stone heart, etcetera." Lindsey took a sip of coffee and continued, "Lukas was pulled from the line-up, but we got nothing yesterday. Jon and Steve thought they would talk to Katrina. She's got no previous and has been very quiet. She works at Abberley General as a healthcare assistant."

As soon at her partner returned with DI Blackman, Dove could see the interview hadn't been successful.

Her boss shook his head. "You two go and talk to Martin Cartwright now, but Katrina is clean as far as I'm concerned, unless we turn up something new. Dove, are you sure you're okay to work? Do you need to take a day to sort stuff out?"

"No, I'm good, thanks." She smiled, aware she must look like crap.

An hour later Dove was driving to Martin Cartwright's flat while Steve sat in the passenger seat, scrolling through the files in his iPad.

"We can place Evan Houselow at the car crash scene, so he's going to be charged, but we can't charge him for Sarah because we don't even know it was murder and there is no evidence to suggest he was involved. *If* he was there, or if Leo or Lukas is our perp and followed her, maybe threatened her, and she stumbled backwards, she hit her head and he placed the stone and legged it." Dove was trying to put it all together out loud, and her exhaustion wasn't helping her brain to function at all. She was beginning to feel like she needed a gallon of caffeine just to stay awake.

"Way too many ifs for this stage of inquiry. And we're constantly getting distracted. Great that the NCA are in on the drugs bust at the garage, but it doesn't help us with our victims at the moment, does it?" Steve agreed.

Dove drove in silence for a while, still thinking through the case.

Steve broke her contemplation. "Evan is the only one with a clear motive. Both women helped to send him down, and now he comes out and wants revenge. It's simple."

"It's never simple," Dove told him. "Why would one of his kids, who also sent him down and hates him, now help him kill Alice and Sarah?"

195

Steve sighed. "Do you honestly believe either of the twins is behind all this?"

"No idea, but it makes sense that someone opened a whole Pandora's box of secrets, and it all seems to have kicked off from that, doesn't it? Lily dies, Evan is out of prison. Gemma still bothers me. She knows a lot more than she's telling. I think she's going to need to come down to the station for an interview. We're not getting anywhere with the softly-softly approach." Dove gave in to her coffee cravings and indicated left at the roundabout.

"She seemed to get really upset about the Benny Milward case . . . Could she hate the system enough to be Evan's partner in crime?"

"No way, she hates him more and she loves those kids she looks after. I get the impression it's all about the kids for her, any kids."

Dove joined the queue in the drive-thru, paused as they placed their order, then resumed her rundown as they waited for the food to arrive.

"Hopefully Martin can shed some more light on all this," Dove suggested, biting into a burger and chips, before swigging her steaming hot coffee, burning her mouth.

DI Marks called while she was finishing the last salt-encrusted chip.

"DC Milson? I was just checking you had seen we might have an overlap on one of your suspects. I saw DCI Franklin is SIO, but I can't get hold of him at the moment, and I had your number to hand."

"Go on." Dove was intrigued, switching her phone to loudspeaker so Steve could hear the conversation.

"We have a mispo that's just landed on our desk. An eighteen-year-old art student went missing from her shared flat last week. Her parents say she quite often goes AWOL to remote places to paint, as do her friends, but they got worried when they couldn't contact her. Her name is Mae Gardner, and she features DJ Darkness quite heavily on her socials. Her friends say she was a bit of a fan and followed his social media obsessively for the last year or so, ever since she saw him play in Benidorm."

"Leo Windsor."

"Quite. You had him and his brother in for a line-up the other day."

Dove brought the DI up to speed on the two Windsor brothers, and she rang off, promising to try DI Blackman for liaison on the two cases.

Steve parked outside Martin Cartwright's address, pulled an energy drink out of his bag and flipped the ring pull. "I need a caffeine hit." He gulped his can of fizzy liquid and chucked the empty into the car door.

* * *

Martin was a tall, dark-haired man, with a shy smile and wire-rimmed designer glasses. His T-shirt was designer too, and his house was extremely clean and tidy. He lived in Lymington-on-Sea, in one of the long rows of terrace houses that stretched up to Junction Road.

Despite the fact that he had been interviewed at the station twice, he didn't seem to be defensive or angry. Dove quickly agreed with the previous assessment that he was a bit of a follower, not particularly street-bright, and therefore had been easily assimilated into the Bensons' business, without knowing quite what he was doing.

"I can't take it in . . ." He ran his hands through his hair. "I still can't quite believe what's happened recently. I sometimes wake up in the morning and think everything is normal and then it hits me Mum and Dad are dead."

After a few more soft questions, Dove got straight to the point. "We are really sorry for your loss, but we are still investigating the murder of your mum and the suspicious death of Sarah Whitmore. I spoke to your dad's carer, Connie, and she says you and your dad were turning out his loft last month. You burned a whole load of paperwork?"

"It was just old stuff. Dad was always a bit of a hoarder, and Mum was the neat one," Martin said carefully.

Steve summarized what Gerald had told them. "Is it possible your parents were involved in taking at-risk children, probably babies, from their parents over a period of years when they both worked at Arrowhill Hospital?"

Martin stared at them. "I . . . oh my God . . . I don't know if that is true, but when we were clearing out Dad's loft, he kept on about some papers we couldn't burn. He said it was really important we had a record, and he took a small box away from the bonfire."

"Did you see what the papers were?"

"Not clearly. They looked like a load of old birth certificates, maybe some legal paperwork, and a spiral-bound notebook."

"When we spoke to your dad, he was . . . confused," Dove said. "He did tell us about the case they were involved in back in 1998, involving a two-year-old . . ."

"Benny Milward. My mum has a scrapbook full of clippings from the inquest. Hang on, I've got it here somewhere." He went into another room and Dove heard cupboard doors bang. "It was with all her stuff. I haven't . . . I mean, I can't go through everything just now. It's too much to deal with, and I know Jack Whitmore feels the same . . ." His face crumpled slightly, and he paused, fist clenched, before he seemed to regain control. He passed over a battered book with a faded red cover. "She has others from other child abuse cases, too . . ."

"Did your parents talk about the Houselow/Windsor case?" Dove asked.

Martin turned several pages of the scrapbook and pointed to clippings from Evan Houselow's trial. "Both my parents seemed to have left the past behind, and I had no idea it haunted them so much," he sighed. "They seemed really happy. Dad with his garden and Mum with her new job and her caravan. Of course, Dad got to the stage where he needed a live-in carer, but I paid for that." He caught their eyes. "Not through drugs."

"It's okay, Martin, we know you've already been interviewed about that," Steve reassured him.

"Yeah, I still can't believe they set me up like that," Martin said, anger finally showing through his calm facade.

Dove couldn't imagine how he was feeling. His parents dead within days of each other, his mates dropping him in it with a drugs scam and now he finds out his parents have some kind of possible vigilante secret past.

"And you have no idea where the box your dad removed may have gone?"

Martin shook his head, but Dove noticed he didn't quite meet their eyes. "If you know something," she said quietly, "it could help us find out who killed your mum."

He ignored this, instead pointing to a large cardboard box in the corner of his living room. "Those are other scrapbooks of other cases. There are eighteen in total. Seems like they were a bit obsessed with following the cases in the newspapers, but Mum was absolutely devoted to her babies. She loved her job, and when she finally retired she was always saying it wasn't the same."

Dove carefully loaded the cardboard box into the car as Steve passed Martin his card.

"All right, thanks, Martin, we'll have a look at the scrapbooks if that's okay?" Steve said as they departed.

Dove indicated out onto the main road and sent a questioning glance in her partner's direction. "Gerald's house?"

"Definitely."

The cottage on Knob Hill was empty, waiting for Martin to attend to his father's personal effects. A full search would only be possible with a team, and as Gerald had died of natural causes, his house and garden were not being treated as a crime scene.

"The bonfire was at the side of the house," Dove said, as they waded through clumps of cow parsley and dandelions.

The patch where the bonfire had been lit was blackened and a few charred magazine covers and papers still fluttered around the edges of the burnt logs. Dove poked gently at one with her toe. *Railway Weekly*.

"Where would he hide a box? Martin said he didn't see where he put it."

Dove walked further round the garden, her boots brushing against the remains of a herb garden, releasing the scent of lavender and rosemary as she walked. On the far side of the garden, half hidden by weeds and trees, was a shed.

"Where else would you put your valuables?" Steve suggested as they crossed the overgrown lawn.

The shed wasn't locked but had a simple rusty hook-and-eye latch. Dove slipped on a pair of gloves and opened the door. The scent of musty earth and mildew hit her, and she wrinkled her nose.

Inside, the shed was bare apart from a neat stack of seed trays, a pile of plant pots and a few garden implements. The two small windows on one side were covered in green mould and a huge clematis was threatening to engulf the whole structure.

"Now what?"

"Pessimist. We look for the box," Steve told her. "It's worth a shot. Connie saw them working in the garden, and the path to this shed has been kept cleared."

After a few moments Dove discovered a shoebox underneath a large plant pot. "This must be it. Let's have a look."

"Birth certificates? They aren't real, though, look at this . . ." Steve picked one up and peered at the faded lettering. Printed across the front was a red SAMPLE stamp. "These are just printouts from the internet or something."

Dove and Steve began to flick through the documents. There was also a bundle of reports signed off by Sarah Whitmore.

It all looked official enough, with stamps and typewritten records. But a closer inspection seemed to reveal a mix of genuine documents and fakes. A few of the fakes were extremely bad, with ink running and duplicated lines. There was also a record of assessments and actions taken to protect a number of local children deemed to be at risk.

"So who was our forger? And who wrote the list?" Steve asked, squinting at the faded writing.

"And who made the decision which children should be taken from their parents?" Dove added, as she jabbed a finger at a list of names and dates. Halfway down, with a green tick, was the name Cara Windsor.

CHAPTER FORTY-EIGHT

"What the hell?" Steve said, picking it up. "The tenth of August . . . That's just before Lily's mystery baby allegedly went missing."

"It's also a week after Evan was attacked and a month before his children decided to report his abuse." Stunned, Dove was trying to sort through the facts in her head. "Does it say anything else about what happened to these kids? Did they actually do this and get away with it?"

"No, it just documents what was happening to them . . . The eldest was five years old and the youngest, I suppose Cara Windsor — but Cara's birth was never registered, was it?" Steve looked as stunned as she felt.

It appeared the gang had been efficient and methodical. There were certificates and documents. No photographs. There was a business card for David Weston at the adoption agency and the spiral-bound notebook listed names and addresses, and notes beside each name.

"I wonder why none of the adoptive parents queried the speed of the adoptions," Steve said. "And the adoption agency — did they know about this?"

"It all looks official, doesn't it? They must have known someone who was a top-class forger. But I still can't believe they actually did this. There isn't anything to say they actually went through with the whole plan, is there. No missing kids were flagged."

"Apart from Cara Windsor?"

Dove looked up. "She wasn't named in the reports relating to her supposed disappearance. I can't believe Martin didn't look at this box, didn't follow his dad and sneak a peek."

"Call him," Steve suggested.

Dove looked up his number on her phone. "I can't imagine how hard this must be for you," Dove said gently when Martin answered. She summarized the contents of the box and there was silence on the other end. "Martin?"

"You're saying they abducted babies? My parents were criminals?"

He didn't sound nearly shocked enough. "Not necessarily. Martin, did you know about this? Did you follow your dad when he hid these documents?"

Another pause.

"Come on, Martin," Dove asked him urgently. "Did you tell anyone else about this, about what you discovered?"

"Yes, I did. I took the box home to look through properly. It was . . . it was such a shock, but I needed to talk to someone who knew me, who knew my parents. I told my ex-boyfriend, Leo Windsor."

"When did you tell him?"

"The day after I found the papers. About . . . a month ago. I was off work. I'd taken a long weekend."

"How did he react?"

"He came straight over to my place, and we talked it all through."

"Did he show a particular interest in any of the paperwork?"

"No, I don't think so, he was just as shocked as I was. Of course, we were shocked his family were on there, and he said . . . he said he needed to talk to Lukas and Katrina." Martin's voice was shaking now, and Dove thought it was easy to see the real reason he hadn't shared his find with the police. He was afraid his ex-boyfriend was involved in the killings.

"Martin, I can understand this must be hard for you, but why couldn't you have told us this a few days ago?" Dove asked him, leaning against the wall of the shed, letting her exasperation show.

"Because I . . . I don't know. I took the box back to the shed and hid it back where Dad must have put it. I guess I'm still processing it all, and I saw Leo's name on there, so it became personal. I didn't want him to get in any trouble either. And Lukas, and Katrina. I know them through Leo. They're doing well, sorting life out and I didn't want any of them hurt. And before you say it, there is no chance any of them killed my mother. They just wouldn't."

Blind denial, thought Dove. At least that seemed to be an honest answer. "You do know Leo has already been interviewed by us in connection with this case?"

"No, I didn't. After I showed him all the papers, we had one conversation. He said he needed time to come to terms with his past. I regretted showing them to him. I thought it might bring us closer together again, but he said he needed to talk to his sister. After that he ghosted me." Martin's voice broke. "I'm not sure how to deal with any of this."

Dove ended the call, went back inside and looked again at the page in the notebook. A longlist of children waiting to be saved. Leo, Lukas, Max and Katrina were all on the list. But next to each of their names was a small red x.

CHAPTER FORTY-NINE

They took the box back to the car, and Dove trawled the file for contact details for Katrina Bentley. "You and the DI only just spoke to her, and she didn't say a bloody word about any of this."

Dove tapped out the number, fuming. Katrina wasn't answering her mobile phone. "She must be protecting her brother, otherwise she would have at the very least mentioned Leo was dating Alice's son!"

"She works at Abberley General as a healthcare assistant," Steve reminded her. "Let's ring them and see if she's on a shift."

"How did she seem when you and the boss spoke to her?"

"Fine. Very together, dedicated to her job, no red flags and a rock-solid alibi for both incidents," Steve said. "Bloody hell, we could have saved hours of work if either she, Martin or Leo had mentioned this little treasure trove. I suppose Lukas knows all about it too."

"Martin said Leo was going to tell them. Which incidentally puts all three of them in the frame for Alice's murder. Did they know Alice took their baby sister? Leo could easily have taken photos of the documents when Martin showed them to him."

A quick call to the hospital informed them Katrina was indeed working today and was on shift until 2 p.m.

They drove to Abberley General. In stark contrast to its predecessor, the hospital was a towering block of concrete and glass, with some of the best facilities in the Southeast.

"Katrina Bentley?"

She was walking briskly across the staff car park towards the canteen when they approached and she faltered, her dark blue eyes wary. "Who wants to know? Oh, it's you."

"Sorry to bother you again. This is DC Milson, also from the Major Crimes Team. Can we ask you some questions?" Steve smiled at her.

"I guess so." She slipped her bag off her shoulders and took out a bottle of water. "I'm really tired, I've just come off a twelve-hour shift."

"Which ward do you work on?" Dove asked.

"Mayflower, mostly. It's the maternity ward. But I'm central bank staff, so I go all over the place, wherever they are short-staffed," Katrina told them, taking a sip of her water.

In the bright sunlight she did look exhausted, with dark shadows under her eyes, and her dark, glossy hair coming down from its tight pleat at the back. She put the bottle away and brushed a few strands awkwardly behind her ears.

"We could grab a coffee in the canteen if you'd rather?" Steve looked towards the staff canteen, which was next to the car park.

"I'm good. What do you want to know?" she asked.

Feeling like it was Groundhog Day, Dove ran through the where, who and how, listening as Katrina said she didn't know who Sarah and Gerald were and she had been working all three nights in question. But she did say she knew Alice Cartwright.

"How do you know her?"

The woman hesitated. "I think I've seen her around the hospital. She used to work at Arrowhill and I think she's one of the volunteers on Mayflower Ward. We have volunteers who just help out and do the evening drinks and that kind of thing. You know, a trolley with tea, coffee and Horlicks," she added.

Steve stared at her in disbelief. "Come off it, Katrina. Your brother was dating Martin Cartwright, who is Alice Cartwright's son, and he's already told us about the paperwork."

Fear and confusion flitted across her face. "Poor Martin. Leo said he was going through hell. I know Alice was murdered. It's really sad but . . ." She bit her lip and the police officers waited.

Katrina said nothing more until Dove prodded, "Did Martin tell you what he had found?"

She nodded, and took a long breath. "It was so . . . strange. I mean, Alice was so normal and caring, and so good at her job. She kept in touch with everyone and was just a really good person." Katrina's eyes filled with tears, "Oh God, I'm afraid I might have caused her death."

"What do you mean?" Dove asked gently.

"Well, Leo said Martin was in such a state about her death and what he had found, and Leo was asking all kinds of questions about . . . well, everything. I tried to calm him down, but he went on about Evan knowing something about our sister . . ."

"And Cara Windsor. I take it she did exist? Was she your sister?"

Katrina's eyes filled with tears again, and this time they flowed unchecked down her pale cheeks. "No. She was my daughter."

CHAPTER FIFTY

Down at the station for a formal interview, Katrina sat clutching a cup of tea, shivering as though the room was freezing.

"Cara was my baby. I was fourteen and I found out I was pregnant during the summer holidays." She looked up at them, eyes red-rimmed with tiredness and tears. "I'd been in the vans a couple of times so it could have been anyone, really. I told Gemma Rogers. She was our babysitter, and I knew she would understand because she had her first baby at fifteen."

"Go on," Dove said gently.

"Gemma knew a midwife, Alice, and she promised she would keep it under the radar, but I couldn't tell Lily and Evan. I didn't want a baby at fourteen, maybe not ever." She took a deep breath, steadying herself with both hands clinging to the edge of the table.

"Alice told me she might know of a way out, and I jumped at the chance. There was no future in dodging Evan, hoping my baby wouldn't become a recipient of his violence. Gemma told me we could keep it a secret, and they would take the baby and have it adopted."

"She actually told you that?" Steve asked.

"Yes. Then it could stay a secret and I could finish school and get a job, move away somewhere . . . Lily nearly ruined everything. She suspected I was pregnant, and I told her about the baby. It was a huge mistake. She offered to raise it herself, got really excited and started to make plans to leave Evan with all us kids."

"Did Evan know you were pregnant?"

"No. I couldn't tell Lily I was giving up my baby, so I went along with both plans, and I waited. Alice told me more about their racket, and without knowing why, I began to feel resentment. Why hadn't they taken me? I had been at risk for years, and now I was proof they should have taken action. Anyway, Alice said she had found a lovely family to take my baby on."

"Did Evan suspect you were pregnant?" Dove asked.

"No. Lily was ruining everything, though, babbling about her baby, until Evan shouted at her and told her she'd better not be up the fucking duff again or he'd kill it as soon as it came out." She finished her drink and squeezed the empty paper cup so tightly it folded in on itself, her knuckles white with effort.

"Go on," Steve said gently.

"I knew what I was going to do then. I had her at Gemma's house at two a.m. Things went wrong for a bit, and I was so . . ." She caught herself. "The baby was breech, but because I hadn't had any scans or anything nobody knew."

"And you had no pain relief?"

"No, but eventually my baby was born, and she was beautiful." Katrina's expression changed but she quickly shut down the emotion. "Anyway, I stayed at Gemma's for three days. Cara was beautiful and healthy, and I caught myself thinking 'what if . . . There was help out there for both of us if we asked for it, but I felt I couldn't ask. I was confused and terrified, and suddenly there was this whole new life depending on me to do the right thing."

"At this stage nobody knew except you, Gemma and Alice?" Dove said slowly. They had been bang on, Gemma was right in the thick of it. "Your brothers?"

"Not my brothers. I knew she had told Sarah, because she was in on it. I liked her but she was kind of no-nonsense.

Alice and Gemma gave me every chance to back out of the adoption plan, but I knew I had to be strong."

"How did Lily take it when you told her?"

Katrina hunched forward in her chair, elbows resting on the table, her eyes bloodshot and exhausted. "She just collapsed, went all quiet. I felt like I was letting her down. She told me that I was wrecking everything, and this was our big chance to get out. But . . ." She looked around the room, seemingly searching for words. "Lily said all these kinds of things and I think she meant them. She would be full of energy and plans, tell us we were going to leave Evan, start afresh, but it never came to anything. I heard Evan say he would kill my baby, and that was enough for me."

"So your brothers didn't know?"

"Lily told them she was having the baby, so it was kind of hard. In the end, after Alice's husband came and took Cara away, Lily went mad and swore she'd had the baby and it had been abducted."

"Nobody backed her up?"

"No. I told my brothers Lily had been mistaken, she wasn't pregnant after all. I don't know what they thought, but they knew we shouldn't say anything. They must have guessed, but I was in such a state . . . Soon afterwards, Evan thought I'd been sleeping with some boy, and he beat me so hard I almost passed out."

"Someone spread the word that Evan was responsible for Lily's baby disappearing. Do you know who did that?"

"I don't, but I think . . . I think it might have been Gemma. She loved us all and she was fighting for us. Leo once asked me about our sister, and what did I think happened to her. We were drunk at his house, and I nearly told him. I'm sure they must all have suspected. But I didn't. I couldn't. I think I did let slip she had been called Cara or maybe he heard me and Lily arguing . . . I told him to leave it and leave Cara alone."

"Do you think, having seen the paperwork, that Leo now blamed Alice for the loss of the baby he believed to be his sister?"

"I don't know . . . Evan was locked away and we got on with our lives, until two things happened. I suffered a miscarriage with my boyfriend, Alexandro, and had to spend a week in hospital. And then Lily died. She sent me a text the day before she did it, telling me of her intentions, and blaming me for the loss of the baby. I was already raw from the miscarriage, and to do Lily justice she never grassed on me. I wonder if she somehow didn't take in what had happened, whether in the end she believed her own version of events."

Dove leaned back in her chair, stunned and devastated for the woman sitting in front of them. "Just to recap, Leo, and Lukas now know about the papers linking Cara to Alice and Gerald Cartwright, and Sarah Whitmore?"

"I believe so, but they each know some of the truth. Evan must have been raging if he realized the truth. I think it's only me and Gemma who know what really happened, and Gemma isn't mentioned in the papers so I don't see how anyone can know about her. They say everyone has a different story, don't they? And only half of it is ever true." Katrina put her fingers to her forehead and closed her eyes, as though exhaustion had finally beaten her.

* * *

"Wow." Dove leaned against the wall by the coffee machine, completely drained. "How is Katrina managing to hold it all together?"

DI Blackman was putting his phone away as he peered out of the door. "You two still here? We're having Leo and Lukas brought in now."

"Do you think Gemma is in danger? Could that be why Alice was calling her the night she died? Did Martin give her a hint of the paperwork he had found?"

"Or could we be looking at three different people, three different deaths, all for different reasons?" Steve reasoned. "This adoption racket must have opened a whole can of worms."

CHAPTER FIFTY-ONE

Steve's phone rang as they turned back into the office, and he had a quick conversation before ringing off with a grim expression on his face. "That was Gemma Rogers. She says she's found something she thinks we need to see. She doesn't want anyone else to come so her neighbours aren't spooked by police, but it's behind her house."

"Cryptic," Dove remarked. "Behind her house is the gym and the lake where someone claims to have seen Evan carrying the baby. I wonder if Evan knows that she framed him?"

"And that she was instrumental in taking Cara from Katrina. She was trusted by everyone and on site, as it were, the whole time."

"Shit, yes! She hates Evan so this would have been a double score for her. Rescuing a child and making it look like Evan killed the baby."

"She sounded a bit freaked out. Let's see what she has and then bring her in. We can ask her to back up Katrina's story."

They parked the car round the back next to the derelict car garage and found Gemma beckoning them from her back garden.

The usual swarm of kids were playing happily, and Gemma spoke in a low voice. "I didn't want to worry the kids, but you need to see this." She led them to another door cut into her garden fence, and led the way through. "Come on, and hurry up."

Dove peered through the fence. The dirty, scum-covered lake was poisonous emerald green, and the gym building sprawled right to the water's edge. To her left was the haulage yard, which was empty apart from two huge HGVs, a large Portakabin in one corner and the dust and gravel swirling around the lorry tyres. A huge metal shed stood open, and Dove could see boxes and freight containers stacked in neat piles. The smell was of oil and exhaust fumes.

"It's just past those trees," Gemma said, leading them quickly along the rough grass, along the perimeter of the yard where a dense growth of scrubby trees and brambles was decorated with Coke cans and crisp packets.

Steve followed her and Dove was right behind him. As he took a step forward, he was roughly hauled away behind the trees.

Dove just had time to call out before she was also attacked, tape over her mouth and many strong hands securing her arms and legs. "*Gemma*!" She could sense Steve struggling nearby, but the abduction was swift and practiced.

She was half dragged, half carried from the daylight to the semi-darkness of a warehouse. Terror made her struggle harder, kicking out and trying to protest, but the tape securing her mouth held firm, and she struggled to breathe as terror took over.

Phones, watches and radios were quickly stripped off, bagged and removed and they were both patted down. Hands lingered and she shrugged them crossly away.

In the semi-shadows a face peered down at her. "Hallo, pigs."

Someone else ripped the tape from her mouth and she turned to make eye contact with Steve. His expression was calm, but he was breathing fast, and blood trickled from the corner of his mouth.

"What's going on?" Steve asked reasonably, despite the bruise already forming on his left cheek. "We're with the

Major Crimes Team. I spoke to Andy last month. He knows me."

"Andy's not here today," another man said sharply.

"You from the drugs squad?" the taller man snapped out. Dove couldn't see his face because it was in shadow, but he towered over her.

"No. We don't care about your business dealings. This is about the woman who was recently murdered in this area, Alice Cartwright." Steve was still doing well, Dove thought. She was fighting a panic attack. Memories flooded back into her brain and to her horror she felt tears well in her eyes. *Chip, chip, chip* . . . But there was no gravestone, no stonemason, and this was here and now. She was older, wiser and had the tools to fight back.

Slowly, as the men were focused on Steve, she felt herself unfreeze. The blinding, breath-taking panic was abating slightly as survival mode took over.

"Yeah, I saw that. Andy didn't do it." The man considered and then added, "Neither did we. It wasn't our drugs in the car neither."

Dove bit her lip and forced herself to contribute, "Nobody is saying he did, or you did. We do have some information Andy might be interested in hearing, as we happen to be on the premises now."

Steve opened his mouth to speak again but the tall man waved a wrench, bending closer, and tapped Steve's bruised cheek. "Shut up. We've heard what you had to say. Only she can speak now and only when we ask questions."

Dove moistened her lips and, risking a whack with the wrench herself, said "Can we see Andy? I really need to give him this information." Her previous training as a source handler hadn't left her, even though it had been three years since she'd last found herself dealing with organized crime gangs. The language was the same, the only difference now was she had no false identity to hide behind, no cover story to protect her.

She sensed anger, but uncertainty. Her own mind was still whirring. Why would Gemma lead them into a trap? Was she afraid they had discovered she had been working with Alice and Sarah, or that she had let Gerald walk away from her house with Cara?

Making eye contact with Steve, she saw him shake his head slightly, warningly, but was unable to translate his movement. The concrete floor was oily, with a coating of dirt. It had been a slick capture, she had to give them that, but now, with wrists and ankles bound, the men were hardly going to apologize and release them.

She thought about her previous training. If a gang went as far as snatching a police officer, the chances were that officer was not coming back breathing. *Fuck.*

One of the men left the group and she could hear mumbled conversation. Of course, if it wasn't Andy, someone else would be right there, listening, deciding what to do. It was a familiar tactic in the game. *Double fuck.* She felt a sudden chill in her heart as a new, lower voice entered the conversation.

She hoped it wasn't bloody Joey sitting listening, fresh from his prison cell. But even then, if she could get him to come out so she could start a conversation, she was prepared to leverage any information she had to get them out of here unharmed. Drugs, there must be something they wanted to know about the Bensons' part in the investigation. Could she trade some information for her and Steve's lives?

Before she had a chance to try, the tall man came back and spoke to the others. "Get them in the truck."

They were swung to their feet, and Dove, seeing her worst fears were being realized, kicked out hard with both tied ankles, using her captor as a prop. In the corner of her vision, she saw Steve wrestling with one of his captors. Sweat was pouring down her face now, and there was a rip as someone grabbed at her shirt, missing her shoulder.

The grunts and occasional swear word were punctuated with the sickening thud of fists on flesh, and Dove, twisting and kicking out, saw her partner was now on the floor. They were holding him down and even as she lunged forward one of the men hit him across the knees with an iron bar. His cry of pain was cut off abruptly.

"I thought I said put them in the bloody lorry." A broad, muscular man in his sixties, with a white vest and oil-smeared overalls stripped to his waist, appeared from the back. His face was expressionless and his eyes cold and dark.

Dove knew the Nicholls family, and he bore enough resemblance to the others for her to guess this was indeed Joey. She was bewildered by the extreme treatment of two police officers, though. Joey had a reputation for being dangerous, violent, but not stupid — why go crazy over this? "Your men are making a mistake. Joey, we're officers from the Major Crimes Team, and we aren't interested in your business," she repeated, forcing herself to speak calmly even as she fought for breath, her arms cruelly pinned behind her back. "We know Andy and we've got some information for him."

He looked slowly around at the carnage, eyes blank, then appraising. "Get them in the lorry. She's a woman, for fuck's sake. Can you really not manage a girl between you?" he laughed.

She knew there were other family members, and desperately tried to remember any old intel, anything they might use. Nothing. The recent case, then? What had Gemma said about Lily? Instinct delivered a name to her lips. "Joey, we want to talk to Andy about Lily." It was a desperate last attempt and for a split second she swore a flash of emotion slipped across his face. Anger.

"Andy went soft over that woman. If you ask me, it's a good thing that she topped herself." Then his expression changed, all feeling gone. "Get in the truck. I'll talk to you later. I'll teach you not to question my business when you've just had me banged up for nine months on a fucking made-up charge."

He spat on Steve's prone body and scowled at his men. "I had a tip-off of my own. I know exactly what you're really doing here, and what you want. See? It's not just you lot who get information."

CHAPTER FIFTY-TWO

She must have wanted to meet us, fumbling her way around in an unfamiliar world. But I could see the fear in her face when she saw she wouldn't be leaving this place for a while.

It's funny how I thought I had found my missing piece of the jigsaw, but all she can really relate to is my false world of social media triumphs and fame.

I just need to decide how to make it finish. So funny, everyone wanted to find Cara secretly. I know they did.

Evan, desperate for an entry into my world, for my money, has talked about everything I asked him to. Some of it is bullshit, but some of it is the truth I needed to know, that I craved when I was younger.

It still amuses me now to think my mother had the guts to have a relationship with Andy Nicholls. It pisses me off she didn't have the guts to stay with him and leave bloody Evan. It explains why Kat has the look of a Nicholls. Her blue eyes and dark hair are so different to Lily or Evan. Evan must have known.

And Cara? She is the spitting image of Kat, with long, curly dark hair. How did she come to university in Brighton? I thought the stars were aligning to bring us back together. But it was all a mistake.

Her career plans seemed to be to carry on doing what she was doing, maybe apply for a reality TV show, and see where it took her.

I reminded myself she was young, possibly a bit spoiled. None of the things that touched her touched me and vice versa.

I bring her food, water and allow her to use the toilet. It's a bucket, but it'll do. When I brought her here, I wasn't thinking straight, after a few lines of coke and a few beers. My one thought was to hide her.

Now, as I stare into her eyes, I can tell she hates me, and she is scared of me, of what I might do to her. I've seen that same look in Kat's eyes, in Lily's eyes, when they stared at Evan, dodged his blows. It makes me ashamed of what I have done.

And Evan helped me. He was so keen to help, I should have known it wouldn't end well. Nothing with him ever does. He knew how much I wanted to find Cara, and when I showed him the photos, he said he thought it was her.

I was so wrapped up in my own happy ending, I forgot who I was dealing with. Not someone I hated and feared, not someone I wrote letters to in prison pleading for information on my lost sister, but an actual person who seemed to understand, to also be invested in what I was doing.

My life could have been so different.

I expect that's what Lily thought too.

CHAPTER FIFTY-THREE

Dove opened her eyes to darkness, the smell of blood and something else . . . like the air on a frosty morning, all sharp and tingling to the senses, filling her nostrils. She cautiously wriggled her fingers. The bonds were tight around her wrists and ankles. As she extended her legs carefully her bare feet hit a warm human body.

"Steve?" she whispered into the blackness.

He groaned next to her. "Fuck me, I've got a headache."

Panic was threatening to overcome her again, but she forced herself to focus, to remember how she could de-escalate the mounting panic inside her mind. *Five things I can see* . . . No, that was no good, she couldn't even make out where the hell they were. Her fingers explored the metal ridged floor. Were they actually in a truck? *Four things I can hear.* That was better. Her other senses were adjusting. Voices outside, the noise of another HGV reversing, her own breathing and Steve's groans as he tried to manoeuvre himself into a sitting position.

Her heart had calmed to racing instead of threatening to burst out of her chest by the time Steve spoke. "Now what do we do? I can't believe even the Nichollses are stupid enough to take on two police officers. It'll give them trouble and a spotlight they don't need. Joey is mad as hell. Why would Gemma do this?"

"I don't even think Andy was there. We only saw Joey, didn't we? What if this is about the drugs, though? Perhaps Gemma was pressured into setting us up?"

"Or maybe she's just terrified we got too close to her and she's getting us out the way the best way she knows."

"Right. And we walked straight into it." Steve's tone was bitter, and she could hear him shifting uncomfortably on the lorry floor.

"What could a child protection racket and dead midwife possibly have to do with the Nichollses? Bloody Gemma. What the fuck is she playing at?" Dove was silent for a moment. "We need to offer something. Some kind of information."

"So let me get this straight. They roughed us up because they think we are a threat because we know something. But actually, we don't know shit, and our case doesn't remotely threaten any of their stuff they've got going on."

"Pretty much sums it up. But Gemma wants us out the way, so we've hit a nerve somewhere. Could she be our killer?"

There were voices outside, laughter, and the side door was flung open, throwing a thin sliver of light across the truck. Several men slid inside, pulling themselves up by the handrails. They were laughing.

Joey Nicholls had long had a reputation as a vicious bastard. Dove knew of him from her time on the Unit. Her stomach clenched and her scars seemed to sting as a reaction to being once again at the mercy of an organized crime gang. How had this gone from a slightly bizarre but fairly normal murder investigation to being locked in a truck with these thugs?

There was a sharp click, and a light came on. The door was banged shut behind the men, who were jostling and laughing.

"Now what are we going to do with our two trespassers?" Joey asked. The others quietened, but Dove could sense the atmosphere was tense.

"I'll keep this one for myself." A thickset blonde man jabbed a thumb at Dove. She ignored him, maintaining eye contact with Joey.

"Have we met before, darling?" he asked now.

She really hoped they hadn't, but there had been some county lines crossovers at one point. They said Joey never forgot anything. She could recall a case involving a CHIS who had run a school-age drugs ring that had connections to the Nicholls brothers, but Dove felt fairly confident that they hadn't met when she was using one of her aliases.

"No, we haven't. Joey, I'm not sure what your drivers were thinking when they tackled us, but we're investigating the murder of Alice Cartwright, a local midwife, which I don't believe has anything to do with your family or business."

"You spoke to Evan Houselow." He came closer, like an evil snake sliding across the floor, and beside her she felt Steve tense.

"We spoke to him in connection with the case. This is part of our murder investigation and I repeat, not a threat to you or anything to do with you. We know Evan was working for Kevin and Jay Benson. What do you want to know?"

He nodded slowly. "What do I want to know? Everything. Everything is my business. That's how we got where we are today. Because I see everything and I hear everything, and you have got under my skin already. That doesn't happen very often with me and women."

She held her breath, hoping they weren't creating too much of a bond. But she had offered information on a rival dealer. A rival dealer with presumably a bigger backer. "The Bensons took part of a shipment that came in a while back from South America."

"Keep talking."

She did, repeating what DI Blackman had told them. Nothing that would harm the investigation, nothing that Joey could interfere with, but sometimes all they needed was the information.

"Your drivers clearly acted without orders and now you've come back and found two police officers in one of your trucks," Steve said reasonably, but Dove could see how pale he was, how his words came out through teeth gritted in pain and she saw sweat beading on his forehead. "You need to just release us and reprimand your men. It was a mistake they made, but we'll overlook it. I know Andy and I've seen he's making a go of the business. We don't care what's going on, or what Gemma might have told you, but you need to let us go."

There was a pause as Joey turned to look at Steve, and then nodded sharply at the tall man next to him. The man hit Steve on the side of the jaw, knocking him out across the floor of the truck.

Dove caught her breath, trying to recall anything that might save their lives. In another life she had been in constant danger, had been in this exact situation before. *Come on, Dove, you're stronger than they are.*

"I'm not interested in any more talk." Joey came close and ran a finger down Dove's cheek. "I like her, but I can't keep her. Too dangerous." He pulled her face around, tipped her chin and kissed her hard.

You have got to be fucking kidding. Dove's brain screamed obscenities, and she tried not to gag, unable to do anything to avoid his mouth. The onlookers laughed, but someone muttered something about just getting on with the show and there was a reluctant rumble of agreement.

Suddenly it was over, and Joey laid her gently onto the floor and for an agonizing few seconds stared down at her. She didn't breathe, didn't move, didn't make eye contact.

Outside an alarm was sounding, and the men leaped up, laughter leaving their faces as they filed out of the lorry. Joey was last out and he turned to pull the light cord. He winked at Dove. "Shame I can't stay. We would have had a good time, darling."

The side door was slammed shut and the lorry began to move forwards, rumbling over the uneven ground as it presumably passed through the gates, making a right turn. They must be heading for the main road.

I'm still alive.

"Steve?"

Tears streamed down Dove's cheeks, and she sobbed into the darkness. Present terror and past memories colliding. She reached out blindly to find her partner, relieved he was still breathing, but worried her fingers encountered stickiness as she explored his face.

Last time her team had come to find her, had arrived in time to save her. This time, Gemma would no doubt be happy to point her colleagues in the wrong direction.

She shivered, aware suddenly of how cold it was getting. Dove wriggled upright, leaned against the jolting metal sides, but a while later she had to move as the intense cold seemed to be eating away at her body. Why was it so bloody cold?

In the darkness she couldn't see her breath in the icy air as the lorry rumbled onwards, but she felt it. Exploring further, she discovered the interior wasn't encased in white plastic insulation, as she had assumed when the light was briefly illuminating their prison. It was a refrigeration lorry. And the temperature was dropping as the system warmed up.

CHAPTER FIFTY-FOUR

Dove jerked out of a doze, her cheek numb where it had rested against the side of the lorry. She was shaking, and Steve had regained consciousness.

"What did I miss? Snowfall?" he asked, in a feeble attempt at humour. His voice was cracked and low, and he cleared his throat several times. "I'd kill for some painkillers and a blanket."

"Haha. How are you feeling?" Dove wriggled nearer but was immediately thrown off balance as the lorry went over a bump in the road.

"Fine, apart from freezing to death." He inched round so his back was against the side of the lorry. "Any ideas which direction we're headed?"

"M25, maybe? We turned onto a motorway before I dozed off. Christ knows how long ago that was, though." She was suddenly aware she was slurring her words and the fear jerked her fully awake. "I'll try and get closer. Body heat. I still can't believe this is happening. Joey's lost it completely."

He gave a weak laugh but didn't object as she leaned against his shoulder.

* * *

They sat in silence, dozing, shivering until at last the lorry, after a series of turns, slowed and stopped. There was no sound of a loading depot outside. A door banged and there was the sound of another vehicle, then of quick, lowered voices. Another door banged, and then there was nothing.

"Have they left us to it?" Steve's teeth were chattering now and the shivering was turning to whole-body shaking.

The noise of scraping and wind made them both jump. "What the hell . . . ?" Dove realized it must be trees on the roof. She began to struggle with her ties again. Now the lorry was stationary, and they weren't being thrown around like peas on a drum, she began edging towards where she had seen the light cord dangling.

Getting her balance in the darkness, with both feet tied, was tough. She fell numerous times, numb from the cold and bruising, but eventually manged to stand and hop over, jumping and grabbing the cord with her teeth to yank it down. The first three times she missed, and she sat in the darkness almost crying with frustration and cold.

At long last she got a firm grip on the cord, and let herself fall, allowing her body weight to turn the light on. It almost wrenched all her teeth out, and as she lay on the ground, blinking in the light, she ran a cautious tongue around her mouth. Blood, and soreness, but nothing missing, and they had light.

"Well done," Steve said through gritted teeth.

She was horrified by the sight of him, even knowing she probably didn't look much better herself. Her partner's face was swollen and bruised, one eye almost closed. His skin was pale, and his lips had a bluish tinge. She winced as her gaze encountered his injured limb. "How's your knee feeling?"

"Well, I won't be doing any gymnastics anytime soon, but I don't think there is anything broken." He seemed to gather himself, making a huge effort. "We need to get out of here. It isn't getting any warmer, even though the engine is switched off. Maybe it isn't linked to the refrigeration system?"

Dove explored every inch of their prison. No way out of the back doors, but there was a small door leading into the driver's cab. It was locked but when Dove shoved her shoulders against it there was some small movement. She rattled it again, throwing herself against it, careless of the pain that ripped across her shoulders, the cramp and bruising making her body scream inside.

"We need to both attack it." She looked doubtfully at Steve. "Can you move any further this way?"

He gritted his teeth against the pain and cold, wriggled down on his front, and began to drag himself towards her using his elbows. Despite the cold, beads of sweat were running down his pale cheek and Dove found herself wincing at every movement.

Eventually he was beside her and she began to push the door again. "See? It's like it hasn't been totally fastened, or the mechanism didn't click into place for some reason."

He nodded. "Let's do it."

On a count of three they both smashed against the door, Dove throwing herself against the top half, Steve taking the bottom half. It moved. Encouraged, they did it again.

The door gave a little, revealing a tiny way through. Halfway up, there was a hook holding it steady.

"Can you get that?" Steve was slumped on the floor again, panting.

"Yes," was all she said, trying to catch her breath. Of course she bloody well could, she told herself. It was that or die in here.

Standing on her tiptoes, she leaned back against the door and, bending her elbows, slid her hands up as far as the middle of her shoulder blades. Thank God for regular yoga classes keeping her supple, she thought, as her fingers fumbled with the hook and eye. The intense concentration, the cramp in her arms and legs, were blocked out by the need to escape.

The hook clicked up and fell away as she tumbled through the driver's door and fell straight onto something warm and alive.

Or maybe not alive. "Jesus, Steve, it's one of the drivers." She examined his face.

"Is he still alive?"

"Yeah, big lump on the back of his head, but he's breathing."

Steve had dragged himself through the door now, bumping over the man's legs, desperate for the warmth of the cab. "Can you kick the door shut? Keep the cold out."

"I'm still hoping with the engine shut off the cooling system should gradually be shutting down too." Dove kicked the door to their prison shut anyway, both feet together, boots thudding against the panelling.

"He has a phone," Steve said, after some exploratory pokes with his fingers. "Back pocket . . . Hang on . . . Got it."

"Signal? Battery?"

"You look while I press buttons. Bloody hell, if he'd had a knife this would have been easier."

Outside more tree branches creaked, and the wind was squally and spattered with rain. At each noise, Dove jumped, and her heart rate accelerated.

"It's an iPhone, right? You direct my fingers to make an emergency call."

She wrenched once again uselessly at her bonds. The cramp in her arms had turned to merciful numbness as she concentrated on Steve's movements.

"Okay, you got it . . . More to the left. Can you feel the button on the side?"

They waited as the call connected and Dove felt a rush of emotion almost overwhelm her as the 999 call handler asked for their location.

Having described their predicament and the location as well as they could, including the fact they had their hands tied behind their backs so they would have to just keep the line open to answer any further questions, they slumped back to back, exhausted.

It seemed to be hours before noises woke them from their doze.

Sirens and blue lights flashing, and the thought of warmth and a knife to untie their bonds. Dove almost burst into tears again and Steve just grunted, his head lolling back against her shoulder.

She had herself under control by the time the first uniformed officer entered the cab. "You took your time."

CHAPTER FIFTY-FIVE

"Hallo, Gemma," Dove smiled sweetly at the other woman as the police officers entered the room.

Gemma's frozen expression told her everything she needed to know about her guilt. Her solicitor, a wizened little man with an immense shock of grey hair, smiled and politely introduced himself.

Preliminaries out of the way, DI Blackman began the questioning.

"I don't want to say anything that's recorded," Gemma said obstinately. "Where's that other bloke? Where's Steve?"

Her solicitor spoke in a lowered voice and her scowl deepened. "I don't know where they dug you up from."

"DS Parker is currently in hospital, recovering from his injuries," DI Blackman said helpfully. "Let's start with DS Parker and DC Milson's visit to your home. I believe you pointed them in the direction of Joey Nicholls. Why did you do that?"

"Everything I said was true." She fidgeted, tapping the table with her fingers, drawing circles. Her long blonde hair fell forward, hiding her expression.

"You said you had found something you wanted to show us," Dove refreshed the woman's memory."

"Oh, yeah, that wasn't true."

"So why did you want two officers beaten and removed from the area?" DI Blackman asked.

"I didn't know that would happen. It wasn't me, anyway, it was Joey. He threatened me, and he knew I'd had the pigs round. Andy's away for a couple of days and Joey wanted to know what was going on." She looked up, annoyance and something that might have been sadness crossing her face.

"Could you not have told him the truth? That one of the victims was a friend of yours and we were just investigating the case?"

"Yeah, I did."

"You didn't, Gemma, because Joey thought we were drugs squad and after his stash, which some of his drivers appear to have been keeping going while he's been inside. Andy might be going straight but Joey is clearly going his own sweet way," Dove told her.

"No comment. I don't have to talk to you, you know. You caused trouble for me, I caused trouble for you. All right, I admit it, but Joey had me terrified."

DI Blackman studied her carefully. "You were all packed up and ready to leave when my officers arrested you. And it didn't just look like a little holiday. You have everything except the kitchen sink."

"I was going away. I knew what would happen when the case was solved. You were getting too close. If it came out that I helped Alice take kids, that I was on the inside, I would have been lynched," she snapped.

"Where were you going?" Dove asked. After a few hours' sleep, a jug of coffee, a hot meal and a shower she had been determined to be part of Gemma's interview. A couple of painkillers washed down with the caffeine hit were wearing off already, though. She shifted painfully on her hard plastic chair. "Come on, Gemma, you weren't coming back, were you?"

"One of my kids has got a driving job up in Liverpool. He's a good boy and he's happy to take me with him. I didn't want to go, and I've always done the right thing by my kids. They are my everything."

"Gemma, we understand you were trying to help the children, but you weren't arrested for that. You just turned two unarmed police officers over to a criminal gang. That was not only dangerous, but also a crime."

Dove scribbled another note on her pad, ignoring the 'no comment'.

"You ruined everything! We did the right thing back then and we shouldn't have to pay for it now," Gemma said, anger making her cheeks flame and her fists clench.

"Did you, Alice Cartwright, Gerald Cartwright and Sarah Whitmore take children illegally from their homes and arrange for and facilitate illegal adoptions?" DI Blackman put in.

"No comment." Gemma's voice broke slightly, and her eyes were wet, a tear sliding slowly off her long black lashes, trickling down her cheek.

"Gemma, we have evidence you were involved in the illegal adoption of Cara Windsor."

"Katrina needed help. The baby . . . The baby was the last thing she needed in the situation she was in. Evan threatened to kill the baby and Lily was a mess." She pressed her lips tightly together and glared at the police officers.

"Go on."

"I don't know where Cara went after Gerald took her away. I didn't need to know because I trusted Alice. Whatever else they might have done, I didn't know anything. I looked after Kat, and I looked after her baby. She didn't want anyone to know she was pregnant." Gemma studied them. "You can't know what it's like unless you've lived it yourself. She was fourteen, she'd been raped, and she was pregnant. She trusted me."

"You could have asked for help, come to us, to child protection, social services, any number of shelters and charities," DI Blackman said, but his voice was gentle. "There is help available."

Gemma didn't snap back, but she nodded slowly. "Didn't feel like it at the time, and I was worried Kat was going to do something stupid. It seemed like the perfect solution."

"And you have no idea what happened to Cara?"

"No, but she will have been safe, far safer than she would have been with Lily and Evan, or even if she went through the proper authorities. It would have been too late, like it was for Benny."

"And today? What did you tell Joey to get him all riled up?" DI Blackman changed the subject.

"I told him one of the drivers had grassed him up to the Bensons and that you two suspected he was involved in their drugs bust. Everyone knows their place got raided. He thought you were going to put him back inside and went apeshit." Gemma sighed. "He's got worse in the last few months and now anything triggers his crazy moods. Once you light the fire, he won't listen to anything, won't try and reason stuff out. That's how I knew he wouldn't even think about what he was doing, taking out two police officers."

"I can imagine," Dove said. "And we walked straight into a trap. No wonder Joey treated us like we were on a drugs raid."

"He didn't say anything to me, I just told him you were coming and what you might know," Gemma told her dismissively. "I haven't done anything wrong. You can't charge me with anything. I know my rights."

"You deliberately sent us into danger and lied to us during the course of this investigation. I believe that's called perverting the course of justice."

"That's your job. You should be used to it." But her eyes were wary, and her painted lips dry.

Once again, she began to tap on the tabletop with her long pink nails. Each nail had a rose drawn on it in black ink. Tiny flowers vivid against the neon background. Dove realized she was drifting again and jerked herself back from a haze of exhaustion and pain.

DI Blackman wrapped up the interview, and he and Dove walked back up to the office.

"She went to a lot of trouble to set us up," Dove said, moving stiffly as her limbs complained from the previous day's brutal treatment. "I mean, did she really think we would just vanish, and nobody would notice? It's the opposite of the carefully planned scene around Alice, and to a certain extent, Sarah."

"Harder to remove two active police officers while they're on duty without anyone noticing," DI Blackman said, a serious expression in his grey eyes.

Dove ignored his tone, hoping she wouldn't start crying or anything stupid. It had been hard enough telling Quinn earlier. "I'm just going to ring Steve and update him, if I've got five minutes?"

"Don't tell me DS Parker is sat up in his hospital bed waiting for your call?"

"He is. He wants to know what's going on." Dove knew she would be exactly the same herself and was faintly surprised by the question until she saw the gleam of amusement in the DI's face. He rarely showed any humour and the strongest emotion she ever got from him was sadness, but he never spoke about anything personal at work, or his past.

Some people were like that, keeping it all hidden away, separating personal life and work and nothing ever met in the middle. She knew because she used to be like that too, keeping her emotional walls high. She had to be like that. But she had changed, and all because she'd changed jobs.

Steve answered immediately, his voice quick and eager, as though he wasn't currently confined to a hospital bed. "What happened?"

She summarized the conversation with Gemma.

"This case just gets more and more bizarre," Steve said. "But I think she's telling the truth. She has everything to lose by digging up the past, and everything to gain by things staying quiet."

"How are you feeling?"

She could hear the shrug in his voice. "Okay, I guess. Turns out my kneecap is shattered, and they are going to need to do some reconstructive surgery."

"That's crap." Dove was horrified.

"It is, and then physio . . . But they seem pretty optimistic." His tone was upbeat, but Dove could detect a note of worry.

"Steve, it will be okay. I've been there and it changed my life, but it won't change yours. Scars on the outside, maybe, but you'll be back running round the beach with the kids by the end of summer. How's Zara?"

"Okay. She said her mum has offered to come and take the kids out so she can work. Her business is doing really well now, so it isn't the money . . . It's just— you know. It's what we do."

"Yeah, this job gets in your blood. But you can come into the office as soon as you feel up to it?"

"I might even get a secondment to a unit that doesn't have any physical exertion." The wry amusement in his voice made her glad. "Perhaps I should try Cybercrimes, ready for when my girls start growing up and are let loose with phones and tablets."

"Hey, don't make plans yet, mate, stick with us for a bit."

She ended the call feeling slightly better. At least Steve seemed to be on the road to recovery.

CHAPTER FIFTY-SIX

"I thought you'd be pleased! I've found Cara . . . I've found our sister."

Bewildered, horrified, I enter the room slowly, my heart thudding frantically against my ribs. I love my brothers beyond everything, but they also scare me sometimes. Their minds go places I would never want to follow.

The girl sitting on the chair, looking terrified, does indeed look very similar to me, is around the right age as my daughter would be now, but I feel no connection, and I know in my heart that my darling brother has fucked up. This girl, this stranger, is not his sister any more than she is my daughter.

She is just a random girl off the street. And she is terrified of all of us.

"Leo, I know you think this is right, but it isn't. I . . ." I'm lost for words, and I see him turning his mobile phone over and over in his hands. He is so damaged, my little brother. Lukas is more balanced, has managed to come out of it, I think, but Leo, I am so afraid for him.

I remind myself that the love and the bond we share, everything we have been through together, is surely enough to get us through this.

"Leo, I need to tell you something. You need to know something, and I should have told you years ago . . . I thought you might have guessed."

We leave the girl and step into the other room, shutting the door firmly on her anguished face.

I tell him, knowing I will also have to tell Lukas, knowing I could maybe have stopped the killings. That is the hardest thing of all.

CHAPTER FIFTY-SEVEN

"Dove, for God's sake go home and recover! You can't do anything here," Lindsey told her.

"I was just waiting to hear whether Katrina and her brothers were picked up," Dove said, slumping in her chair. An hour later and all three siblings had vanished and there was no news from the SIO investigating Mae Gardner's disappearance. Mae was a key person in their own investigation now. A missing person connected with a suspect, so potentially in serious danger herself.

The incident board now had Katrina and Mae's photographs tacked up side by side. The similarity, even accounting for the age difference, was eerie.

Dove stared at the photos, as her mind ticking over possibilities. The two dark-haired girls smiled at the room. They could have been twins.

When the room started to spin, Dove gave up for the night and drove to their borrowed apartment on the marina. She drove extra slowly, aware of her exhaustion. The last thing she needed now was to cause an accident.

The underground car park gave her the creeps as she locked her car and started to walk towards the lift. Her footsteps seemed to be magnified across the whole car park, all the empty lots and the darkness of the ramp leading up to street level.

"How are you feeling now?" Quinn raised an eyebrow as she finally came in the door, struggling a little with the unfamiliar locks.

"Shit, obviously. Thanks." She took a full glass of wine and breathed in the heavenly smell of pizza.

"Most people would have stayed at home for a few days after their hospital check, even if physically they were just about okay. You didn't just fall of a push bike, you were abducted and beaten," he pointed out.

She could tell he was pissed off. "I'm really sorry, Quinn, I just . . . I needed to look her in the eye and ask her why she put us in danger. It was like . . . It was like proving to myself that this time, I was strong enough to push through. Not like last time."

He shook his head. "Neither of these episodes are your fault, and I can see why this would shake up all sorts of memories."

Dove put her arms around him. "It's all right, I'm not going to crack up again. I was just trying to explain why I needed to stick around after the doctors signed me off."

Her fiancé sighed. "It's tough seeing you get beaten up and hurt, especially when I can't do anything to prevent it."

"It doesn't happen often," she started, before realizing the irony in what she had been about to say, and hastily shutting her mouth.

He glanced up from mixing a green salad, a trace of amusement hanging on his lips, but he said nothing.

Neither did Dove. After another hot shower, which felt like the best thing ever, she crawled into bed next to Quinn, revelling in the warmth, in being able to stretch out her legs and arms.

"I hate to bring it up, but I'm a bit freaked out I might have to give evidence in court against the firebug stalker," Quinn admitted into the darkness.

Dove slipped an arm around him, snuggling close. "You've testified in court before."

"That was work and that was when I was absolutely sure it wasn't my fault."

"How could the fire possibly be your fault?"

He said nothing, but she could tell he was looking at her, head turned on the pillow.

"Quinn?"

"I still feel like an idiot. Maybe if I hadn't even spoken to her . . ."

"Don't be stupid. The issue is with her, and we now know she has a previous record. Hopefully she will get the medical help she obviously needs," Dove said firmly.

"Right."

He didn't sound convinced, but his breathing soon slipped into a deeper, slower rhythm and Dove knew he was asleep. She stayed alert in the unfamiliar surroundings of the plush apartment bedroom, going over the current case in her mind, sifting information.

She was half tempted to sneak out of bed and check her laptop. Maybe she might have missed something? Certainly, she probably hadn't been functioning quite as well as she could have been after the Joey Nicholls treatment.

A pang of concern and guilt for Steve, tucked up in his hospital bed, followed, but as she drifted off to sleep, she allowed exhaustion to take over. The bed was warm and soft, and she was safe. That was all that mattered.

CHAPTER FIFTY-EIGHT

I stare down at them, lying side by side in the back of the old van.

Neatly bound and gagged, they've been here for a few hours now, and in the wilderness of the site, the acreage beyond the hospital buildings, I found a spot behind the entrance to the morgue.

I still can't believe Evan was there that night too. He was half a mile away from me the whole time, as the crow flies, and then he fucked up by shooting at police officers.

Instead of being organized, the whole thing turned into a shitshow, and I was terrified as I ran from the caravan, leaving the dead body behind. The other woman's voice, her knocking on the door, panicked me into hurrying. It was like coming out of a dream. I had been so angry at her for not telling me what I needed to know.

It was much the same way when me and Lukas attacked Evan years ago, after he came back. We were drunk then and just felt like hurting him. We'd been through so much and he deserved a taste of what we had been through. I remember taking a stone heart from my pocket and shoving it in his mouth, half hoping he would choke.

So now I know what happened, but my burning question is still why. Why did they take the others and not me? That's why it felt good to hurt Alice, and she never gave me a proper answer. Like Lily, she could have saved me. Lily was weak and now I know my own sister has betrayed me, giving the baby who would have saved us to strangers.

I was left behind. They didn't think I was suffering enough, special enough, whatever. But the anger has passed, and now I look down at the two women in the car and I feel sick. What have I done?

CHAPTER FIFTY-NINE

With the investigation still in full swing, Dove spent the day sorting through paperwork, trying to get a handle on the missing women and Leo. The search area had been widened and become a multi-county operation. Community groups, neighbourhood watch and anyone with the slightest link to the case was being contacted.

"They got a last hit on Mae's phone, in the vicinity of Leo's address, before it went dead," Lindsey said. She picked up a cup and took a mouthful of tea, made a face and put it down again.

"Lukas must know something," Dove said in exasperation.

"DI Blackman and Maya are with him now, but he's been working, I checked." Lindsey went back to her screen.

How could three people just vanish? With a whole combined force of various teams from up the coast, extra support staff from their own area and the public and community groups out looking for them? Dove gritted her teeth in frustration. A headache was throbbing behind her eyes and her bruises from her encounter with Joey Nicholls, who was also in custody, were beginning to niggle again.

At least the news on Steve was good. The X-rays had been reviewed and the damage wasn't as extensive as they had initially feared.

By late afternoon, with heavy rain thundering on the windows, the office was still buzzing with information coming in. Another media appeal for information had resulted in a flood of calls, which meant the admin support teams were flat out, sifting through genuine sightings and information, as well as contributions from the crackpots who always joined in with any investigation.

Evan was being questioned about his possible involvement in Mae's abduction, after Lukas had inadvertently provided information leading to a link between Evan and Leo on the night she went missing.

Dove yawned and flexed her fingers over her keyboard. She was keen to give Lukas a shove in the right direction — he seemed like a good kid, and he had also hinted he might know some names relating to the previous case that he had been too afraid to confess at the time.

Names that might potentially get the cold case reopened and lead to a prosecution of the child abuse ring? Dove shrugged to herself. That was getting way ahead of herself, but she hated the thought of those bastards getting away with it. She was fairly sure Evan, faced with even more prison time, would be persuaded to talk.

By 8 p.m. Dove called it a day and started the drive back to the marina. Typically, there were roadworks set up on the exit road into the one-way system, and after sitting at a red light for ten minutes, Dove did a U-turn and headed to the apartment via the longer route.

Her phone rang with no caller ID, and she answered on speakerphone. "DC Milson."

"It's Katrina Bentley . . . Um, Katrina Windsor." The woman's voice was faint, and the crackle on the line was appalling. "We're in a wrecked car near a derelict building, I don't know where. Me, Mae . . . and Leo is here too. He's . . ."

The line went dead and Dove instantly tried to call back, slamming the back of her hand on the steering wheel in frustration when the call didn't connect. Fuck! Where were they? She called the DI. Thank God she had given Katrina her card.

"Send me the number. Why call you and not just 999?"

"I don't know. I gave her my card with my mobile number. She must have put it in her phone. Perhaps she thinks Leo won't . . ." She stopped as she realized she was talking to empty air. Dove heard him shouting across the room, relaying the new information. Why had she gone home?

By the time he was back she had two thoughts. "The old cement works or the Arrowhill site. Lukas knew both places and we found Leo riding his bike at the cement works."

"Where are you?"

She glanced at her satnav. "Two minutes from Arrowhill if I cut back across Leaf Hill."

"Go there and wait for backup. We'll send a team to each place."

Dove arrived at the Arrowhill site, parked up and studied the entrance. No other cars, and the light was on in the security guard's hut. She got out, taking her torch, and walked over, avoiding the worst of the puddles, turning her head slightly sideways to avoid the downpour.

She knocked on the door, loudly, and there was a sudden movement from inside. "Police!"

The security guard peered out. It was the same man who had been on duty when she and Steve had visited the site.

"Oh, it's you. Everything all right? I did send you the link to that girl . . ."

She cut him off and relayed the information that there would be a team arriving shortly. "Have you noticed anything wrong here tonight? Any vehicles? Any trespassers?"

His expression said the weather was shit and he had been sitting in his hut watching YouTube videos. His laptop was open on the small desk inside, and she could see the screen. YouTube videos and other videos.

The door was still partially open, and they both heard the scream. A woman. No words, just a sound of terror.

Dove ran to the barrier, squinting into the darkness, as the security guard lumbered after her, switching on a powerful torch.

As she stepped cautiously around a pile of rubbish, she thought she heard a shout further on, past the hospital building itself. They passed a collection of scrapped cars, the ones in the YouTube videos where the kids had been using them as parkour props.

The scream came again. This time the sound ripped through the darkness from the left side of the building and Dove glanced back at the road. No sign of backup yet.

"Let's go!" The guard was right beside her. "You said your backup is coming, but what if it's too late for her?"

More screams, and Dove agreed. A life was in danger. "Call 999 and tell them what's going on. Leave the line open."

Together, they began to jog towards the screams, avoiding ruts and brambles, ducking their heads in the rain. Dove was in the lead, and she could hear Dan talking to the 999 call handler. She stopped and listened.

The sounds came from behind the building. Shouting now, a man's voice. Leo. She could see movement now, someone walking around two burnt out cars, waving his arms, gesticulating to match the anger in his voice.

Then he leaned into the back seat of the car and the screams started again. Dove was barely aware of moving forward and certainly not aware her companion wasn't by her side.

As abruptly as they had started, the screams stopped. Was she too late? But the man — she caught enough of a glimpse through the shadows and the rain to tell it was Leo — was now running away from the scene, disappearing behind the derelict storage shed.

She inched forward until she could see inside the back seat of the car.

Lying on the back seat, arms and legs bound with white extension cords, were Mae and Katrina. Both were breathing fast, wriggling furiously as they tried to break their bonds, but seemed unharmed.

"Katrina? Mae? Are you hurt? What happened?"

Before the women could answer, Dove became aware of a figure behind her, and the sudden pain as a knife slid into her back.

"You shouldn't have called her!" Leo screamed at his sister. His blonde hair was ghostly in the shadows, face contorted with fear and fury. "I would never have hurt you. You know that!"

Dove, breathing heavily, had pitched forward, and was now leaning against the car, one hand feeling for the wound, pressing as hard as she could. Where was the bloody security guard?

Katrina was now in a sitting position, ignoring the knife, speaking calmly to her brother. "Leo, you need to stop this. It's going to be okay. You need to just calm down. I'll . . . I'll be with you, all right?"

There was a frozen moment where the siblings stared at each other, fear and distrust souring the air. Dove inched round so her back was against the car door, adding to the pressure on her wound. Fuck. The pain was making her weak, and her hand was hot and sticky. She tried to breathe slowly, carefully, but each movement of her chest was agony.

Dove felt the situation de-escalate slightly, but unfortunately Mae, possibly finding her voice after Katrina had spoken, screamed at him. "It's not my fault, or anyone's fault! It's just life and you need to deal with it and move on. I'm not your fucking sister and the police are here now!"

Leo pushed Dove aside and grabbed his captives by their wrist bonds, the knife flashed but Leo struck the younger woman with his fist instead, a hard vicious blow that knocked her back against the car, but not before she had made a grab for the knife. They struggled briefly before he hit her again and she was quiet.

Breathing fast, Leo pulled Katrina out of the car and slashed with the knife.

"Leo, please, you don't need to do this," Dove managed, but he barely looked at her. All his focus was now on his sister. He hadn't hurt her, Dove realized, instead he had cut her bonds.

"Kat, you need to help me, for fuck's sake" His voice was desperate, and he was still holding her arm.

"I can help you, but you need to stop running. It's over," Katrina told him, reaching out and holding both his arms, shaking him gently. "Leo, you need to stop." She looked wide-eyed and horrified at Dove, back at Mae huddled silently in the car. "Leo?"

From behind them lights were flashing, illuminating the darkness, and sirens and shouts were coming from the main gates.

With a heart-wrenching sob, Leo whirled, pushing Dove to the ground, and making her groan with pain. A thud of footsteps racing into the darkness, and both Katrina and her brother were gone.

"Mae?" Dove hissed through her teeth. Someone was shouting her name. Lights flashed blue and white, while the rain still pounded down, oddly refreshing on her burning skin. The pain tore at her body. There were exclamations, a needle in her arm and she drifted away.

CHAPTER SIXTY

I thought if I found Cara, I might be at peace and it would make everything okay. She was always supposed to be our talisman, the person who saved us. Lily told me so herself, over and over.

Now I realize that maybe she isn't the answer to my problems. She isn't even my sister, and the baby was Kat's all along. I can't even begin to process that.

I don't know, will never know, where the real Cara is. But it isn't her fault they took her instead of me. That's where the real pain lies and always has done. That and the broken promises. When you're a kid and someone offers you a dream, you believe them, especially if the person making the promises is your own mum.

It could have been me with a different life, a different person with a new name. Instead of shivering on a cold beach, I could be going home to a loving family. My career might not have imploded, leaving me without a job.

Lukas says that was my fault. He says I lost focus and it's always been up to us to make our own way in life. But I didn't realize I was lost until it was too late. Lukas is me, but he isn't me. Our bond as twins is special and vital, but my bond with Kat was the same until I found out about the baby.

She gave Cara away, and I don't want to hate her for that, but she also contributed to the broken promises. It could have all been so different.

We ran until we couldn't go any further. The darkness cloaked our movements and once the panic gave out, I was just numb. None of it seemed real.

Kat pushed me down into the hedge once when a helicopter flew overhead, bright light moving slowly over the ground just metres from where we were huddled.

We could hear shouts and vehicles racing up and down the coastal roads we were crossing. Kat was supporting me, and I was just so tired. She urged me on, her arms around me. I could feel the sweat on her body, the hammering of her heart and her breath on my cheek. I knew she was terrified, but she was taking care of me, as she always has.

* * *

The last part of our journey was the hardest, the treacherous path down the cliffs to Claw Beach. At last, I began to feel pain, and when I looked down a few minutes ago, I realized my left side was sticky with blood. Unconsciously I had my hand clamped to the wound, and whenever we stopped, I know Kat would pull a little tighter on the makeshift bandage she had fashioned out of her white shirt.

I close my eyes now and rest my cheek against the pebbles. Kat's gentle voice washes over me and her hand in my icy one is warm and soft. I smile inside, and my mouth twitches, I'm so relieved I can still love her.

The sea whispers and the waves dance up and down the beach, the lacy froth stretching close, but not quite touching. We are out of the wind, in a tiny cove sheltered by high rocks. I am cold, but I am safe.

It could have been so different . . .

Or maybe not.

CHAPTER SIXTY-ONE

"Did you get them?"

"You're back. Thank God for that!" Quinn squeezed her hand.

She blinked at him, slowly finding her bearings. Hospital, the smell of disinfectant, her fiancé's face pale and exhausted. It was still dark outside. "Did they get them?"

"No, not yet."

"Is Mae okay?"

"Fine. She's got a black eye, and she's traumatized after the abduction, but she'll be fine. From what Steve said, Evan has been charged in connection with the drugs offences, and Leo will be charged with the murder of Alice, but he'll probably get away with manslaughter in Sarah's case."

"And Kat?" Dove shut her eyes again as the room began to spin. She moved a hand to scratch her face, and her back burned with pain. "What time is it?"

"One in the morning now. You haven't been out long, and you're all sewn up now. In answer to your other question, Steve said they reckon Kat is with Leo. He said there's a massive search op underway, so they'll catch up with them soon. Why the hell did you go back to Arrowhill?"

"I wasn't going there on purpose, but Katrina rang and said she needed help . . ." She ran through the series of events in her head. "The security guard thought it was hilarious. He thinks I fancy him." She smiled blearily. "I waited at the gate for backup but then I heard a girl scream, and I just ran. The security guard, he's called Dan, he said he was following."

"He fell over and broke his ankle, about ten metres from his hut." Quinn rolled his eyes. "Well, you are a complete fucking idiot and I thought you were dead."

"Sorry."

He smiled back, "I'm used to it by now. Neither of us have very safe jobs, do we?"

"Define safe."

"Chef?"

"Too many knives."

"Good point. Anyway, I'm sure your lot will soon be in to interview you, now you're back in the land of the living. Are you okay if I go back to the apartment and take a shower?"

She realized then that he was still slumped in the chair in his bloodstained T-shirt and trousers.

"They called me while they were bringing you in. I was with you as soon as you came through the doors," he grinned at her. "Made a great mess of my new T-shirt. That's the last time I'm listening to Gaia and buying designer — not with you around."

She grinned back, a little feebly. Everything hurt so much, and it felt like days had passed since she had been stabbed, not mere hours. "You can be the one to tell her that."

"I must ring them both. I'll do that on the way home. Ren was here until six, and Gaia only went home half an hour ago."

"Love you." She surprised herself. She didn't often say that kind of thing.

He bent over, careful not to disturb the wires and tubes in her arms. "Love you too, babe."

DI Blackman and Steve were her next visitors, the latter moving deftly on his crutches.

"How are you feeling?" her boss asked, standing by the window, leaning with one shoulder against the glass pane. He looked at his watch and had his phone in one hand. "I was on my way past when they called to say you were awake."

"Crap, obviously." She grimaced as she moved. "So where are they now? Kat and Leo?"

"Still running is my guess," DI Blackman answered. "We have concerns for Katrina's safety. Mae was able to tell us Leo seemed to be furious with her. Is there anything else she said to you, or to Mae, that might give us an idea where they are headed?"

Steve, slumped heavily into the vacant chair next to her bed, was following the conversation intently.

Dove considered. "No, not really, and nothing we don't already know. I don't understand why Katrina ran away with Leo. She was tied up too when I saw her, and he cut her loose. Why would she try to save him?"

"He didn't use his car to get away. It was parked behind the building housing the two scrap vehicles." The DI's expression changed. "We also found a collection of stone hearts and tools for carving and painting in the same place. Over thirty boxes of these stone hearts."

Dove shivered, but she felt a pang of sadness, too. Leo had been thrashing around like a cornered animal when she encountered him. Something had changed between the coolly calculated attack on Alice, the mess-up that had led to Sarah's death, and tonight's chaos.

"Mae said Kat was horrified when Leo showed her what he'd done, abducting her and tying her up. She said the siblings went in the kitchen and talked for ages, and they were both crying. Kat was trying to persuade Leo to turn himself in," DI Blackman added, "We've got a watch on all their addresses and Lukas is down the station. He's in bits. Mae also said Katrina was already tied up in the car when Leo brought Mae out there, so she guessed they had an argument about her and he attacked his sister.

"Lukas doesn't know where they went, and he's off his head with worry, says Leo has been behaving erratically for months now." The DI was looking out the window at the darkness, his shoulders set and tense. "There's a full search team out. We'll get them."

"No. He went on about how he didn't want to hurt anyone. He was terrified, angry and I would say remorseful," Dove said thoughtfully. "Which he should be after three dead and a bit of knife practice on me. I could be wrong, but I think he's been fixated on his sister for years, and now he finally manages to bust the whole thing wide open, finds out who and why and meets the girl, who isn't his sister, and then his other sister tells him the baby was her daughter . . . It would be too much for anyone to take in. Christ, what a mess."

"So then, what now?" Steve asked.

"I honestly don't think he knows either. My impressions are that he was chaotic, disorganized and lashing out in his panic," Dove said, flicking through her memory of the preceding hours. "But Kat hasn't done anything except help Leo escape. Unless he's taken her hostage. She could still be in danger."

"The thought did occur to us—" DI Blackman's phone rang, and he picked up immediately, listening intently before offering a curt goodbye. He turned back to Steve and Dove, "We have a sighting on the traffic cam on Bay Road from half an hour ago. It's not a great picture, and it's brief, as they run across the road and vanish into the woods above Claw Beach, but it looks like our suspects."

His phone beeped and he showed them the grainy video footage of the small figures, emerging from the bushes in a moment with no traffic, running, staggering to the other side.

When Dove next awoke, the first thing she saw was her sisters. Ren smiled at her, amber eyes bright with relief. Gaia was sipping coffee from her refillable container, gaze fixed on Dove's face.

"Great, you are alive!" Gaia remarked dryly as Dove licked her dry lips and tried to sit up. "For Christ's sake don't move, you're covered in stitches." She leaned over and passed Dove a plastic cup filled with water.

"Thanks."

"Are you in much pain?" Ren asked, ever the practical sister. She patted a bag and added, "I got you some toiletries and bits. The bag Quinn brought had a summer dress and a tube of sun cream." She grinned suddenly, "But he also brought a massive box of chocolates for you."

* * *

Dove's phone rang an hour later, and she guiltily slipped it onto her pillow. She had made Lindsey promise to keep her updated, couldn't rest until she knew Katrina was safe and Leo in custody.

"What's happening?"

Lindsey's voice came loud and distorted. "It's bloody windy up here. We got another sighting saying they had made their way up towards the Downs. Someone called in to the info line with a description."

"And?" Dove's hand was clenched on the phone. She thought of the vast chalk cliffs that separated the beach from the Downs.

"Misdirection. It was a couple off on a romantic jolly." Lindsey sounded disgusted. "The teams are going back onto the beach and the lifeguard is out."

"Thanks for letting me know."

Dove lay back against her pillows, frustrated she wasn't out searching, would miss the conclusion, and also terrified Katrina was now a hostage. The cliffs and the sea in darkness were a dangerous place to be, even if your brother wasn't a killer.

253

CHAPTER SIXTY-TWO

The waves are calm tonight. The chill of late spring makes me shiver, hugging my arms around my body. It's less than four hours since I ran from Arrowhill, dragging my brother along with me. We ran and then walked, hiding and ducking away from the populated areas. Long before I reached the coast I was exhausted, my bloodstained clothing clinging to my sweaty body.

I didn't notice how badly he was hurt, and I swear he never said a word. It took me back to my childhood role, when it was my job to get the twins to school, feed them, keep them out of Evan's way . . .

Past Claw Beach there are caves, and the coastline gets more rugged. A good place to hide. I didn't have a plan, but if I did it would have involved walking into the sea and not stopping until the cool waters closed over my head. My own brother has killed people. The thought still makes me gasp out loud, and I start to shiver again.

I force myself to go over the truth as I know it. He kidnapped a girl off the street, hit her, and stabbed a police officer. And he killed Alice.

When Alice was murdered, when I saw it in the papers, I admit I wondered, and when Sarah died that part of my life started to come back in my nightmares. I never thought my brother would be involved, though. Evan, yes, he was out of prison, and I could have possibly seen how he might have gone after those women, but he never knew my secret.

He may have suspected. Perhaps Lily was doing me a favour after all, keeping the focus on herself. Or perhaps that's going too far.

I can't explain why Leo suddenly snapped, other than I guess after so many years of keeping it all hidden, his mind couldn't take it anymore. Evan being released from prison, Lily taking her own life, losing his job in Spain. Sometimes all these little things can join together and became unbearable.

I never knew he wrote letters to Evan asking what had happened to Cara, but I can imagine how much it took for him to write them. Equally, I can imagine how much Evan enjoyed not answering them, keeping a little bit of power over the boy he had bullied and beaten.

Did they really take any other children? I gave Cara up because I knew she would have a better life. It could have been me with a different life, a different person with a new name. Instead of shivering on a cold beach, I could be going home to a loving family. Or maybe not.

I often think that when I'm present at a birth. I love my job, I realize, suddenly, blindingly. I love my job, and I hope I can still go back to my life, the one I have built so carefully for myself.

I have a few friends, although I accept that I probably won't have any by the time this comes out. And a boyfriend. We are not together but he still called me last week to see if I was okay.

I have realized I still love him, too, and I was wrong to keep pushing him away. I take a deep breath of the cold night air, and let it go, imagining breathing all the darkness from inside my mind, releasing it out to sea, where it fades into the night air.

Leo said he pulled the knife without thinking. His instinctive reaction to danger is always to fight back now he is an adult. He said he was carrying it to scare her, to make her talk, not to kill her. But they struggled and rage and terror took over.

The staging of the baby doll, the planning bothers me a lot. He wanted to send a message to her, to them all, to start something that in his mind could only end one way. And he went out with the heart and the bracelet and his plans. He says, too, that he wasn't going to put the objects in her mouth, but when she died, he felt like he was waking from a dream, and he knew it was the right thing to do.

She wouldn't tell him anything at all about Cara, and when he asked her who she chose to take she just said they couldn't save everyone, and she was sorry. That's what has really been eating at his soul, ever since he saw those little red crosses next to our names. We weren't chosen.

Alice's ex-husband, Gerald, he was clearly having a medical episode when Leo arrived to confront him. He says he tried to question him, but the old man raved about trees and magnolias and boys and girls sleeping at peace. So he called an ambulance.

He isn't all bad, my brother, he just needed to know the answers to his questions.

And Sarah . . . I think, having read the paperwork, that it was her idea, not Alice's or Gerald's. Leo said she was angry, but then she was terrified when he tried to question her. She fell backwards and hit her head. Leo was desperately asking questions, always asking questions, as she died. He was horrified at what he had done.

I understand what happened with Benny Milward, I see why they were doing what they did, I think, but that doesn't make it right.

So now I have my own choice to make. I can face up to the crimes that have been committed and try to make them understand how I didn't mean for any of it to happen, but that much of it is my fault, or I can walk out into the English Channel.

There is a body on the stones a little further up. My brother, who died in my arms in the darkness and the shadows, his blood seeping into the beach, his face peaceful at last. His hatred for me was back for a while as he told his story, and then it was gone, and I knew I was forgiven.

"I'm sorry I hurt you. Didn't mean to . . . I love you, Kat." In the shadows his cheeks looked rounder, his smile more innocent. The hardness and the angular set of his chin changed, and I saw the softness and sweetness he had radiated as a toddler, struggling around after me as I sought to make sense of my own life, to keep him safe.

"Love you too, Gumball." It was my old nickname for him, after he used to steal those giant gumballs from the machine on the pier. When I got older, I used to steal them for him. To make him happy and to see him give his sudden, rare smile. To make life a little more bearable.

"Tell Lukas . . . Tell him why I did it, Kat?"

"Of course I will," I soothed him, pushing his hair back off his forehead. His skin was so cold and clammy.

I wanted to call an ambulance, to stem the blood flowing from his body, to save his life, but he begged me not to. He would go to prison for killing Alice, for indirectly killing Sarah, for abducting Mae.

My phone had no signal, and I could tell he didn't have much time left. If I had left to seek help, he would have died alone.

He said he wanted to go while he still had music in his head and pebbles under his fingers, the still night air on his cold face.

My heart was tearing apart, my tears fell so fast that his face was blurred. I gathered him in my arms.

"Goodbye, Gumball."

I stand up, feeling the breeze ruffle my hair. I'm starving, and even my bones feel exhausted. But as I stand, considering, I realize the decision has almost been made for me. The sickness, the emotion. The test I bought from the chemist last week. It seems like years ago. And now I have two paths to follow. A crossroads, but I am in control. It's not like before, I remind myself.

I slide my hands gently down to my belly and cup the soft swell gently, as though I can already feel the baby. I walk forward, the stones are sharp on my bare feet and the icy water swirls around my ankles.

There is just a glimmer of light on the horizon, right where the sea meets the sky.

CHAPTER SIXTY-THREE

Dove watched the next aircraft take off, listening to the commentator talking about the history of the air show, the bio of this particular pilot. Jess's twins, Alex and Charlie were eating strawberries, side by side in their red buggy. Charlie was clutching at the balloon string, half an eye on his food, the other on the shiny helium balloon that danced on the wind.

Quinn was talking to a couple of mates at Chromium Ambulance who were providing event cover today. The noise of chattering crowds, the smell of cut grass and the drone of the aerobatic plane as it went into a series of barrel rolls were a perfect background to the May Bank Holiday weekend, Dove thought.

"It's a shame about Leo, but I'm glad the sister was okay. Any luck with the missing kids?" Jess asked.

"Nope. Cara may or may not still be alive, and if she is, I haven't been able to find any records of her changing her name. It's a tough one. I think the general consensus is that this now has go on the back burner. It's a lot of money to put into a cold case, isn't it?" Dove replied, bending down to tuck the handle of the changing bag under the buggy. Alex gave her a gummy grin and she smiled back, without a thought. The ache wasn't there anymore.

"What about the other kids they had adopted?"

"Well, there isn't any proof they actually went through with any of the other names on their list. All first names and it will take someone ages to try and join the dots."

"Would you want to be the one to break the news to the adoptive parents that their kid isn't who they thought they were? And what about the biological parents . . ." Jess had a serious expression in her sharp blue eyes as she bent over her sons.

"I know. I sort of hope they don't find out," Dove admitted.

"How are you feeling about the wedding?"

"Yeah, good . . . Jess, would you adopt again?"

"In a heartbeat. These boys are my whole world." She looked shrewdly at Dove. "Why? Are you still thinking about kids?"

Dove fixed her gaze on the dot on the horizon that was the plane leaving the airfield. The commentator started to introduce the next one. "I don't know. Quinn says he honestly doesn't mind what we do. He'd love kids, but he's also happy if we don't ever have any."

"He's a gem. A grumpy bastard, but a gem," Jess commented.

"He is. You know, I think a lot of it was not having the choice anymore. I sort of took it for granted that it would always be my choice, my decision and when that is taken away from you . . . Now, I look at kids, at your two, and think maybe I wasn't meant to be a mum at all. And it doesn't hurt to say that."

"Hmmm . . ."

"Okay, maybe a bit, and perhaps I'll change my mind. But the point is, if we decide to have kids, I can't carry them, I won't give birth to them. There's no ticking clock in terms of fertility or anything. It's just if the time is right."

"I guess. If you do go ahead, don't leave it so long you're practically retiring, though. I'm thirty-nine and the night feeds nearly finished me off. I go to work for a rest now," Jess told her, laughing.

"That's what Steve said about his girls." Dove grinned at her.

"What happened with Eden? You mentioned she had concerns about a friend and her kids?"

"Turns out her friend was really struggling and had picked up an extra shift at the supermarket to try and turn her finances around," Dove said, sipping her Pimm's. "Her boyfriend walked out, and she didn't know how she was going to eat for the next week, let alone keep her kids in nappies and baby clothes."

"So Eden got her some help?"

"She did." Dove shot her friend a glance. "This friend also tried to make money with some YouTube videos before she had kids, but nobody was interested, so she left it for a while before doing one last video of Arrowhill. Eden said she checked back and found she has loads of followers and can monetise her channel, so that's another income source."

They both watched the next aircraft do a low flypast, before it began to climb ahead of a loop-the-loop. It flew higher and higher above the trees, and then seemed to hang in space.

For a moment, Dove thought it looked a little low for the top of a loop. The little plane began to drop, close enough to the south side of the crowd, but far enough away that the trees suddenly hid it from view. She held her breath in horror, expecting the worst, before the plane reappeared. Those tiny moments that could change your life in a flash. But this time it hadn't happened.

Jess was watching her curiously. "What's up?"

"I was just thinking how quickly things can change, how our jobs are always going to be on that knife-edge of danger."

Jess pushed her designer sunglasses back on her head, her smooth blonde bob hardly moving in the spring breeze. "You love it." But her eyes followed the plane as the pilot launched into a series of barrel rolls. "I know what you mean, but you can either live and take chances, or stay tucked away, hoping nothing will go wrong."

"Katrina says she's going to train as a midwife. She is truly amazing. All that going on and she is just carrying on with what she was going to do before her brother went on a killing spree." Dove bent down to pick up a dropped beaker. "Oh, and she's found out she is pregnant."

"Wow. That's a lot to process. She is one strong lady."

"I know. She said she's feeling very positive about getting to know Andy Nicholls. From what Gemma said, he's a nice enough bloke, and it can't have been easy growing up in Joey's shadow."

Jess pulled out a tube of sun cream and started to smear some on her exposed shoulders. "You said Joey is having medical treatment?"

"Yeah, he collapsed in custody, and they found a growth on his frontal lobe on the scan. The doctors said it would explain why he has been getting more violent and suffering irrational episodes, and why he thought it would be okay to take out me and Steve."

She decided to change the subject. "I can't believe I'm getting married this year." Dove took the sun cream from her friend. It was great to be spending some time with Jess away from work, and although there were still questions to be answered on the case, it was time for some respite.

She still felt a bit odd about the wedding, especially given that she had suspected Quinn of cheating. Marriage wasn't the sort of thing she had ever wanted to do, and part of her still wondered if it was a good idea. The tiniest, hidden-away part.

"It's awesome. And of course, you have the best women all organized, so we'll sort out the wedding planning, too." Jess was supremely confident in her part.

Dove looked over as Quinn finished his conversation, saw her watching and started to walk slowly back across the grass towards her, smiling.

THE END

AUTHOR'S NOTE

I can't believe this is the fourth book in the Detective Dove Milson series!

Huge thanks to all my wonderful readers for sticking around to see what happens next. Without you I wouldn't be writing at all.

Thanks also to my amazing publishers, Joffe Books, who have been publishing my books since 2017 and continue to do such an incredible job of looking after us all.

Special mention to Elodie, who has been editing and proofreading the series since the beginning, and always does an amazing job. She also writes really nice comments in the margins lol.

My lovely agent, Kate Nash, also deserves a bottle of wine (possibly a whole vineyard!) for her patience, her professionalism and for working so hard for all her authors. I am so lucky my books and I have found a home at the Kate Nash Literary Agency.

A large chunk of this book was written during an eleven-hour flight to and from San Diego, California. A plane is an old favourite place to write. Thank you to the wonderful British Airways crew for keeping my caffeine levels topped up!

Thank you to my professionals, for answering my endless questions on police procedure (Eric and Dee) and on midwifery (Maggie), and also to fellow writers Lisa, Hayley, Debbie and Laura for providing gin/shoulders to cry on/kicks up the bum — all administered as necessary!

To the book bloggers, the libraries, the bookshops, the tour managers and everyone behind the scenes who helps get our books out into the world, a heartfelt thanks.

Finally, thank you to my lovely family, for putting up with me tapping endlessly on my computer, and supporting me as I hang onto my dream.

D.E. White

ALSO BY D.E. WHITE

DETECTIVE DOVE MILSON MYSTERIES
Book 1: GLASS DOLLS
Book 2: THE ICE DAUGHTERS
Book 3: THE ABBERLEY BEACH MURDERS
Book 4: STONE COLD KILLING

RUBY BAKER MYSTERIES
written as Daisy White
Book 1: BEFORE I LEFT
Book 2: BEFORE I FOUND YOU
Book 3: BEFORE I TRUST YOU

Thank you for reading this book.

If you enjoyed it please leave feedback on Amazon or Goodreads, and if there is anything we missed or you have a question about, then please get in touch. We appreciate you choosing our book.

Founded in 2014 in Shoreditch, London, we at Joffe Books pride ourselves on our history of innovative publishing. We were thrilled to be shortlisted for Independent Publisher of the Year at the British Book Awards.

www.joffebooks.com

We're very grateful to eagle-eyed readers who take the time to contact us. Please send any errors you find to corrections@joffebooks.com. We'll get them fixed ASAP.